TWELVE
DEAD MEN

Center Point
Large Print

Also by William W. Johnstone
with J. A. Johnstone and available from
Center Point Large Print:

Those Jensen Boys!
Brotherhood of Evil
Rimfire
Will Tanner: U.S. Deputy Marshal
Tyranny
The Trail West
Black Friday
A Stranger in Town

Also by J. A. Johnstone and available from
Center Point Large Print:

Crossfire
Brutal Vengeance
Hard Luck Money
Bullets Don't Die

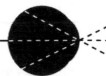

**This Large Print Book carries the
Seal of Approval of N.A.V.H.**

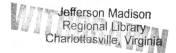
THOSE JENSEN BOYS!

TWELVE DEAD MEN

William W. Johnstone
with J. A. Johnstone

CENTER POINT LARGE PRINT
THORNDIKE, MAINE

PUBLISHER'S NOTE
Following the death of William W. Johnstone,
the Johnstone family is working with a carefully selected
writer to organize and complete Mr. Johnstone's outlines
and many unfinished manuscripts to create additional novels
in all of his series like The Last Gunfighter, Mountain Man,
and Eagles, among others. This novel was inspired by
Mr. Johnstone's superb storytelling.

The text of this Large Print edition is unabridged.
In other aspects, this book may vary from the original edition.
Printed in the United States of America on permanent paper.
Set in 16-point Times New Roman type.

ISBN: 978-1-68324-417-2

Library of Congress Cataloging-in-Publication Data

Names: Johnstone, William W., author. | Johnstone, J. A., author.
Title: Twelve dead men : those Jensen boys! / William W. Johnstone ;
with J. A. Johnstone.
Description: Center Point Large Print edition. | Thorndike, Maine :
Center Point Large Print, 2017.
Identifiers: LCCN 2017015295 | ISBN 9781683244172
      (hardcover : alk. paper)
Subjects: LCSH: Large type books. | GSAFD: Western stories.
Classification: LCC PS3560.O415 T95 2017 | DDC 813/.54—dc23
LC record available at https://lccn.loc.gov/2017015295

The Jensen Family
First Family of the
American Frontier

Smoke Jensen—*The Mountain Man*

The youngest of three children and orphaned as a young boy, Smoke Jensen is considered one of the fastest draws in the West. His quest to tame the lawless West has become the stuff of legend. Smoke owns the Sugarloaf Ranch in Colorado. Married to Sally Jensen, father to Denise ("Denny") and Louis.

Preacher—*The First Mountain Man*

Though not a blood relative, grizzled frontiersman Preacher became a father figure to the young Smoke Jensen, teaching him how to survive in the brutal, often deadly Rocky Mountains. Fought the battles that forged his destiny. Armed with a long gun, Preacher is as fierce as the land itself.

Matt Jensen—*The Last Mountain Man*

Orphaned but taken in by Smoke Jensen, Matt Jensen has become like a younger brother to Smoke and even took the Jensen name. And like Smoke, Matt has carved out his destiny on the American frontier. He lives by the gun and surrenders to no man.

Luke Jensen—*Bounty Hunter*
Mountain Man Smoke Jensen's long-lost brother, Luke Jensen, is scarred by war and a dead shot—the right qualities to be a bounty hunter. And he's cunning, and fierce enough, to bring down the deadliest outlaws of his day.

Ace Jensen and Chance Jensen—
Those Jensen Boys!
The untold story of Smoke Jensen's long-lost nephews, Ace and Chance, a pair of young-gun twins as reckless and wild as the frontier itself . . . Their father is Luke Jensen, thought killed in the Civil War. Their uncle Smoke Jensen is one of the fiercest gunfighters the West has ever known. It's no surprise that the inseparable Ace and Chance Jensen have a knack for taking risks—even if they have to blast their way out of them.

Chapter One

"Nice, peaceful-looking town," Chance Jensen commented as he and his brother approached the settlement.

"Think it'll stay that way after we ride in?" Ace Jensen asked.

"Why wouldn't it?"

"I'm just going by our history, that's all. Seems like every time we show up in a place, hell starts to pop."

Chance made a scoffing sound. "Now you're just being . . . what's the word?"

"I was thinking *crazy*," Ace said.

The brothers drew rein in front of a livery stable at the edge of town, halting Ace's big, rangy chestnut and Chance's cream-colored gelding in front of the open double doors.

Not many people would have taken them for twin brothers, despite the truth of their birth. When they swung down from their saddles, Ace stood slightly taller than Chance and his shoulders spread a little wider. Dark hair peeked out from under his thumbed-back Stetson. The battered hat matched his well-worn range clothes and the plain, walnut-butted Colt .45 Peacemaker that stuck up from a holster on his right hip.

A flat-crowned brown hat sat on Chance's

lighter, sandy-colored hair. He preferred fancier clothes than his brother, in this case a brown tweed suit and a black string tie. A .38 caliber Smith & Wesson Second Model revolver rode in a shoulder holster under the suit coat, out of sight but handy if Chance needed to use it . . . which he could, with considerable speed and accuracy.

Both Jensen brothers possessed an uncanny ability to handle guns that had saved their lives —and the lives of numerous innocent people—in the past.

A tall, rawboned man in late middle age ambled out of the livery stable to meet them. He wore overalls and a hat with the brim pushed up in front. Rust-colored stubble sprouted from his lean cheeks and angular jaw, and a black patch covered his left eye. "Do you gents for somethin'?"

"Stalls and feed for our horses," Ace said.

The liveryman studied the mounts for a second and nodded in approval. "Nice-lookin' critters. Be four bits a day for the both of 'em."

Ace took two silver dollars from a pocket and handed them over. "That'll cover a few days. My brother and I don't know how long we'll be staying here in . . . ?"

"Lone Pine," the liveryman said. "That's the name o' this place. Leastways, that's what they call it now."

"Did it used to have another name?" Chance asked.

A grin stretched across the man's face. He chuckled and said, "When it started, they called it Buzzard's Roost."

"That sounds a little sinister," Ace said.

"Just a wide place in the trail, back in them days. Couple saloons and a store. Owlhoots all over New Mexico Territory—hell, all over the Southwest—knew you could stop at Buzzard's Roost for supplies and a drink and maybe a little time with an Injun whore, and nobody 'd ask any questions about where you'd been or where you planned to go. Folks who lived here would forget you'd ever set foot in the place, happen the law come lookin' for you."

"So it was an outlaw town," Chance said.

"And now look at it," the liveryman said with a sigh that sounded somehow disapproving. "Place is plumb respectable these days."

That appeared to be true. Lone Pine had a business district that stretched for several blocks, lined with establishments of all sorts. Saloons still operated, to be sure, but so did restaurants, mercantiles, apothecaries, a blacksmith shop, a saddle maker, lawyers, doctors, a newspaper—the *Lone Pine Sentinel, LEE EMORY, ED. & PROP.*, according to the sign painted in the office's front window—and even a shop full of ladies' hats and dresses.

Dozens of residences sat along the tree-lined cross streets. Lone Pine appeared to be a bustling settlement in pleasant surroundings, at the base of some foothills that rose to snowcapped peaks in the west, with green rangeland lying to the east.

Ace spotted a marshal's office and jail a short distance along the main street, too. With any luck, he and Chance wouldn't see the inside of it during their stay in Lone Pine.

He planned to hold on to that hope, anyway.

"The way you talk about Buzzard's Roost makes it sound like you were here during those days," Chance said to the liveryman.

"Oh, I was. I surely was."

"But you weren't one of the owlhoots." Chance grinned.

"Nope. Didn't have nothin' but a piece of ground with a corral on it in those days, but I rented out space in it to anybody who come along, no matter which side o' the law they found theirselves on. Had to, or risk gettin' shot. Slowly but surely, things begun to settle down, and I made enough *dinero* to start buildin' a barn." The man jerked a knobby-knuckled thumb over his shoulder at the structure behind him.

"It looks like you've done well for yourself," Ace said. "I'm Ace Jensen, by the way. This is my brother Chance."

"Crackerjack Sawyer," the liveryman introduced himself.

"Surely Crackerjack isn't your real name," Chance said.

"Castin' doubts on a fella's name ain't too polite," Sawyer said, his eyes narrowing.

"My brother didn't mean anything by it." Ace cast a warning glance at Chance. "Sometimes he talks before he thinks."

"Well, as it happens, that ain't the name my ma called me. 'Twas Jack. But I'm from Georgia, and when I come out here back in the fifties, some folks called me a cracker. That sorta got put together with my name, and it stuck."

"We're pleased to meet you, Mr. Sawyer."

"Jensen . . ." the liveryman repeated slowly, frowning. "Since you was bold enough to ask me about my name, I'll ask you boys about yours. Are you related to Smoke Jensen?"

The brothers got that question fairly often, since just about everybody west of the Mississippi — and a good number of those east of the big river—had heard of the notorious gunfighter and adventurer Smoke Jensen. Those days, Smoke was a rancher in Colorado, but he hadn't exactly settled down all that much, as Ace and Chance had good reason to know.

"Don't encourage him," Chance said to Sawyer. "My brother thinks Smoke Jensen is some long-lost relative of ours."

"As a matter of fact, we've crossed trails with him several times, and his brothers Matt and Luke, too," Ace said. "They're friends of ours, but as far as we know we're not related to them."

"A long time ago—must be goin' on ten years now—Smoke come through Buzzard's Roost. Rumor had it he was on the owlhoot then, but come to find out later the charges against him weren't true. He already had a rep as a fast gun, though. Some other hombres who were here fancied themselves hardcases and tried to prove it by bracin' Smoke." Sawyer shook his head. "Almost quicker 'n you can blink, all four of 'em wound up dead in the street. Never seen the like of it, in all my borned days."

"That sounds like Smoke, all right," Chance said.

"Well, we're not looking for any trouble like that," Ace added. "We're just planning on spending a little time in a nice, peaceful town before we move on."

Sawyer snorted. "Drifters, eh?"

"Let's just say we haven't found anyplace we want to settle down in yet."

"Lone Pine's peaceful enough these days . . . most of the time."

"Meaning some of the time it's not?" Chance asked.

"Bein' respectable and law-abidin' don't sit well with some people. Steer clear o' Pete McLaren and his bunch, and you'll be fine."

"Where do they usually hang out . . . so we can avoid them?" Ace said.

"Harry Muller's Melodian Saloon." Sawyer

pointed. "Two blocks up, on the far corner."

"Is it the biggest and best saloon in Lone Pine?" Chance wanted to know.

"Well . . . I reckon most folks 'd say so."

"But there are other saloons in town," Ace said.

"Yeah, three or four."

"If we want to wet our whistles, we won't have any trouble finding someplace to do it. If you'll show us the stalls where you'll be keeping our horses, we'll take them in and unsaddle them, Mr. Sawyer."

"No need to do that. I got a couple hostlers who'll take care of it. Just get any gear you want off of 'em. We'll take good care of the critters for you."

Ace and Chance took their saddlebags off the horses and draped them over their shoulders, then pulled Winchesters from sheaths strapped under the saddle fenders.

Ace considered the state of their finances, then said, "How about a hotel? Maybe not the best in town, but decent enough to stay in."

"The Territorial House," Sawyer answered without hesitation. "Next block, this side of the street."

"We're obliged to you."

Ace and Chance walked up the street to the hotel, which turned out to be a two-story, whitewashed frame building with a balcony along the front of the second floor. They stepped up onto the boardwalk and went into a lobby with a threadbare rug on the floor and a little dust gathered in the corners. An elderly man with white hair, a bristly white mustache, and hands that trembled a little checked them in.

"Mr. Sawyer down at the livery stable recommended your place," Ace commented as he slid a silver dollar across the counter while Chance signed the registration book for them. It was actually cheaper for them to stay there than it was to keep their horses at the livery stable.

"That old Reb?" the hotel man said.

Ace didn't know if he was the owner or just a clerk.

"I'm surprised he sent any trade my way. I was a Union man." He drew himself up straighter. "Colonel in the 12th Illinois infantry. Colonel Charles Howden."

"Mr. Sawyer said he came out here to New Mexico before the war."

"Yes, and then he went off and fought in the Battle of Glorietta Pass for the Confederates. Forgot to mention that, didn't he?"

"It's been quite a while since the war ended, Mr. Howden," Chance pointed out.

"Colonel Howden, if you please."

"Of course, Colonel," Ace said. "If we could, uh, get the key to our room . . ."

"Certainly." Howden took a key from the rack and handed it to Ace. "Room Twelve, on the second floor. I hope you enjoy your stay, Mister . . ." He looked at the registration book and read their names upside down, a talent most people who worked in hotels acquired. "Jensen."

The name didn't seem to mean anything to him.

The brothers went upstairs, left their saddlebags and rifles in Room Twelve—which, like the lobby, showed signs of wear and was a little dusty—and then came back down and strolled out onto the boardwalk in front of the hotel.

"Reckon it's late enough in the day we could find someplace to get supper," Ace said.

"We *could,*" Chance said, "but think how much better supper would taste if we had a drink first."

"You weren't thinking about that Melodian Saloon Mr. Sawyer mentioned, were you?"

"He said it was the biggest and best in Lone Pine," Chance replied with a smile, "and it's right over there." He pointed diagonally across the street toward the building on the far corner.

"I'm going to have a hard time talking you out of this, aren't I?"

"More than likely," Chance agreed. "Anyway, that troublemaker the old-timer mentioned— what was his name? McLaren? He's probably not even there right now."

Chapter Two

Pete McLaren laughed. "Shoot, Dolly, you might as well stop tryin' to get away. You know I like it when you put up a little fight."

The blonde put her hands against Pete's chest and pushed as she tried to squirm off his lap. He just tightened the arm around her waist, put his other hand behind her neck, and pulled her head down to his so he could press his mouth against hers.

Dolly Redding let out a muffled squeal and tried even harder to get away for a few seconds. Then she sighed, wrapped her arms around Pete's neck, and returned the kiss with passionate urgency.

He let that continue for a minute or so and then pulled his head away and laughed raucously. "You see, fellas, I told you this little hellcat couldn't resist me for long!"

The four other men at the table in the Melodian Saloon joined in Pete McLaren's laughter. Like Pete, they were all young, in their twenties, and dressed like cowboys, although the lack of calluses on their hands indicated they hadn't had riding jobs lately. Exactly how they got the money they spent there and in other saloons was open to debate, although nobody was going to

16

question it too much if they knew what was good for them.

Dolly pouted. "Pete, you shouldn't make sport of me. Just 'cause I work in a saloon don't mean you shouldn't treat me like a lady!"

"Nobody's ever gonna accuse you of bein' a lady, Dolly, but hell, if I wanted a lady, I'd be chasin' after that Fontana Dupree. I like my gals, well, a little on the trashy side. Like you."

That provoked more gales of laughter from Pete's friends. Dolly just looked embarrassed as a blush spread across her face. She didn't deny what Pete had said about her, though.

To tell the truth, Dolly Redding was a good-looking young woman, and she hadn't worked in saloons long enough to acquire the hard mouth and the suspicious lines around her eyes that most doves displayed. She still had a faint flush of . . . well, innocence would be stretching it too far, but maybe remembered innocence would describe it.

Some of her thick, curly blond hair had fallen in front of her face while Pete was kissing her. She tossed her head to throw it back and told him, "I'm just sayin' you should treat me a little better, that's all. Maybe I ain't a lady now, but I might be someday if I work hard enough at it."

"Oh, you work hard at what you do. I'll give you credit for that," Pete said with a leer on his handsome young face.

The other men at the table thought that was hilarious, too.

The commotion in the corner drew a few disapproving frowns from the saloon's other patrons. The hour was early, not even suppertime yet, so the Melodian was only about half full.

A burly, bald man in a gray suit leaned on the bar where he stood at the far end of the hardwood. He glared at the table where Pete McLaren and his friends were working on their second bottle of whiskey since they'd come in an hour or so earlier.

A young woman with light brown hair framing a face of sultry beauty came out of a door at the end of the bar and paused beside the bald man. The silk gown she wore wasn't exactly churchgoing garb, but it was more decorous than the short, low-cut, spangled getups worn by Dolly Redding and the other girls who delivered drinks in the Melodian.

"What's wrong, Hank?" the brunette murmured.

"Ah, it's just that blasted McLaren kid and his pards again," Hank Muller said as he continued to scowl. "I hate to see Dolly gettin' mauled like that."

"It sort of comes with the territory, doesn't it?"

Muller looked sharply at her. "I make no bones about what goes on here. The girls know what's expected of 'em, and they don't kick about it. Pete McLaren's too rough about it, though. Too sure of himself. Ah, hell, Fontana, maybe I just don't like the kid and the rest of that bunch."

"You're not the only one," Fontana Dupree said. "Want me to try to distract them?"

"Well . . . I don't suppose it'd hurt anything to try."

Fontana smiled and nodded. She left the bar and walked over to a piano sitting next to a small stage in the back of the barroom. At a table close by the piano, a small man with thinning fair hair sat reading a copy of the *Police Gazette*. An unlit store-bought cigarette hung from the corner of his mouth, bobbing slightly as he hummed to himself and studied the etchings of scantily clad women in the magazine.

Fontana put a hand on his shoulder. "Come on, Orrie. It's time to get to work."

Quickly, he closed the *Police Gazette* and sat up straighter. "Uh, sorry, Miss Dupree. I didn't figure we'd be starting this early—"

"It's all right," Fontana told him. "How about some Stephen Foster?"

"Sure." Orrie stood up from the table and went to a stool in front of the piano. He put his fingers on the keys and looked up at Fontana as she took her place beside the instrument. When she nodded, he began to play, and a moment after the notes began to emerge, crisp and pure, she started singing a sad, sentimental ballad in a voice even more lovely than Orrie's playing.

Chance Jensen stopped in his tracks. "I think I'm in love."

He and Ace had just pushed through the batwings and stepped through the corner entrance into the Melodian. Ace almost bumped into his brother, then moved aside so he could look past Chance. He heard the singing, and judging by Chance's intent, love-struck expression, Ace figured he was staring at the singer.

She was worth looking at, Ace thought, slim and lovely in a dark blue gown. Creamy skin and features that compelled a man to look at them twice in appreciation. A small beauty mark near the corner of the young woman's mouth gave her character and didn't detract at all from her attractiveness.

"She sings like a . . . a nightingale," Chance said.

"Just how many nightingales have you heard singing?" Ace asked.

"Well, then . . . a mockingbird. Only prettier."

"She *is* prettier than any mockingbird I've ever seen," Ace admitted.

"That's not what I—Ah, just shut up and let me look at her and listen to her."

That didn't seem like such a bad idea. They had been in their saddles for quite a few miles and Ace wouldn't mind sitting down. An empty table stood not far away, so he took hold of Chance's arm and urged him toward it. "Come on. You can see and hear her just as well from over there."

Chance didn't argue. He went with Ace without taking his eyes off the young woman standing beside the piano in the back of the room.

Ace was more interested in taking in all their surroundings, however, not just one small part. As they sat down, he let his gaze travel around the saloon. Checking for trouble like that was just a habit he had gotten into. The Jensen brothers might be young, but they had run into more than their share of ruckuses.

Most of the customers in the saloon appeared to be townies, cowboys from some of the spreads to the east, or miners from diggings up in the hills.

A group of men at one table caught Ace's eye. They wore range clothes but had a certain indefinable hard-bitten air about them that set them apart from the usual breed of puncher. For one thing, they all wore gun belts and holstered revolvers.

So did he and Chance, Ace reminded himself. That didn't mean there was anything wrong with them, just that sometimes they needed to be armed.

The bunch at that table was loud and boisterous even though the young woman at the piano was singing. One of them had a blond saloon girl on his lap and was pawing at her as he laughed. She looked a little uncomfortable, but she wasn't trying to get away from him.

The racket had started to annoy Chance and he frowned. "Don't those fellows know you're supposed to shut up and be quiet when a lady's singing? How can they not be in awe of such a beautiful voice?"

"They've probably guzzled down enough rotgut they don't care," Ace said.

"I don't care how drunk they are, they need to pipe down."

"Maybe so, but it's not our job to make 'em do it."

Chance looked like he wanted to argue, but he sighed and turned his attention back to the young woman. From time to time, he cast an irritated glance toward the noisy table across the room.

Chance wasn't the only one whose nerves those hombres were getting on, Ace realized a moment later. A bald, broad-shouldered man standing at the bar was glaring at the rowdies, too. He caught the blonde's eye, lifted a hand, and used his thumb to point at the table where Ace and Chance sat.

That had to be the boss. Crackerjack Sawyer had mentioned the saloonkeeper's name, and after a moment Ace recalled it—Hank Muller.

The blonde finally managed to wriggle free of the man who had her on his lap. She said something to him and stepped back quickly out of his reach when he tried to snag her again. Picking up a tray from an empty table nearby, she hurried across the room toward the Jensen brothers, looking relieved and worried at the same time.

As she came up to the table, she put a smile on her face. "Hello, boys," she said, trying to sound bright and cheerful but not quite managing it. "What can I get you to drink?"

Ace could tell that took an effort. "Beer for both of us." It was all they could really afford, and besides, neither of them was much of a heavy drinker, although Chance had cultivated a fondness for fine wine when they had enough dinero for it.

The blonde nodded. "I'll be right—"

A heavy footstep sounded behind her and she let out a little gasp as a man's hand grabbed her shoulder.

He hauled her around, revealing himself to be the hombre from whose lap she had escaped. "You'll get right back over to our table where you belong," he said, giving her a shove in that direction. "If these saddle tramps don't like it, that's just too damn bad!"

Chapter Three

Chance sprang out of his chair instantly, and Ace was just a second behind him.

"I don't really care what you call my brother and me," Chance said in a taut, angry voice, "but

23

you'd better apologize to the lady for treating her so rough."

"Lady?" the man repeated with a cocky, arrogant smirk on his face. "I don't see no lady here, only a saloon floozy who ain't no better than she has to be."

Ace said, "Mister, you're just making us like you even less."

The man laughed. "You reckon I give a damn about whether you like me?"

The blonde said, "Please, Pete, I told you I'd come right back after I got these boys their drinks—"

"I don't want any trouble in here, McLaren," Hank Muller interrupted her from the bar.

So the hombre gazing defiantly at them was Pete McLaren, Ace thought. The old-timer at the livery stable had mentioned him. From the sound of what Crackerjack Sawyer had said, McLaren was the biggest troublemaker in Lone Pine.

"Stay outta this, Muller," McLaren snapped. "This is between me and these saddle tramps."

"Really," Chance said. "Do I *look* like a saddle tramp?" He gestured to indicate his suit, which was of good quality even though it wasn't particularly new.

McLaren sneered again. "No, you look more like a damn, four-flushin' tinhorn, if you ask me."

Chance clenched his fist as he took half a step toward McLaren.

At the same time, the four men who had been sitting with McLaren got to their feet. They had been content to let their leader—as McLaren seemed to be—sally forth alone, but now that combat seemed to be imminent, they clearly didn't want to miss out on any of the action.

"Take it easy, Chance," Ace said quietly.

Five to two wasn't very good odds. They would buck those odds if they had to—they were Jensens, after all. Related to the famous clan or not, they didn't run from a fight, but Ace understood why Hank Muller didn't want such a ruckus breaking out in his saloon.

"As if the way you treated this girl isn't bad enough, you ruined a beautiful song," Chance said with a nod toward the piano and the lovely brunette who stood beside it.

She had stopped singing and the piano player had stopped tickling the ivories when the confrontation began, just like the rest of the saloon's customers had halted their drinking and talking to watch the unfolding drama.

The brunette smiled at Chance's compliment, but the expression vanished a moment later when McLaren chuckled coarsely and said, "Beautiful song? You mean that caterwaulin' that was going on a minute ago?"

Ace heard the hiss of Chance's sharply indrawn breath. McLaren had pushed him too far by insulting the singer.

25

Chance lunged forward, fist whipping up toward McLaren's face.

McLaren was fast. A few years older, he had more experience at brawling and jerked his head aside so Chance's punch went harmlessly past his ear. Stepping in, he hooked a left into Chance's midsection and then hammered a right into his chest.

Chance went backwards, his legs tangling with his brother's as Ace tried to charge into the battle. As they struggled to hang on to their balance, McLaren's friends sprang to the attack. Hank Muller bellowed for everybody to stop, but they ignored him. Customers at nearby tables scrambled to get away from the violence.

Ace and Chance got loose from each other, but only in time to be hit again. McLaren bored in on Chance, pounding him and making him retreat against one of the tables, while one of McLaren's companions punched Ace in the jaw and knocked him halfway around.

That gave one of the other men the opportunity to grab Ace from behind and pin his arms back. "Thrash him good, Lew!" the man called to his friend.

Grinning, the man who had already hit Ace once moved in, fists cocked to deal out punishment.

Ace was a little groggy from the blow to the jaw, but his instincts were still working. As Lew closed in, intent on handing him a beating, Ace jerked both knees up and lashed out with a double-footed kick that landed on the man's chest and sent him flying backwards. Lew crashed down on a table that collapsed with a splintering and rending of wood.

Ace's kick also made the man holding him stumble backwards in the opposite direction. He tripped and fell onto his back on the sawdust-littered floor, pulling Ace with him. Ace landed on top of him. Thinking clearly enough, he rammed an elbow into the man's belly and rolled to his feet.

Chance had recovered his wits and pushed off the table he was leaning against. He lowered his head and tackled McLaren as the hardcase tried to crowd him. They staggered around in a circle as Chance smashed a couple punches into McLaren's kidneys, figuring he ought to do whatever it took to win—especially when he and his brother were outnumbered more than two to one. He continued the punches, even though he knew Ace would have considered such blows to be dirty fighting.

McLaren bellowed in pain and anger, got his hands on Chance's chest, and shoved the younger man away. He threw a roundhouse punch that Chance leaned away from.

Getting his feet back under him, Chance put his own experience to work. He jabbed a right into McLaren's mouth that made blood spurt. He followed it a split second later with a left that rocked the man's head back, turning the tide of battle for a moment.

One of the other men snatched up a chair and brought it down on Chance's head. The crashing blow sent him to his knees. McLaren caught his balance, kicked Chance in the chest, and knocked him over on his back.

Ace grabbed the chair-wielder by the shoulder, jerked him around, and slammed a right to his jaw. The other man in McLaren's bunch clenched his fists together and swung them in a clubbing blow to the back of Ace's neck, knocking Ace off his feet. He landed facedown next to his brother, who was lying on his back.

"A nice, peaceful-looking town, you said," Ace groaned as he tried to push himself up.

Chance rolled onto his side. "How was I to know we'd wind up in a fight?"

Ace didn't bother answering that. He climbed onto his feet and helped Chance up. McLaren and the other four men were all standing, too, bunched together about fifteen feet away with angry glares on their bruised, bloody faces.

That pause was just a breather. The battle was about to resume.

"Everybody hold it right where you are, damn it!" The bellowed command came from the saloon's entrance, where a man stood just inside the batwings, which were still swinging back and forth a little behind him. As if his loud, harsh, gravelly voice wasn't enough to attract attention, the twin barrels of the shotgun he held looked as big around as cannons to anybody unlucky enough to be in front of them.

"Thank God you're here, Marshal," Hank Muller said. "I've already had a table and a chair busted up. There's no telling how much damage these hellions might have done if they'd kept fighting."

"Who are you calling hellions?" Chance asked resentfully. "We were just trying to help that girl who works for you."

Before Muller could reply, the newcomer stalked farther into the saloon, keeping the scattergun leveled in front of him. The customers who had tried to get away from the fight shrank back farther to make sure they were out of the line of fire.

The lawman was a medium-sized man of middle age. His clean-shaven face was tanned to the color of old saddle leather and seamed with numerous wrinkles, especially around the mouth and eyes. Thick white hair stood out in sharp contrast to the old black hat he wore. A marshal's badge was pinned to his vest. All it took was a glance to see that he still had all the bark on him, despite his years.

"I want to know who you *hellions* are," he said

to Ace and Chance. "I know McLaren and his pards, but I don't reckon I've ever seen you two before."

Ace did the introductions. "I'm Ace Jensen and this is my brother Chance. We just rode into town a while ago. Mr. Sawyer down at the livery stable will confirm that, and so will Colonel Howden at the Territorial House."

"Didn't take you long to start trouble, then, did it?"

The young woman at the piano spoke up. "They didn't start it, Marshal Dixon. McLaren and his friends did."

"That's a damn lie," McLaren said.

The brunette's face flushed angrily and she took a step forward.

The marshal told her, "You'd best just stay out of it, Miss Dupree."

Chance nodded toward the blonde saloon girl. "McLaren was roughing up that young lady, Marshal. My brother and I wouldn't have stepped in otherwise."

McLaren sneered. "There you go with that *lady* business again. You see any *ladies* in here, Marshal?"

Dixon didn't answer that.

McLaren went on. "Anyway, I didn't hear Dolly complainin' about the way I was treatin' her. Did you need somebody to protect you, Dolly?"

The blonde swallowed hard. "I . . . I guess it was all right . . . What you did, I mean, Pete. I know you wouldn't really hurt me."

"Damn right I wouldn't." McLaren cupped a hand under her chin. "You're my gal, ain't you?"

"I—Sure I am, Pete."

A disgusted look crossed Chance's face. Ace felt the same way. Even though the girl called Dolly hadn't liked the way McLaren was holding her on his lap, she was still smitten with the handsome young hardcase. Both Jensen brothers could tell that by the look in her eyes.

"Muller, who threw the first punch?" Marshal Dixon asked the saloonkeeper.

Muller didn't look happy about it, but he couldn't very well refuse to answer the lawman's question. Besides, there were plenty of witnesses who had seen the same thing he had. "That oung fella there did"—Muller pointed to Chance—"but McLaren provoked him by insulting Fontana."

"Doesn't matter," Dixon said. "Nobody appointed these two the defenders of fair womanhood." He jerked the barrels of the Greener to motion Ace and Chance toward the entrance. "You two are gonna spend your first night in Lone Pine in the calaboose."

Chapter Four

Ace was tempted to make some other sarcastic comment about what a peaceful place Lone Pine was as the cell door clanged shut behind them a short time later, but he didn't. For one thing, he didn't blame Chance for the predicament they were in. Pete McLaren was such an obnoxious son of a gun Ace knew *he* would have taken a punch at the varmint sooner or later if Chance hadn't beaten him to it.

Anyway, it wasn't Lone Pine's fault. The Jensen brothers seemed to carry trouble with them, wherever they went.

In the aisle between the iron-barred cells, two to a side in the stone-walled cell block behind the marshal's office, Dixon tucked the shotgun under his left arm. "For what it's worth, boys, Pete McLaren's a scoundrel, and he and his friends would be locked up right now, too, if I had my druthers."

"You're the law in this town," Chance said with a bitter edge in his voice. "Can't you lock up whoever you want to?"

"Not without cause. You haven't denied that you threw the first punch."

Chance gripped the bars and scowled.

Ace said, "We regret our part in the trouble, Marshal, but I've got to tell you . . . in the same situation, I reckon we'd do the same thing again."

Dixon's wrinkled face creased even more as he smiled. "I don't doubt it for a second. You young fellas got that look about you. When the Good Lord made you, He didn't put any backup in you, did he?"

"Not so's you'd notice," Ace said.

"What happens now?" Chance asked.

"You two cool your heels in there overnight. In the morning, there'll be a little hearing, and I reckon Judge Ordway will assess disturbing the peace fines on both of you, along with damages for what happened to Hank Muller's saloon. Pay up and you'll be free to go."

"That may be a problem," Ace said. "We don't have a lot of money."

Dixon shrugged. "Then you'll be guests of the town for the next thirty days, unless I miss my guess."

Chance groaned, went over to the bunk bolted to the wall, and sank down on one end of it. "Thirty days behind bars," he said miserably. "I don't know if I can stand it."

Ace sat down at the other end of the bunk. "We may not have any choice. I figured you'd win enough playing poker for us to replenish our supplies before we rode on."

"Yeah, that was my plan, too."

Dixon said, "I've found it doesn't pay to make too many plans. Life's always got some surprises in store."

Ace couldn't argue with that.

Marshal Hoyt Dixon was sitting at his desk in the office a short time later, using a thumb to pack tobacco in his pipe, when his night deputy Miguel Soriano came in.

"Everything's quiet in town, Marshal," Miguel reported. "I hear there was a ruckus at the Melodian. I would have given you a hand, but I was clear at the other end of town. Didn't hear any gunfire." He was a stocky young man whose dark hair and eyes and olive skin testified to his Spanish heritage.

In Lone Pine, the gringo settlers and the descendants of the families that had been there since the territory was part of Mexico . . . and Spain before that . . . got along well, mostly.

"There wasn't any," Dixon said. "Just a bunch of young fools beating on each other." He scratched a kitchen match on the sole of his boot and used it to light the pipe. When he had puffed it into life, he leaned back in the chair and inclined his head toward the cell block door. "Got a couple of 'em looked up back there. Young fellow named Jensen, who threw the first punch, and his brother."

"Rumor had it Pete McLaren was mixed up in it, too," Miguel said with a frown.

Dixon nodded solemnly. "He was. And when you get right down to the nub, it was McLaren who started it by manhandling Dolly Redding and then insulting Miss Dupree's singing."

The deputy's frown turned into an angry glare. "I'll bet Dolly stuck up for Pete, though, didn't she?"

"She did. You didn't expect any different, did you?"

Miguel let out a disgusted snort and shook his head.

Dixon had wondered before if Miguel was a mite sweet on Dolly. It was possible. He spent a considerable amount of time at the Melodian when he wasn't on duty. Hank Muller had half a dozen girls working for him, and it could have been any one of them who had caught the deputy's eye.

Or maybe Miguel just liked the whiskey Muller served. It was the best in town, after all.

Dixon smoked for a moment in silence, then shoved up from the chair. "I reckon I'm going home, now that you've made the rounds. I don't think those two back yonder will give you any trouble. To tell you the truth, even though I had to lock 'em up, they strike me as decent lads. Just a mite too hotheaded and rambunctious for their own good."

"That describes a lot of people." Miguel smiled. "It used to describe me until you sort of took me under your wing, Marshal."

"I'd say you're still a work in progress, Deputy," Dixon commented dryly. He left the office, smoke from the pipe wreathing his head as he stepped out onto the boardwalk.

In a private room at the Melodian, Pete McLaren threw back the whiskey in his glass and grimaced as the fiery liquor stung his lips where Chance Jensen's fist had split them. "I'm gonna get even with those two sons o' bitches if it's the last thing I do," he vowed.

"They're locked up and you ain't," Lew Merritt said as he poured a drink from the rapidly emptying bottle of Who-hit-John they had brought with them. He rubbed his chest. "Anyway, I'm the one who got kicked. Feels like a mule kicked me and stove in some of my ribs."

"You wouldn't be able to bitch so much if you had busted ribs," Vic Russell said with a grin.

The other two men at the table, Larry Dunn and Perry Severs, chuckled at Russell's gibe.

All five of them had a bit of a glow from the booze they had already consumed, but they weren't finished with their drinking, not by a long shot. McLaren picked up the bottle, drained the last few drops into his glass, then stood up.

A little shaky on his feet as he walked over to the door, he told himself it was from the whiskey, not from the way he'd been hit by that Jensen bastard.

The room didn't have any furnishings except the table and chairs where they had been sitting and an old sofa against one wall. An oil lamp sat on a shelf and cast its flickering glow, which barely reached the corners. Hank Muller sometimes held private, highstakes poker games back there. When McLaren had announced that he and his friends were going to be using the room for a while, Muller hadn't objected. The saloonkeeper had figured there had already been enough trouble for one night.

McLaren jerked open the door and looked around the smoky room. Dolly stood next to a table where several burly, bearded miners sat. She was smiling as she talked to them.

And that annoyed McLaren. "Dolly," he called. "Get your pretty little rump in here. And bring another bottle with you when you come."

She abandoned the miners without hesitation. That made McLaren feel a little better. She might bitch and moan about the way he treated her—that was just second nature for women, he had always found—but she still came whenever he called her.

She'd keep it up if she knew what was good for her.

He left the door open a few inches and went back to the table. Severs had gotten out a greasy pack of cards he carried around and started shuffling them. "Deal you in, Pete?"

"I got better things to do than play cards with you coyotes." McLaren picked up his glass and drained the little bit of whiskey that was in it.

Dolly came in carrying a fresh bottle.

He held the glass out to her and ordered, "Top that off, then leave the bottle on the table."

"Sure, Pete." She did what he'd said, then looked at him and asked, "Anything else?"

"Yeah." He caught hold of her hand with his free hand and dragged her toward the sofa. "C'mon over here with me."

"Pete"—she tugged away from him in a futile effort to escape his grip—"I'm still working."

"You really think Muller's gonna complain if you stay in here for a while?" McLaren laughed. "Hell, he's lucky every stick of furniture out there didn't get busted up, and he knows it."

"But all your friends are here—"

"They're playin' poker. They ain't gonna be payin' a lick of attention to us." He raised his voice. "Ain't that right, boys?"

Mutters of agreement came from the men, none of whom lifted his gaze from the cards Severs had dealt.

McLaren guzzled down the whiskey, then threw the glass across the room. Dolly gasped as it shattered against the wall. McLaren fell back on the sofa and pulled her with him. She sprawled across his lap.

He put a hand behind her head, buried his fingers in the thick, curly blond hair, and kissed her. He was none too gentle about it, and when he took his mouth away from her, she gasped again.

"When Pete McLaren kisses 'em, they *stay* kissed, by God." McLaren was happy. He'd had a good fight but had dodged jail for a change, he was pleasantly drunk, and he had a pretty girl in his lap, powerless to stop him from doing anything he wanted to her. Life was good.

Almost.

Back in the foggy chambers of his brain, a desire for revenge on those two strangers still smoldered. They had meddled in his fun, and they had to pay the price for that. Everybody else in Lone Pine knew better than mess with him, and the Jensen brothers had to learn that lesson, too.

He ran a hand over the soft, rounded curves of Dolly's body, relishing the warmth of her flesh.

She swatted ineffectually at him. "Pete, please don't," she whispered. "Those other fellas can see—"

"I told you they're not payin' any attention to us. And you don't have some tinhorn saddle tramp to come to your defense like some knight in shinin' armor, now do you? Bet you liked that, didn't you?" He closed his hand harder on her.

"You liked havin' some handsome stranger willin' to fight for you, didn't you?"

"No, Pete. I . . . I never even thought he was handsome. I didn't really look at him—"

"Might as well not have. All he was interested in was that Fontana Dupree. Why would anybody look at a calico cat like you whenever she's around?"

"You . . . you like to look at me, Pete."

"That's because I know what you are and how to treat you. And you like it, don't you?" He squeezed hard again. "Don't you?"

"I . . . guess I do."

"Kiss me and prove it."

She leaned in and brought her lips to his, and it was easier, not as rough.

That was how you broke a woman, McLaren thought. Hard and then soft, over and over again until she didn't have any will of her own left, just a hunger to please. He knew Dolly would do any damn thing he told her to, whether the other fellas were in the room or not.

He kept getting distracted, though, by thoughts of Ace and Chance Jensen and the grudge he carried against them. He brushed his lips against Dolly's ear and whispered, "You know those fellas who wanted to help you? I'm gonna make those sons of bitches wish they'd never been born."

Chapter Five

"Hey, Marshal!" Chance yelled as he gripped the cell door's bars. "You out there, Marshal?"

The cell block door swung open. The young man who came from the office wasn't Marshal Hoyt Dixon, though. "What's all the commotion back here?" His hand rested on the butt of his holstered revolver. A badge was pinned to his flannel shirt.

"You must be the night deputy," Ace said from where he was sitting on the bunk.

"That's right. Miguel Soriano's my name, and I like for this jail to be nice and peaceful at night. That means not a lot of carrying-on."

"We had to get your attention some way," Chance said. "We have an intolerable, inhumane situation here."

Deputy Soriano frowned. "And that would be . . . ?"

"There's only one bunk in this cell, and it's too narrow for more than one person. I'm fond of my brother, you understand, but not to that extent."

Ace said, "I suggested we flip a coin for the bunk and the loser could sleep on the floor, but Chance pointed out there are three other empty cells in here, each with its own bunk, so it seems reasonable to move one of us."

The deputy's eyes narrowed with suspicion. "This is some sort of trick. You fellas are trying to break out of here."

"Not at all," Ace said. "We'll give you our word on that, if you'd like."

Miguel's frown didn't go away, but he rubbed his blunt chin as he thought about the suggestion. After a moment he said, "The marshal told me he figured you two were decent sorts."

"That didn't stop him from arresting us," Chance said.

"Marshal Dixon follows the law. According to that, you fellas started that fight in the Melodian. It wouldn't matter to the marshal if he liked you or not."

Ace said, "Yeah, he explained all that. But doesn't it sound to you like he'd trust us enough to let one of us move to another cell?"

Miguel mulled over the idea for another minute or so, then said, "I'll get the keys. But I'll tell you right now, try anything funny and I'll shoot."

Chance held up both hands, palms out. "No tricks. You have our word on that."

Miguel went back into the office, then returned a moment later with a ring of keys in his left hand. He unlocked the cell directly across the aisle and opened the door, then drew his gun with his right hand and pointed it at the Jensen brothers standing at the bars. "Both of you back up as far as you can." His thumb was looped over the hammer of the Colt. "All the way against the wall beside the bunk."

They backed away from the door.

Satisfied, Miguel stuck one of the keys in the lock and turned it. "Now one of you—and I don't care which one—can come out. Make up your mind who's moving, though. If both of you take a step, I'm liable to start shooting."

"Take it easy, Deputy," Ace said. "I'll change cells. That all right with you, Chance?"

"Sure. It doesn't really make any difference."

Keeping his hands in plain sight and not making any sudden moves, Ace went to the cell door, swung it open, and stepped directly across the aisle into the opposite cell.

"Close it," Miguel ordered.

Ace did so, putting himself securely behind bars again.

Miguel pushed shut the door of what had just become Chance's cell and removed the key from the lock.

"See, no trouble," Ace said. "We don't want to give anybody an excuse to keep us locked up any longer than necessary."

"Pay the fine the judge hands down in the morning and you'll be free to go."

Chance sighed and shook his head. "Easier said than done."

It wasn't the first night the Jensen brothers had spent behind bars, but that didn't make it any more pleasant. The mattress on the bunk was thin and hard, and the lone blanket in each cell was scratchy. Neither of them could completely forget that iron bars stood between them and their freedom, and that chafed at their spirits.

Eventually they slept, and when Ace woke up the next morning, he smelled the enticing aroma of coffee brewing. Judging by that, it was good coffee, too.

A tall, lantern-jawed man with a loose-jointed gait ambled into the cell block carrying a tray. A badge was pinned to the black vest he wore over a collarless white shirt. "Mornin', boys," he greeted the prisoners with a friendly grin. "Got some breakfast here for you from the Lone Pine Café. You're in for a treat. That ol' Scandahoovian who runs it rustles up some mighty good grub."

"You must be the marshal's other deputy," Ace said as he moved to the door.

Across the aisle, a fuzzy-haired Chance was sitting up, yawning and rubbing his face as he tried to come fully awake.

"Yes, sir, that's me," the newcomer said. "Norm Sutherland's the name. When I took over for him this mornin', Miguel, I mean Deputy Soriano, told me about splittin' the two of you up. Seemed like a good idea to me. No need for crowdin' when we ain't got an excess o' guests."

Since Ace was standing by the cell door, Deputy Sutherland slid the tray through the opening to him. On it was a plate heaped with flapjacks and bacon. "You can eat that without a fork. I'll get the other tray, then bring each of you a cup of coffee."

"We've stayed in hotels with worse service," Chance said.

"Worse food, too," Ace said around a mouthful of flapjack.

The coffee tasted as good as it smelled. It didn't come from the café. Deputy Sutherland had brewed it on the potbellied stove in the marshal's office.

The deputy propped a shoulder against the jamb of the open cell block door, sipping from a cup of his own. "I hear you boys tangled with Pete McLaren and his bunch."

"That's right," Chance said. "They're the ones who ought to be locked up in here, not my brother and me."

"Well, I reckon Marshal Dixon did what he thought was proper. Never knowed him to do otherwise. But the judge'll sort out all o' that in a little while. The marshal will be here around nine to take you over to court." Sutherland took another sip of coffee. "Just between us fellas, though, I don't blame anybody for wallopin' Pete McLaren. You can tell that varmint's got it comin' just by lookin' at him."

"He was manhandling one of the saloon girls, and he was rude to the young woman who was singing."

45

"Well, gettin' manhandled now and then is sorta part of a saloon gal's job, I reckon, but there's such a thing as bein' too rough. McLaren's got a reputation for treatin' gals poorly. Of course, he treats just about ever'body poorly except for those no-account pards of his."

"This was a girl with blond, curly hair," Ace said.

Sutherland nodded. "Dolly Redding. Not a bad sort. Not as brittle around the edges as most o' that kind. Not yet, anyway."

Since the deputy seemed to enjoy talking, Chance asked him, "What do you know about the singer?"

"Really good-lookin' gal with brown hair and a little mole on her face? That's Fontana Dupree. Wouldn't surprise me if that isn't her real name, but it's what she's gone by ever since she showed up in Lone Pine so that's what ever'body calls her. When she sings, it's like a little bit o' heaven."

"You won't get any argument from me about that," Chance said.

Sutherland grinned. "Fell in love with her as soon as you laid eyes on her, didn't you? Well, I wouldn't get your hopes up. Most fellas around here fall in love with her right off. It don't get 'em nowhere. Fontana's friendly to ever'body but don't get too close to nobody. She don't do nothin' but sing in Hank Muller's place, neither. Nobody takes her upstairs. Her singin' and the way she looks is enough to draw fellas in there, so I reckon Muller's satisfied with the arrangement."

"Maybe I'll get a chance to talk to her sometime," Chance hoped.

"You just go on thinkin' that," Sutherland said, "for all the good it'll do you."

Ace and Chance had finished their breakfasts and were lingering over the coffee when Marshal Dixon came into the office. They heard the front door open and close, and then the grizzled old lawman appeared in the cell block doorway, followed by Deputy Sutherland.

Dixon had the key ring in one hand and a shotgun tucked under his other arm. "You fellas ready to go to court?"

"We're ready," Ace said, although his reply was somewhat dispirited. They might be able to scrape up enough money to pay their fines if the judge didn't come down too hard on them, but throw in the damages to Hank Muller's saloon and it was unlikely they'd be able to manage that. They might have to throw themselves on the mercy of the court.

Dixon handed the keys to Sutherland and stepped back to cover the prisoners with the shotgun while the deputy unlocked the cells. Ace and Chance straightened up their clothes, swatted at hair made unruly by restless sleep, and put on their hats.

"I don't think you boys plan on trying anything," Dixon said, "but just in case I'm wrong about you, I'll have this Greener pointed at you the whole way. You'd do well to remember that."

"It's hard to overlook a shotgun, Marshal," Chance said.

"We're not going to give you any trouble," Ace added.

Dixon marched them out of the building, leaving Sutherland to hold down the fort. The town hall, where the judge would hold court, was almost directly across the street.

Ace felt a lot of eyes on them as they crossed the street. He couldn't blame the townspeople for gawking at them. Life on the frontier was monotonous. Anything out of the ordinary, even something as simple as a couple hombres facing charges for disturbing the peace, would attract quite a bit of attention.

Something about the sensation he felt at the moment was different, though, Ace realized as the hair on the back of his neck stood up and the skin prickled. It wasn't just ordinary curiosity that he was feeling.

It was more like somebody had painted a big fat target right in the middle of his back.

Chapter Six

Pete McLaren's lips pulled back from his teeth in a snarl as he watched Marshal Dixon escorting the Jensen brothers to the town hall. McLaren stood at the window of a second-floor room in the Melodian with the curtains pulled aside enough for him to look through the gap. He wore only the bottom half of a pair of long underwear.

His head throbbed from all the whiskey he had put away the night before. His vision was a little blurry, but he could see well enough to make out those damned Jensens. He had a clear angle at them and could have put bullets in their backs. They never would have known what hit them.

McLaren didn't want that, though. He wouldn't mind seeing them dead, but he wanted them to know who was responsible.

Besides, if he picked up his revolver from the dresser where it was lying and gunned them down, he'd have to get out of Lone Pine in a hurry. True, the marshal was an old codger, one of the deputies was a grinning half-wit, and the other was a greaser, but taken all together they might be able to cause some trouble for him. McLaren didn't want that yet. He had plans.

"Pete, come on back to bed," Dolly urged

sleepily from the tangle of sheets where she lay with her blond hair spread out over a pillow.

McLaren glanced over his shoulder. He could see the curve of a pale, smooth-skinned hip protruding from the covers. It was a tempting sight. He looked out the window again and saw that Dixon and the prisoners had reached the town hall and were going in.

A woman crossing the street toward the town hall caught his attention. The angle of her path told him she could have come from the saloon. Her trim shape and brown hair made him realize he was looking at Fontana Dupree, even though he couldn't see her face.

What was that snooty bitch up to this morning, he wondered?

Well, it was none of his business.

When Dolly said in a pouting tone, "Peeete . . . ," he let the curtain fall closed and turned away from the window.

A quick step took him to the side of the bed. His hand flashed out, the palm landing with a rousing *crack* on that bare hip. Dolly yelped and jumped.

McLaren grinned when he saw the red mark his hand had left on her skin. "Now that you're awake good and proper . . ."

Judge Alfred Ordway was a scrawny little gent with thinning hair, pince-nez spectacles perched on his nose, and a sour look on his face. Ace had a bad feeling as soon as he got a good look at the judge.

Ordway seemed like the sort of fellow whose only pleasure in life would be handing down harsh punishments to those unlucky enough to come before him in court. He sat behind a table at the front of the room. Two tables were arranged before it for the prosecution and the defense, and several rows of chairs had been set up for spectators, as well as a railed-off jury box to one side.

It was just a simple hearing so there were no spectators or jury or even a prosecutor . . . just the judge, the marshal, and the two prisoners.

Marshal Dixon herded Ace and Chance up to the open area between the defense and prosecution tables and told them in a quiet voice, "This'll do."

Ordway continued studying some papers on the table in front of him for a moment longer, then looked up, grasped the gavel lying beside the papers, and rapped the table sharply. "Court's in session," he said in a voice as sour as his expression. "I see by these documents before me that these two young men are charged with disturbing the peace."

"That's right, Your Honor," Dixon said.

"Said charges stemming from an altercation at Henry Muller's Melodian Saloon."

Even though it wasn't really a question, Dixon said, "Yes, sir."

"Were they fighting each other?"

"No, sir. It was these two against Pete McLaren and his friends—um, Russell, Merritt, Severs, and"—he hesitated a moment—"Dunn. That's the other one's name."

"Yes, I'm familiar with all of them. They've appeared before this court in the past on a variety of charges." Judge Ordway squinted through his pince-nez. "I must say, I'm a bit surprised not to see them, since they were involved."

"According to all the witnesses, this fella here threw the first punch, Your Honor," Dixon said with a nod toward Chance.

Ordway sniffed. "State your name, young man."

"It's Chance Jensen, Your Honor."

Ordway glared at him. "Are you trying to tell me that your mother named you *Chance?*"

"Um, no, Your Honor, my real name is Benjamin Jensen, but I've never really used it."

Ordway looked at Ace and snapped, "And you?"

"William Jensen, sir. But I've always gone by Ace."

Ordway leaned back in his chair and said, "It's not relevant to the case, but this is my courtroom, so I'll ask . . . why in heaven's name?"

Ace glanced at Chance, then said, "You mean, why are we called Ace and Chance? Well, you see, Your Honor, our mother, um, passed away when we were born. We were raised by a friend of hers, and he's the one who gave us those nicknames. We never really knew anything else."

"This friend of hers . . . I take it he was a gambling man?"

Ace wondered if that was going to make the judge even more disposed not to like him and Chance, but he had to answer the question honestly. "Yes, sir, he was. But he always played a straight game."

"And taught us to do the same," Chance added, which Ace thought might not have helped that much.

"All right, but your names are being entered in my records as William and Benjamin Jensen. Now, do you have anything to say for yourselves?"

Chance said, "Just that there were . . . what do you call 'em? Mitigating circumstances, Your Honor. That's it. Mitigating circumstances." He paused while Judge Ordway waited. "What I mean to say is, Your Honor, I might've thrown the first punch, but that fella McLaren had it coming."

"I've no doubt about that, but it's our duty as civilized citizens of society to allow duly established authorities to deal with those who 'have it coming.'" Ordway looked at Ace. "You stepped in to help your brother, I presume?"

"Yes, sir, Your Honor."

"A somewhat lesser offense, in the eyes of this

court, than striking the initial blow, even though the charges are the same. Therefore, Benjamin Jensen, I find you guilty of disturbing the peace and fine you twenty-five dollars. William Jensen, I also find you guilty of disturbing the peace and fine you ten dollars."

Ace started to breathe a little easier. They had about thirty dollars between them, and he had a spare ten-dollar gold piece hidden in his boot that Chance didn't know about, so they would be able to pay their fines. It wouldn't leave them with much.

Then he remembered there were damages to consider, too, and he had to bite back a groan of despair.

Ordway turned to Dixon. "Marshal, have you established the amount of damages incurred by Mr. Muller in the course of the altercation?"

"I talked to Hank—I mean, Mr. Muller—this morning, Your Honor, and he said fifty dollars would cover it."

"Very well, then. Plus another five dollars for court costs, coming to a grand total of ninety dollars. You may pay the marshal, gentlemen, and you'll be free to go." Ordway picked up his gavel to signal that the hearing was at an end.

"Uh, Your Honor," Ace said before the gavel could fall. "I'm afraid we don't have that much. We can pay the fines and maybe the court costs, but the damages . . . well, we just don't have it."

Ordway looked more than ever like he'd been sucking on a lemon. "In that case, I have no choice but to sentence you to—"

"That's all right, Your Honor," a new voice came from the back of the courtroom. "I'll pay the fines, the damages. All of it."

Ace, Chance, and Marshal Dixon looked around, and Judge Ordway craned his neck to see who had spoken. Fontana Dupree stood just inside the door, wearing a brown tweed outfit much more demure than the silk gown that had been clinging to her the night before. She looked just as lovely as ever as she stood there holding a small, beaded bag.

Judge Ordway cleared his throat. "Miss . . . Dupree, is it?"

She favored him with a dazzling smile. "That's right, Your Honor. I don't suppose you've ever heard me sing—"

"I wouldn't go so far as to say that, my dear."

The judge still had blood flowing in his veins, so Fontana had the same effect on him as she did on every other man, Ace supposed. At least, Ordway looked considerably less prune-faced.

He hadn't forgotten his legal responsibilities, though. "You say you intend to pay what these two young men owe?"

"That's right." Fontana came forward and opened the bag. "Ninety dollars, I believe you said?" She took out four double eagles and a

55

ten-dollar gold piece and dropped them into the palm of a visibly startled Marshal Hoyt Dixon. "I think that's the correct amount?"

Dixon looked down at the coins in his hand. "Uh, yes'm. It sure is."

Chance said, "We can't let you do that—"

"Nonsense," Fontana interrupted him. "It's the least I can do. I know you got involved in the first place because of the way McLaren was treating poor Dolly, but you never took a swing at him until he insulted my singing." Something sparkled in her eyes as she added, "I can't allow such gallantry to go unrewarded."

Chance looked like he wanted to argue some more, so Ace said quickly, "We're mighty obliged to you, Miss Dupree. We'll pay you back just as soon as we can."

"I'm not worried about it. But if you'd like to discuss the matter . . . you can come to the Melodian again this evening." She was smiling at Chance as she spoke.

Ace recognized the look on his brother's face. Chance was in love, or what passed for it, anyway, given his fiddle-footed nature.

Judge Ordway said, "Given that the fines and damages have been paid, this case is closed and court is adjourned." The gavel smacked down on the table. "All of you can get out of here now."

Ace, Chance, and Fontana left the courtroom and stepped out onto the boardwalk.

Marshal Dixon followed them and warned in a stern voice, "You boys don't give me any reason to arrest you again, you hear?"

"Don't worry, Marshal," Ace said. "We're peaceable men. And we intend to be the most law-abiding folks in Lone Pine from now on."

"You do that," Dixon said. "Come by the office and pick up your guns anytime you're of a mind to." With a curt nod he walked off toward his office and the jail.

"That was a noble sentiment you expressed," Fontana said to the Jensen brothers, "but I'm not sure you'll be able to live up to it."

"Why not?" Ace asked.

"Because I think Pete McLaren might have something to say about that. He's not the sort of man who takes it lightly whenever someone crosses him."

"So you think he'll try to stir up more trouble?" Chance said.

"I think you can bet that hat you're wearing on it," Fontana said. "But in the meantime, you're coming to the Melodian tonight to hear me sing again, aren't you?"

"We wouldn't miss it for the world," Chance said with a smile.

Chapter Seven

Ace and Chance walked into the lobby of the Territorial House a short time later.

From his usual post behind the desk, Colonel Charles Howden said, "Good morning, gentlemen. I heard about the unfortunate events of yesterday evening, so I knew you wouldn't be using your room last night. I held on to it for you, though, since you'd already paid for it and left your belongings there."

"Thanks, Colonel," Ace said. "I hope having a couple convicted jailbirds here doesn't bring disgrace on your hotel."

"Oh, far from it!" Howden exclaimed. "I don't think there are many of the so-called respectable citizens of Lone Pine, myself included, who wouldn't have liked to punch Pete McLaren in the face at one time or another."

Chance chuckled. "I got the feeling he's not well-liked around here."

"You can say that again," Howden agreed. "Too many of us have been around long enough to remember when this place was called Buzzard's Roost, and Otis McLaren was the king of the roost."

"Otis McLaren?" Ace repeated.

"Pete's older brother. Although there's enough

difference in their ages it's more like Otis is Pete's uncle or even his father. He was even worse than Pete, if you can imagine that."

"He must've been a real hell-raiser."

"That's right. He was rumored to have been behind all sorts of lawlessness back in those days. A regular road agent."

"What happened to him?" Chance asked.

"Gone," Howden replied with a shake of his head. "No one knows where. My theory is that he decided the pickings were too slim in these parts—he was crooked *and* ambitious—so he took off for greener pastures and probably got himself killed . . . or he went to Washington, changed his name, and became a politician."

Ace laughed. "I'm surprised he didn't take his brother with him."

"Pete was too young at the time, barely more than a kid. Otis probably didn't want to be saddled with taking care of him." Howden leaned on the desk and went on in a confidential tone. "Although . . . I've wondered sometimes if he doesn't send money back to Pete. The boy's never held a job in his life, at least not an honest one, but he always seems to have funds." The colonel straightened up. "Ah, listen to me go on, gossiping like a little old lady. My apologies if I bored you."

"Not at all," Ace assured him.

"Speaking of gossip . . . I believe I saw you

talking to the lovely Miss Dupree when you left the town hall."

"That's right. She was, uh, thanking us for sticking up for her against McLaren last night." Chance didn't want it getting around the settlement that Fontana had paid their fines and damages for them.

Ace understood that and felt the same way, so he just nodded in agreement with what Chance had said.

"Well, if there's anything I can do for you fellows . . ."

"I think we're fine," Ace said. "I figured we'd go on up to the room and maybe get some rest."

"Yeah," Chance said. "Those bunks in the jail aren't the most comfortable place to sleep."

"That's good," Colonel Howden said with a smile. "I don't need any more competition."

Just after midday, both brothers woke up hungry. Since their breakfast in jail that morning had been so good, they went in search of the establishment that had provided it. Colonel Howden gave them directions to the Lone Pine Café.

The place was run by a man named Lars Hilfstrom, with the able assistance of his wife and three daughters, all of them strapping blondes. The café was still open for lunch when Ace and Chance walked in, and they were soon enjoying bowls of hearty beef stew washed down by cups of strong black coffee. The meal was good. It was almost enough to make them forget about the unpleasant things that had happened since they rode into Lone Pine.

Almost.

Even if they *had* forgotten, it wouldn't have lasted. Soon they were reminded of the previous night's events by a tall, skinny gent in a well-worn suit who came into the café, looked around, and then started toward the table where Ace and Chance were sitting.

"Looks like trouble headed this way," Ace said quietly when he noticed the stranger approaching.

"What makes you say that?" Chance asked.

"Look at his fingers. Those are ink stains. That means he's a newspaperman."

That deduction quickly proved to be correct. The newcomer, who wore spectacles and had brown hair, walked up to the table. "Good afternoon, gentlemen. Am I correct in assuming that you're the Jensen brothers?"

"That's right. I'm Ace. He's Chance."

"My name is Lee Emory. I'm the editor and publisher of the *Lone Pine Sentinel.* Do you mind if I join you?"

Ace and Chance were both too polite to say no.

Chance nodded toward one of the empty chairs. "Help yourself."

Lee Emory sat down and told the buxom

Hilfstrom girl wearing a gingham apron, "I'll just have a cup of coffee, Ilsa."

"Yah, Mr. Emory. I be right back."

Emory smiled at Ace and Chance. "You're probably wondering what I'm doing here."

"Not really," Ace said. "You probably want to interview us for your newspaper."

"How did you know that?" Emory asked, looking surprised.

"We've been in a lot of settlements like this," Chance said. "Couple strangers ride in, get in a big fight, and wind up being thrown in jail. That counts as news in a place like Lone Pine, I reckon. No offense to the town."

"It's true, there's not a lot of excitement here." Emory let out a rueful chuckle. "Some weeks it's a real struggle to fill up the pages. Once you get past the births and the deaths, not a lot happens most of the time. But then there'll be a new strike at one of the mines, or a ranch will lose some cattle to rustlers—"

"If it was me, I'd wonder where Pete McLaren was while that rustling was going on," Chance said.

Emory took a sip of the coffee Ilsa Hilfstrom brought to him, then leaned forward. "That's exactly what many of us around here wonder. The same thought occurs to us every time some horses go missing, or a stagecoach is held up, or any other banditry takes place. So far, no one's ever been able to prove anything along those lines."

"What about the county sheriff?" Ace asked.

"There's a deputy responsible for this part of the county, but to be blunt, he's not worth much. I'm pretty sure he got the job because he's somebody's nephew or cousin."

Chance said, "If it's help you want with your owlhoot problem, I'm afraid we're not interested. We're not lawmen or bounty hunters or range detectives."

Ace added, "We're just a couple hombres on our way from where we've been to wherever it might be we're going."

"Still, you clashed with McLaren and his bunch, and like you said, Mr. Jensen, that's news."

"Call me Ace. Mr. Jensen's my pa." Wherever *he* was . . . if he was even still alive. "We never heard of Pete McLaren until yesterday evening, Mr. Emory. We can't shed any light on his activities, and there's really not much to say about what happened in the Melodian."

"McLaren was treating a woman badly," Chance said, "and then he insulted another lady. My brother and I don't take kindly to behavior like that."

"You're talking about the lovely Miss Dupree," Emory said.

"That's right."

"She's quite an excellent singer, from what I've heard. Something of a mystery woman, though."

Chance hitched a shoulder up and down in a shrug. "A lady's got a right to her secrets."

Emory smiled. "I have a sister. I know what you mean. But if I could ask a few more questions . . ."

"Go ahead," Ace told him.

"Where are you gentlemen from?"

"We were born in Denver, but you couldn't say we're *from* there, because we've lived all over, all our lives. Lately we've spent some time up in Montana and then in Colorado. We drifted south from there and wound up here."

"Where do you intend to go next?"

"We haven't made up our minds about that," Chance said. "We don't like to plan things too far in advance. Sort of takes the spice out of life, don't you think?"

"I've always stayed in one place for a good long time," Emory said dryly, "so I wouldn't really know. I've been here in Lone Pine for five years."

"Was it still called Buzzard's Roost when you came here?" Ace asked.

"Ah, you know something of the town's history, then. No, the citizens had already started calling it Lone Pine. Things weren't as settled then as they are now, but the town was starting to put its wild days behind it."

"Seems like Pete McLaren wouldn't mind bringing those wild days back," Ace said.

"I don't suppose he would. He probably feels like he has a legacy to live up to. Have you heard of Otis McLaren?"

"Colonel Howden over at the hotel told us about him. Did you know him?"

Emory shook his head. "No, he had already left town before my sister and I got here. His departure was recent enough, though, that I heard a lot about him. All the respectable citizens were glad to see him go. Actually, he's supposed to have had such a hair-trigger temper that even many of the more disreputable characters in town were happy he was gone. Having Otis McLaren here was sort of like having a panther pacing around town. You never knew when he was going to go on a rampage." The newspaperman leaned back in his chair and smiled. "I must be slipping. I think you two have interviewed me more than the other way around. I have another question."

"Shoot," Chance said.

"An appropriate choice of words, because I wanted to ask you about your last name. There's a famous gunfighter named Jensen, and although they're not as well known, he has a couple rather adventurous brothers, too."

Ace shook his head. "We're not related . . . but as it happens, we *are* acquainted with Smoke, Matt, and Luke."

"Really? Do you have any interesting stories about them you might be able to share?"

Ace thought about the dangers he and Chance had shared with the other Jensens, as well as the wildly exaggerated yarns that drink-addled scribblers spun about Smoke in dime novels. He shook his head and said, "No, the times we met up were all pretty boring. We just sort of sat around in rocking chairs and talked."

"Is that so?" Emory looked like he didn't really believe Ace's answer, but he didn't press the issue. "Well, I suppose I have enough for a story. And of course it may not be over yet."

"What do you mean by that?" Chance said.

"Pete McLaren is the sort who holds a grudge against anyone who defies him. Have you been warned about that?"

"Several times," Chance said.

"Then you know to be on the lookout for more trouble."

Ace glanced at Chance. "That seems to be pretty much what we do all the time."

Chapter Eight

The afternoon passed peacefully in Lone Pine, however. Ace and Chance went to the livery stable to check on their horses and spent quite a while jawing with Crackerjack Sawyer. The old liveryman wanted to know all the details of the brawl with Pete McLaren.

When Ace and Chance finished filling him in on that, Crackerjack asked, "How's that damn Yankee at the hotel treatin' you fellas?"

"Colonel Howden's been very friendly and helpful so far," Ace said. "Although he commented that he was surprised you recommended his hotel to us."

Crackerjack grunted. "Yeah, I'll just bet he was. That ol' blue belly's got it in for ever'body from the South. He don't believe nothin' good can come from any of us."

"The war's been over for quite a while," Chance pointed out. "Most people have stopped holding grudges about it."

"Don't you believe that, son. Folks may *say* they don't hold any grudges, but deep down they do. 'Specially those who went back after it was all over and saw what the Yanks did to their homes. Don't matter how bad they hated the South, they didn't have to take it out on innocent families. I got no problem with soldiers fightin' soldiers, but they made war on women and kids and even livestock, burnin' and lootin' and killin' anybody who happened to be in their way." Crackerjack shook his head. "No, sir, there ain't no forgettin' or forgivin' that, and there never will be."

Having been born during the early days of the war, Ace and Chance were too young to have any memories of the great, nation-rending conflict. Ennis "Doc" Monday, the gambler who had raised them, hadn't been of a particularly partisan bent, so he hadn't supported or condemned either side. He was content to play cards and take anybody's money, be they Yank or Reb.

Because of those factors, the Jensen brothers were happy to let the war stay in the past. They left the livery stable soon after Crackerjack's heartfelt speech.

They spent the rest of the afternoon reading some of Colonel Howden's month-old newspapers and getting caught up on the news of the world. Then, as dusk settled over the town, they strolled up to the Lone Pine Café for supper. The steak, potatoes, greens, biscuits, gravy, and deep-dish apple pie that Mrs. Hilfstrom and her daughters served up were just as good as the stew had been at lunch.

As they stood in front of the café after the meal, pleasantly full, Chance rocked back and forth on his heels. "I reckon I could use a drink now."

"At the Melodian?" Ace asked.

Chance grinned. "Where else?"

They headed in the direction of Hank Muller's saloon. On the way, Ace spotted a familiar figure headed toward them on the boardwalk.

"Deputy Soriano," he greeted the lawman as Miguel came up to them.

"I heard you fellas were out of jail," Miguel said. "Miss Dupree paid your fines and the damages, right?"

"We'd just as soon keep that to ourselves," Chance said, glancing around to see if anyone was within earshot. "And we're going to pay her back."

"That was pretty nice of her, but I can understand why she did it. She doesn't have any more use for Pete McLaren than most of the other folks around here."

"You haven't seen McLaren around this evening, have you?" Ace asked.

Miguel thought about it and shook his head. "Can't say as I have. He and his friends either rode out of town, or they're lying low somewhere. You boys worried about him jumping you?"

"Everybody keeps warning us he's liable to."

"Yeah, that sounds about right. You know, if McLaren and his friends were to attack you, that would give Marshal Dixon and me a good excuse to throw them in jail."

Chance said, "Hey, if they killed us, you could keep them locked up even longer."

"That's right," Miguel said, grinning. "I guess there's some truth to that old saying about there being a silver lining in every cloud."

At the far northern end of town stood a small building that was little more than a clapboard, tarpaper, and tin-roof shack. Inside the front room, which was lit only by a small lamp with a smoke-grimed chimney, were a few crude tables and a plank bar. A grossly fat man named José owned and ran the place, serving tequila as well as whiskey he made himself.

Most men drank the tequila, since the whiskey had been known to give an hombre the blind staggers.

At the moment, only five customers—Pete McLaren, Perry Severs, Larry Dunn, Lew Merritt, and Vic Russell—were in José's. That was enough to almost fill the place up. They had been in the squalid little bar all afternoon, ever since McLaren had snuck down the rear stairs of the Melodian and met the other four there.

Merritt, Russell, and Dunn were drunk. Not fallingdown snockered, but their words were slurry and their movements a little unsteady.

McLaren and Severs had been drinking, too, but their tolerance was higher and they hadn't put away as much tequila.

"It's gettin' dark, Pete," Severs said. "If you're planning on doing anything before those bastards get to Muller's place, we ought to be movin' along."

McLaren tossed back the inch or so of tequila he still had in the dirty glass he clutched. "You're right. We've stayed out of sight long enough. Damn it, we oughtn't to have to hide in Lone Pine. This oughta be *our* town, by God! People have forgot this used to be Buzzard's Roost, and my big brother was cock o' the walk!"

With his multiple chins wobbling, José said from the other side of the bar, "You are not Otis McLaren, amigo. These days, no one is."

Pete glared across the bar for a second before his arm shot out. He grabbed the front of José's soiled apron and jerked him forward. It wasn't easy to budge the man's formidable bulk, but Pete was mad enough he didn't care. "Listen, I know you used to ride with Otis before you got so fat and crippled up, but that don't give you any right to talk bad about me."

"Señor Pete, I-I meant no offense!" José stammered. "I was just saying that your brother, he was a very special man. Tough and hard, the likes of which we no longer see."

"Yeah, well, Otis ain't here and I am, which I reckon makes me the toughest man in these parts!"

"No one would argue that with you, señor. No one with any sense."

Pete let go of José's apron and gave him a shove back away from the bar. "That's more like it. Vic, Lew, Larry . . . come on."

Lew Merritt lifted a bleary-eyed gaze. "Where're we goin'?"

"We talked about it earlier, you damn sot. We're gonna teach those Jensen boys a lesson they'll never forget."

"Oh, yeah," Russell said. "They got it comin', don't they, Pete?"

"They damn sure do," McLaren said. "And they're gonna wish they never heard of Pete McLaren, let alone crossed him."

After saying good evening to Deputy Soriano, Ace and Chance started toward the Melodian again, but they had gone less than a block when a familiar figure stepped out of one of the general stores ahead of them. The mercantile was still open and probably would be for a while yet.

Lee Emory smiled as he saw them. "We meet again." He wore a suit coat and a hat, which he hadn't had on earlier.

He wasn't alone, either. An attractive young woman stood at his side. Ace recalled Emory mentioning a sister who had come to Lone Pine with him, and now that he looked closer, he could see the family resemblance between the two of them, even though Emory appeared to be considerably older.

Ace's hunch was confirmed when the newspaperman said, "I'd like to introduce my sister. Meredith, this is Ace and Chance Jensen. Fellows, my sister Meredith Emory."

She put her hand out in a forthright fashion. "I'm pleased to meet you, gentlemen." Like her brother, she had a bit of an accent that placed her origins as back east somewhere.

She was a lot prettier than Lee Emory, though, Ace thought. Meredith was slender—*coltish* was a good word to describe her, he decided—and had raven hair that framed an appealing face highlighted by sharp, intelligent eyes. He shook hands with her and found that she had a good grip, too.

A few ink stains on her fingers told him she worked alongside her brother at the newspaper press.

Meredith shook hands with Chance as well, then said in a blunt but friendly tone, "Where are you fellows headed this evening?"

"We, uh, thought we'd go down to the Melodian for a while," Chance said.

"An excellent choice. I'm told Miss Dupree has a beautiful singing voice, and even though I've seen her around town only a few times, I know she's quite lovely. I'm sure she's the main reason you intend to patronize the Melodian, but I've also heard that Mr. Muller serves fine libations."

Emory smiled faintly as he said, "My sister has a habit of speaking her mind in no uncertain terms."

Meredith turned her head and looked up at him. "And what's wrong with that, I ask you?"

"Not a thing as far as I'm concerned, Miss Emory," Ace said quickly. "In fact, I find it pretty refreshing."

"You see, Lee, no one likes a mealy-mouthed person."

"No one could ever accuse you of that, my

dear." Emory turned his attention back to Ace and Chance. "We won't keep you from your business."

"We're in no hurry—"

"Well, a little," Chance interrupted Ace.

"It was nice to meet you," Meredith said. "I'm sure we'll see each other again if you stay in Lone Pine for very long. Do you intend to?"

"We, uh, don't really know yet," Ace said.

"Well, I hope you do. Good evening."

Still smiling, Emory nodded. "Night, fellas."

Ace and Chance tugged on their hat brims and moved aside to let Emory and his sister go by. As they resumed walking toward the saloon, Chance glanced over at his brother and said quietly, "She's an odd one, isn't she?"

"I didn't think so at all," Ace said.

Chance looked at him again and laughed. "Good Lord. You're taken with her, aren't you?"

"Miss Emory seemed pretty smart. I always like intelligent folks."

"And easy on the eyes, too. Although not nearly as pretty as Miss Dupree."

Ace just shrugged. He wasn't going to waste time arguing over which of the young women was more attractive when they were both mighty nice-looking.

The Melodian wasn't far. They walked past the darkened mouth of an alley just a few buildings away from the saloon.

A sudden scuff of boot leather against the ground was the only warning Ace had before something crashed into the back of his head and sent him pitching forward to his knees.

Chapter Nine

An arm went around Ace's neck from behind and closed tightly on it. Whoever had hold of him jerked him to his feet and dragged him backwards into the dark, narrow passage between buildings.

The blow to the head had stunned him and caused his brain to whirl madly. For a second or two he couldn't think or even see straight.

Then he heard grunting beside him and boots slapping against the dirt of the alley and realized Chance was under attack, too. One word leaped into Ace's mind.

McLaren!

They had been warned over and over. They had been alert. And yet they had been taken by surprise, and with a sinking feeling, Ace knew why.

He had been thinking about Meredith Emory, and he suspected Chance had been looking forward to seeing Fontana Dupree again. Without them even realizing it, their vigilance had been blunted by pretty faces.

They were in trouble, but that didn't mean

things were over, Ace told himself as his mind began to clear. Not over by a long shot, he vowed. The forearm clamped across his throat kept him from yelling, but he could still put up a fight.

Deep into the alley, a man ordered, "Hang on to them, damn it!" The harsh whisper disguised the voice a little as he said, "Let's get 'em, Perry!"

Ace thought he recognized it as belonging to Pete McLaren.

Tequila fumes from the mouth of the man holding him enveloped Ace's face. He stumbled a little as he dragged Ace along the passage.

The attackers had been stoking themselves up with liquid courage, maybe as long as all afternoon Ace quickly realized. That meant their bellies might be a little tender. He put that theory to the test by suddenly ramming his right elbow back into the gut of the man holding him.

The blow had an immediate effect. The man grunted in pain and then retched, loosening his grip on Ace's throat. Ace twisted free just in time to avoid getting soaked by the vomit that spewed forth.

Ace kept turning and brought his left arm up and back so the elbow caught his erstwhile captor under the chin and rocked his head back. The man fell away, but as he did, the one who had been in front of Ace giving the orders closed in. A punch hammered into Ace's chest before he could get his feet set. He reeled back, and his shoulder blades struck the wall of the building on that side of the passage.

That was good. Nobody could come at him from behind.

A little light filtered into the alley from the street, but not enough for him to make out anything except vague shapes. A few yards away, several figures—Chance and a couple other men—struggled, swaying back and forth.

Drawing Ace's attention back to his current dilemma, the man still in front of him bored in, fists pistoning back and forth.

Ace got his arms up, blocked some of the blows, absorbed the punishment from the others. He snapped out a left jab, aiming almost blindly, and felt a satisfying shiver up his arm as it landed against what felt like his opponent's cheekbone.

The punch made the man move back a step. Ace followed, not crowding too close in case the man was trying a feint, and hooked a right to the body. It landed solidly.

The air in the passage was thick with shadows and the reek of upchucked tequila. Ace ignored the stench and lifted a left uppercut that knocked the man he was fighting off his feet.

A more unscrupulous battler would have rushed in, kicking and stomping while his opponent was down. Ace, more honorable than most, paused to see if McLaren—he felt sure the man was McLaren—was going to get back up.

At that moment, a weight landed on Ace's back and knocked him forward.

The man who had tackled him pinned his arms to his side. "I got him, Pete!" the man yelled, his mouth painfully close to Ace's ear. "Get up and kill him!"

The smell of vomit told Ace it was the man who had grabbed him earlier. With both feet against the ground, Ace caught his balance and shoved hard backwards. Not braced well enough to withstand the force, the man lurched backwards, which allowed Ace to keep driving with his feet and ram his captor against the wall.

That broke him loose. Ace whirled and swung a punch at a dimly seen jaw. His fist landed with a solid thud. The man's head went to the side, and his knees buckled. Ace darted aside to let him fall.

Expecting McLaren to jump him again, Ace twisted to meet the attack, only to catch a glimpse of a silhouetted figure running along the alley toward the street. The man reached the alley mouth and darted to the side. A stray beam of light fell across his face, revealing the bruised, panting features of Pete McLaren.

That came as no surprise to Ace, nor was he shocked that McLaren had lit a shuck when the fight didn't go his way. McLaren was a bully. He wanted the odds on his side, and he didn't like it when anybody stood up to him. He sure wasn't interested in a fair fight.

It wasn't a fair fight Chance was facing, that was for sure. He had gotten loose from the man who'd grabbed him initially, but he had three hombres crowding in, all trying to throw punches at him.

Chance had managed to get his back against the wall on the other side of the alley, though, and his three opponents kept getting in each other's way as they tried to hammer him. As Ace watched, Chance leaned his head away from a punch and the man's fist slammed into the wall. The man howled in pain and staggered back, clutching the injured hand.

Ace was ready. He swung both clubbed fists against the back of the man's head in a pile-driver blow that sent him senseless to the dirt of the alley.

Chance knocked one of the remaining men off his feet with a powerful left, right, left combination, the punches flying too fast for the eye to follow even if there had been enough light in the alley.

The last man in the bunch, caught between the Jensen brothers, had no opportunity to get away. Ace staggered him with a hard punch, then Chance finished him off with a roundhouse blow that dropped him, out cold. Ace and Chance were the only ones left standing, their chests rising and falling heavily as they tried to catch their breath.

"Let's get out of here," Chance said. "It stinks in this alley."

"Yeah," Ace said. "I want to see if we can find McLaren."

"I can't believe we let him get away with jumping us when we knew he was liable to do it!"

"He didn't get away with it," Ace said with a grim smile as they reached the street. "Not yet, anyway. And his pards sure didn't, since they're laying back there and can't even get up."

They looked both ways along the street for any sign of Pete McLaren but didn't see him.

"Blast it. He could have gone anywhere," Chance muttered.

"There's the marshal and Deputy Soriano," Ace said, nodding toward the boardwalk across the street. "Maybe they saw him."

In fact, the two lawmen had taken note of the Jensen brothers and their disheveled appearance and were already starting across the street toward them. Ace and Chance picked up and dusted off their hats that had fallen off when McLaren's friends grabbed them.

"What in blazes happened to you two?" the marshal asked as he and Miguel came up to them.

"Let me guess," Miguel said before either Ace or Chance could answer. "Pete McLaren tried to get even."

Ace pointed over his shoulder with a thumb.

"His four pals are back in the alley, either unconscious or close to it. They grabbed us and dragged us in there and planned to give us a thrashing."

Dixon grunted. "Let me guess. They wound up with more than they could handle."

"We might've gotten a little lucky," Ace said, since modesty was in his nature. "When McLaren saw things weren't going his way, he took off for the tall and uncut."

"I don't suppose you saw him?" Chance said to the lawmen.

"No, but I reckon I know where he'll go," Dixon said heavily. "There's a little cantina on the edge of town run by an old pard of McLaren's brother Otis. More than likely he headed for José's place." The marshal frowned. "You boys willin' to swear out a complaint against McLaren?"

Ace hesitated. He and Chance had always been in the habit of stomping their own snakes, rather than turning to the authorities for help whenever they ran into trouble, but if they planned on staying in Lone Pine for a while, it might be better not to take the law into their own hands.

He wasn't sure about Chance, but he wasn't ready to leave the settlement just yet. Not until he'd had an opportunity to get to know Meredith Emory a little better. He was willing to bet Chance felt the same way about Fontana Dupree.

The same thought process must have been going through Chance's mind, because both brothers agreed at the same time.

"All right, then," Dixon said with a curt nod. "We'll go hunt him up, then. Miguel, can you get those varmints in the alley on their feet and prod 'em over to the jail?"

"Sure," the night deputy replied, "but if you're going to arrest McLaren, I ought to come with you, Marshal."

"That's all right. I reckon these Jensen boys will go along with me. I want all of McLaren's bunch locked up while we've got the chance."

"*Sta bueno*," Miguel agreed, although clearly reluctant to let the marshal tackle the chore of arresting Pete McLaren without him.

Ace, Chance, and Dixon moved off down the street, with the brothers letting the lawman lead the way. Dixon's route took them to a shack on the edge of the settlement where a lantern burned dimly through a filthy window.

The marshal had his hand on the butt of his gun as he opened the door and stepped inside. Ace and Chance went in behind him and saw that the cantina was pretty squalid.

It also appeared to be empty except for the grossly fat man standing behind the bar. Beads of sweat clung to his face and shone in the lantern light.

Ace thought maybe he was sweating because it

was hot and he was fat . . . but there might be another reason, too.

"José, I reckon you know why I'm here," Dixon said with a stern frown on his face. "I'm lookin' for Pete McLaren."

José shook his head. "I have not seen him, Señor Marshal. Not for days."

"That so? Then how come I've had reports him and his pards were in here blottin' up tequila most of the day?" Dixon might have been guessing about that, but the look on José's face confirmed the marshal was correct.

"Where is he?" Dixon asked. "I know you used to ride with the boy's brother a long time ago, José. I don't hold that against you. You've been pretty law-abidin' here lately. Don't let lyin' to me about McLaren ruin that for you."

José's mouth opened and closed a couple times, making his chins wobble, and even though he didn't say anything, his eyes cut sharply toward a couple barrels stuck in a corner of the room.

Watching from behind those barrels, McLaren saw José's reaction just as well as the others did. He came up, kicking a barrel aside, and flame spouted from the revolver jutting out of his fist as it went off with a deafening roar.

Chapter Ten

The gun wasn't pointed toward Marshal Dixon or the Jensen brothers. José yowled and reeled back as blood bloomed like a crimson flower on his grimy apron.

"You damn backstabbin' greaser!" McLaren yelled as he triggered again.

The shot missed. José had already collapsed behind the plank bar. The bullet exploded a jug of tequila sitting on a shelf and sprayed shards of clay pottery around the area behind the bar. José yelped again, so at least he wasn't dead.

Dixon clawed at the gun on his hip. He might be a tough, veteran lawman, but he wasn't fast on the draw. McLaren pivoted toward him, and it looked like he might get another shot off before Dixon was able to clear leather.

In the cantina's close quarters, throwing too much lead around could turn out disastrous, Ace figured. He snatched up a chair from a nearby table and slung it at McLaren.

McLaren's gun boomed a third time, but the flying chair had already crashed into him and knocked his arm up. The slug went well over the heads of Ace, Chance, and Dixon. The marshal had his gun out, but he held his fire as Chance leaped toward the staggering McLaren, caught hold of the gunman's wrist with his left hand, and forced his gun hand up. The next instant, Chance's right fist slammed into McLaren's jaw and drove him off his feet.

Ace kicked the gun out of McLaren's hand and sent it spinning across the room. He and Chance both stepped back as Dixon loomed over McLaren and covered him with a rock-steady Colt.

"Wouldn't take much of an excuse for me to pull the trigger on you, McLaren," Dixon warned. Without taking his eyes off the gunman, he said, "One of you boys check on José. See how bad he's hurt."

Ace did that while Chance drew his gun from the shoulder holster and trained it on McLaren as well. With two guns pointed at him, McLaren didn't dare try anything.

José was groaning as he lay on the dirty floor behind the bar. Ace knelt beside him and rolled him onto his back, which was sort of like trying to right a beached whale. Ace pulled the apron and cotton shirt aside and saw the bloody hole in José's shoulder. A quick check revealed a similar wound in José's back where the bullet had gone out.

Ace told him, "Looks like you're going to be all right, amigo. The slug went through clean and didn't break any bones as far as I can tell. I'm sure Lone Pine's got a good doc who can patch you up."

"We do," Marshal Dixon said. "I'll send for him soon as I get a chance. Although he may already be on the way, if he heard those shots." He motioned with his gun barrel to McLaren. "On your feet. You're under arrest."

"You can't do this," McLaren said as he climbed to his feet. "It ain't right. It's all the fault of these two troublemakers."

"The Jensens?" Dixon snorted and shook his head. "I followed the law the first time around and locked them up, even though I knew you were really to blame for that ruckus in the Melodian. But this time you and your pards jumped them—"

"You've only got their word for that," McLaren said as his jaw stuck out defiantly.

Dixon glared at him. "Maybe so, but I just saw it with my own eyes when you shot ol' José."

From behind the bar, José said in a quavery voice, "I-I will not press charges, Señor Marshal."

"It don't matter," Dixon told him. "You don't have to press charges since I witnessed the crime. That's plenty to put McLaren on trial for attempted murder and send him to Cañon City for seven or eight years."

"No!" McLaren exclaimed. "You can't!"

"I can and will," Dixon said grimly. "Now get movin'."

As they were prodding the prisoner out of the

cantina, Miguel Soriano came trotting up with a shotgun in his hands, followed at a distance by a slender, bespectacled man in a town suit.

"Marshal!" Miguel said. "I heard the shots. So did Doc Bellem."

Dixon jerked his head toward the door. "Your patient's inside, Doc. José's shot through the shoulder, but this young fella took a look at it and said it wasn't too bad."

The physician frowned at Ace. "Do you have any medical training, young man?"

"No, sir," Ace replied, "but I've seen more than my fair share of bullet holes."

"He's patched up a few, too," Chance added with a grin.

Bellem bustled on inside. Miguel joined the group taking Pete McLaren to jail. The shots had attracted a considerable amount of attention, and quite a few people stood along the street to watch the procession.

A number of them wore very satisfied expressions, as if they were happy to see McLaren on his way to the hoosegow. He couldn't have failed to notice that, and it probably fueled his rage even more.

But with four armed men at his back, especially when one of them held a scattergun, McLaren could do nothing about it.

"You get the others locked up all right?" Dixon asked Miguel.

"*Sí*," the night deputy responded. "They were so groggy they gave me no trouble."

"And we've got their ringleader," Dixon said. "Maybe now we can actually finish the job of cleanin' up this town."

Dolly Redding rose up on tiptoes to peer over the shoulder of one of the men who stood at the front windows of the Melodian watching avidly as Marshal Dixon, Deputy Soriano, and the two Jensens escorted their prisoner past the saloon toward the jail. She caught her breath as she saw Pete striding along, his face mottled in rage but apparently unharmed.

A buzz of excited conversation filled the big room. Fontana had been singing when a man had run in and said excitedly that it sounded like a war had broken out down at José's cantina. The tune issuing from the piano had trailed off as Orrie quit playing. Men gathered around the bearer of the news, and when they pressed him, he admitted there had been only three shots, but that was enough to generate quite a bit of excitement. Some of them had been talking about heading down there to see what was going on.

Suddenly, one of them looked out the window and exclaimed, "Here comes Marshal Dixon with a prisoner! By the Lord Harry, it looks like Pete McLaren!"

That caused a stampede to the windows and the

entrance. Some of the customers went out on the boardwalk to watch while others peered over the batwings and through the glass.

Fontana Dupree came up beside Dolly. "Well, you ought to be relieved. Now he can't bother you anymore, at least as long as the marshal's got him behind bars. I hope it's a good long time."

"What? Oh . . . Oh, right," Dolly said. "Pete won't be able to bother me anymore."

Fontana looked at the blonde, eyes narrowing. "Wait a minute. Are you upset that Pete's under arrest?"

"Why would I be? He . . . he's nothin' but a troublemaker. Always has been."

"Yeah, but I know that look in a girl's eyes," Fontana said. "You're sweet on him, no matter how bad he treats you, aren't you?"

Dolly tossed her curly hair and sniffed. "You're loco. Marshal Dixon can lock him up and throw away the key, as far as I'm concerned."

"Uh-huh," Fontana said, clearly skeptical.

Dolly came up on her toes and looked outside again, but the group of men had moved on and was no longer in sight. She sighed. Pete was a bastard, no doubt about that. But Lord help her, he had the touch that reached out to something inside her, something that already longed for him even though he wasn't locked up yet.

She hoped the marshal wouldn't keep him

behind bars for too long. She wasn't sure she could stand that.

Lee Emory was waiting on the boardwalk in front of the marshal's office when they got there.

Dixon asked, "What are you doin' here?"

"Covering a story for the newspaper, of course. It's not every day that the town's biggest troublemaker gets arrested. What did he do, Marshal?"

"That ain't a matter of public record yet. Court's an open proceedin'. You can show up tomorrow and see him charged like anybody else."

Emory smiled. "I'm a newspaperman, Marshal. I have other sources. For example, I saw Dr. Bellem hurrying toward the other end of town with his medical bag. He and I are good friends."

"All right, all right." Dixon jerked his head toward the door. "Come on in."

Ace opened the door and went in first, his gun drawn. Miguel prodded McLaren through the opening next with the shotgun at his back.

As McLaren stepped past Emory, he glared at the editor. "You write a bunch of garbage about me and you'll be sorry, mister."

"You ain't in no position to be handin' out threats," Dixon said. "Keep movin'."

Some of the other bystanders tried to crowd into the marshal's office after them, but Dixon shut the door in their faces. Miguel took McLaren on into the cell block.

Dixon told Emory, "Pete and those no-account friends of his jumped the Jensen brothers here and tried to hand 'em a beatin' to pay them back for that scrape in the Melodian last night. Only they hadn't counted on Ace and Chance bein' such wildcats."

Emory looked at Ace and Chance. "Sounds like I definitely need to interview you fellows. But then what happened, Marshal?"

"McLaren ran off when things didn't go his way. I tracked him down at José's. The Mex and Otis McLaren used to ride together years ago, you know."

"Yes, I believe I've heard something about that," Emory said with a nod.

"Anyway, McLaren was hidin' behind some barrels in the cantina, and he got mad when he realized José was about to give him away. He jumped up and plugged José, then made a try for me. The Jensens stopped him without anybody else gettin' hurt. That's about the size of it."

Emory's eyes widened a bit at the news of the shooting. "How bad is José hurt?"

"He'll live, more than likely. McLaren shot him through the shoulder. Doc Bellem's with him now."

"But that means you'll charge McLaren with . . ."

"Attempted murder, yeah."

Before the conversation could continue, Miguel Soriano came back into the office from the cell block and said to Dixon, "McLaren really wants to talk to you, boss. Says he insists and that he's got a right to."

"I don't know about that, but I guess I'll humor him."

Dixon went into the cell block, followed by Ace, Chance, Emory, and the night deputy. McLaren's four friends were divided evenly between the two cells on the right, Dunn and Russell in the first one, Merritt and Severs in the second.

Pete McLaren was by himself in the first cell on the left, standing at the door and gripping the bars so tightly his knuckles had turned white. "This is your last chance, Dixon. Open this door and let me outta here right now."

"Or else what?" Dixon said.

"Or else you'll be bringin' down hell on this whole town, you old fool. My brother's bound to hear about you lockin' me up, and when he does, he'll come back here and you'll see the buzzards roostin' again, just like the old days!"

Dixon let out a humorless laugh. "That's a pretty far-fetched notion, kid. Otis McLaren is long gone from these parts. Nobody around here has seen hide nor hair of him or heard anything about him for years. Hell, he's probably been dead for a long time. That's the way all no-good owlhoots wind up sooner or later."

"You're wrong, Marshal," McLaren said as his face twisted in a hate-filled grimace. "And you're gonna be damned sorry." He looked at the others in the aisle of the cell block. "All of you are! You're all dead men. You just don't know it yet!"

"Shut up or I'll see to it I forget to give you breakfast in the mornin'." Dixon nodded toward the door. "Come on, gents. Let's let this sorry bunch stew in their own juices."

As they all went out, Pete McLaren screamed obscene curses and threats after them. Miguel Soriano closed the cell block door with a solid thud. The thick wood muffled the vile words, but they could still hear McLaren ranting.

"If he doesn't get tired and shut up after a while, go in and throw a bucket of water on him," Dixon instructed the night deputy.

Emory said, "Those were pretty serious threats he was making, Marshal. Do you, uh, do you think we need to worry?"

"About McLaren?" Dixon shook his head. "He can make all the threats he wants. He can't back 'em up while he's behind bars. And that's where he's gonna be for a long time if I have anything to say about it."

Chapter Eleven

Leaving the jail, Ace and Chance headed for the Melodian again.

"Think we'll make it this time?" Chance asked dryly as they walked along the street toward the saloon.

"Town seems quiet," Ace said.

"It seemed quiet before . . . right up until the time McLaren and his friends jumped us from that alley." Chance shook his head. "It bothers me that they got close enough to do that without tipping us off what was about to happen."

"Me, too," Ace admitted. "Our minds were on other things."

Chance grinned. "Yeah. I hope Miss Duprec hasn't already finished her performances for the night."

No one interfered with the brothers on their way to the saloon, although some of the townspeople they passed gave them long, interested looks. Their run-ins with McLaren's bunch had given them some notoriety in Lone Pine, Ace thought.

When they entered the Melodian, Fontana was standing at the end of the bar with Hank Muller. She caught their eyes and smiled.

Chance took that as an invitation to go over and talk to her. He pinched the brim of his hat as he nodded politely. "Miss Dupree. It's mighty nice to see you again."

"It appears you went through a lot to get here," she said.

Chance gestured toward his slightly rumpled outfit. "You mean this? I suppose I should have cleaned up—"

"I was thinking more about that bruise on your jaw."

"There's a bruise on my jaw?" Chance touched it gingerly with a couple fingertips and made a face. "Son of a gun. There sure is. It's been such a busy evening, I hadn't even noticed."

Muller said, "Any evening that winds up with McLaren and his friends behind bars is a good one, as far as I'm concerned."

One of the saloon girls was walking past him as he spoke. Ace saw the glance she gave him and recognized her as the blonde who'd been on McLaren's lap when he and Chance had first come in the night before.

Dolly, that was her name. She didn't look particularly happy about what Muller had just said. Maybe she had a soft spot in her heart for McLaren, despite the way he treated her. Ace had seen such things happen before.

"I sure hope you haven't finished singing for the evening, Miss Dupree," Chance went on to Fontana.

"I can always manage another tune or two," the

brunette said. "Especially for you boys. After all, we're sort of business partners now, aren't we?"

"Excuse me?" Ace said. "How do you figure that, Miss Dupree?"

"Both of you can call me Fontana. And since I paid your fines and the damages, I figure that gives me, well, a stake in the two of you."

Muller frowned. "If I'd known you were the one who was gonna come up with that dinero, I never would have asked for damages."

"It's all right, Hank," she told him, then laughed. "Anyway, I'll get it back from you in wages, won't I?"

"I reckon you could look at it that way," Muller said with a shrug of his beefy shoulders.

"Now, since Chance is interested in hearing a song . . . and I suppose you are, too, Ace, or you wouldn't be here—"

"Yes, ma'am," Ace said.

"I'll see what Orrie and I can come up with." She walked off toward the piano while Chance eyed her gracefully swaying form with appreciation.

Muller cleared his throat "You fellas want a drink? First one's on the house, considering we've got you to thank for those hellions being locked up."

"Beer's fine," Ace said, thinking that considering the state of their finances, the first drink tonight might also have to be the last one.

•••

Marshal Hoyt Dixon knocked on the door of the brothers' hotel room early the next morning. Ace, being more of an early riser than Chance, was already up shaving. With lather still on his face, he set the razor aside and picked up the six-gun sitting next to the basin.

"Morning, Marshal," he said with a friendly nod when he opened the door and saw who was standing in the hallway.

Dixon looked at the gun and asked, "You always answer the door with a hogleg in your hand?"

"It's sort of a habit, especially when Chance and I aren't expecting visitors." Ace tucked the revolver into his waistband. "What can I do for you?"

"You should've been expectin' me. You got to go to court this mornin'."

Ace's eyes widened slightly. "We're not in trouble again for something, are we?"

"No, but you got to testify at the hearin', kid. McLaren and those other varmints will be appearin' before Judge Ordway in about an hour."

"Oh," Ace said as understanding dawned on him. "Well, that'll give us some time to get breakfast."

"I'll join you, if you don't mind."

"Keeping an eye on us, Marshal?"

"Witnesses have been known to change their

minds at the last minute about testifyin' against Pete McLaren."

"That's not going to happen with me and Chance. You can bet your hat on it."

"I ain't a gamblin' man," Dixon said. "That's why I'm havin' breakfast with you two hombres."

Ace nodded and went to the bed. He gave Chance's shoulder a shake. "Rise and shine. Justice is calling."

Shaggy from sleep, Chance raised his head and gave it a groggy shake. "Huh?"

"We've got to go to court in a little while."

"Plead innocent," Chance said as he buried his face in the pillow again.

Ace grinned. "I'm not sure anybody would believe that, but we're not the ones the hearing is for. We have to testify against McLaren and his friends."

"Well, why the hell didn't you say so?" Chance groused as he started untangling himself from the sheets.

The three men sat down to breakfast a short time later at the Lone Pine Café. They swallowed strong black coffee and dug into their food.

Ace asked, "Quiet night at the jail, Marshal?"

"Yeah, once McLaren got too tired to keep cussin' and ravin'. Miguel said there was no other trouble. My other deputy, Norm Sutherland, has relieved him and is holdin' down the fort now." Dixon took another sip of coffee. "I might as well tell you now. I talked to the prosecutor, Tim Buchanan, and he says McLaren's friends aren't guilty of anything except disturbin' the peace."

"What?" Chance said. "They jumped us and figured on beating us within an inch of our lives. That's got to be attempted murder, or at least assault."

"Yeah, you'd think so, but the way it turned out, you boys gave even more than you got. They could turn around and claim that *you* assaulted *them*."

"So we're penalized for defending ourselves," Ace said with a note of disbelief in his voice.

"The judge will levy the heaviest fines he can, I expect," Dixon said, "but don't count on those boys goin' back to jail once the hearin' is over. Don't worry. They're a sorry lot, but they don't amount to much without McLaren around. Perry Severs is probably the smartest one in the bunch, and he's dumb as a box of rocks. McLaren's the only one who really counts, and he's gonna be standing trial for shootin' José."

"You sure about that?" Chance asked.

"His lawyer, Sol Horton, is about as slick as a snake oil salesman, but he can't change the facts of the case. All three of us saw McLaren plug the Mex. He's goin' to prison, all right."

Ace hoped the lawman's confidence wasn't

misplaced. They finished up their breakfasts and headed for the town hall.

The chairs for spectators were full already, and people thronged on the boardwalk outside so they could watch through the windows and listen through the open doors.

The five prisoners, all in irons, were clustered behind one of the tables at the front of the room. A man with a black mustache and shaggy black brows sat with them. That would be the lawyer Marshal Dixon had mentioned, Ace thought.

At the other table sat a frock-coated man in his thirties who had a high forehead and wavy brown hair. Ace supposed that was Prosecutor Buchanan.

As he looked around the room, Ace saw that Hank Muller and Fontana Dupree were present, as was José. The cantina owner, with his wounded shoulder swaddled in bandages, sat among the spectators just behind the prosecution table.

"You fellas stand over there by the wall," Dixon told Ace and Chance. As they took their places, the marshal went to the front of the room and waited. He called, "All rise!" when Judge Ordway came in.

When the formalities were over and Ordway had gaveled the proceedings underway so everybody could sit down, the prosecutor stood up again and announced, "Timothy Buchanan for the county, Your Honor."

"And Solomon Horton representing the defendants, Your Honor," the mustachioed lawyer said as he got to his feet.

"We'll dispense with opening statements," Judge Ordway said. "Marshal, what are the charges against these men?"

Ace figured the judge knew what the charges were just like everybody else did, but things had to be done a certain way.

Dixon read off the charges from a document he picked up from the prosecution table.

Ordway looked to the prosecutor. "Call your first witness, Mr. Buchanan."

The prosecutor turned to look at Ace. "I call Mr. William Jensen."

It wasn't the first time Ace had testified in court, but he didn't like it and never had. The worry that he was going to say or do something wrong always lurked in the back of his mind, even though he responded with complete honesty to all of Buchanan's questions. It took only a few minutes to cover the events of the past two nights.

Then Sol Horton got to his feet. "Mister . . . Jensen, is it?"

"That's right," Ace said.

"Mr. Jensen, I believe you and your brother were locked up for disturbing the peace night before last, is that correct?"

"Yes, sir, it is."

"And the two of you were found guilty and

fined in this very courtroom some twenty-four hours ago."

"That's right."

"Then why should we not believe you and your brother were equally to blame for the altercation last night? Isn't it perfectly reasonable to believe that the two of you started the fight . . . not my clients?"

"With odds of five against two?" Ace shook his head. "I don't reckon I'd call that idea perfectly reasonable, Mr. Horton."

That answer brought laughter from many of the spectators, a reaction that spread out onto the boardwalk.

Horton flushed with anger. "But it *is* conceivable events could have transpired that way?"

"I suppose it is. But they didn't. They happened just the way I told Mr. Buchanan."

Horton spread his hands. "But you just admitted you might have been mistaken."

"No, sir, I didn't. You can try to twist my words that way, but it won't change the facts."

Horton looked sharply at the judge. "Objection, Your Honor! Witness is not responding to a question. His statement is irrelevant and immaterial."

"Overruled," Ordway said curtly. "You opened the corral, Counselor. You can't complain when the horses come out."

Horton scowled. "No further questions."

Ace left the witness chair and Chance took his place. They went through the process again, except Horton just growled, "No questions," instead of cross-examining Chance. Buchanan had no further witnesses.

Horton got to his feet, but before he could say anything, Judge Ordway pointed the gavel at him and said, "Do you plan on calling all four of those miscreants to the stand so they can spout the same pack of lies?"

Horton looked horrified. "Your Honor, I object. That was clearly prejudicial—"

"That's because we all know what happened, and I'm prejudiced in favor of the truth. In the matter of the disturbing the peace charges, you can call one witness if you want, but that's all."

"This is highly irregular, Your Honor."

"Since it's my courtroom, I decide what's regular or not. What say you?"

Horton blew out an exasperated breath. "The defense calls Perry Severs."

The witness stumbled through an obviously contrived story about how he and his friends were just walking through the alley peacefully when they were set upon by the Jensen brothers.

When Horton was finished with his questioning, Buchanan didn't even stand up. He just drawled, "I don't think there's any need to dignify that with cross-examination, Your Honor."

"I agree, Counselor. In the matter of the

disturbing the peace charges, I find the defendants guilty and fine them seventy-five dollars each."

The amount brought some mutters of surprise and disagreement from four of the defendants, but Pete McLaren himself sat in stony silence. His head moved slowly as he directed hate-filled stares at various people in the courtroom, including Marshal Dixon, Ace and Chance, the two deputies, and the prosecutor and judge. McLaren looked around even farther, toward the front row of spectators. Those townspeople abruptly fell silent as if they'd caught a rattle-snake staring at them.

Judge Ordway looked at the other defendants. "You four are free to go once you've paid your fines." He squared up some of the papers in front of him. "Now . . . as to the matter of the charge of attempted murder against Pete McLaren . . . Mr. Buchanan, call your first witness."

Chapter Twelve

Marshal Hoyt Dixon took the witness chair first. In curt, efficient questions, Buchanan didn't waste any time getting the lawman's testimony on the record.

Sol Horton snapped, "No questions," when the prosecutor was done.

Buchanan started to call José next, but Judge Ordway stopped him.

"I would remind both counselors that this is not a trial, merely an evidentiary hearing to determine if the charge of attempted murder has merit. In the opinion of this court, it meets that standard, and I order that the defendant, Pete McLaren, be held in the Lone Pine jail pending a full trial scheduled to begin . . . let's see. Today is Friday . . . trial will be held at nine o'clock Monday morning."

Horton got to his feet. "Your Honor, you're not even going to allow me to present a defense?"

"You can do that, Counselor . . . at the trial." Ordway picked up the gavel and rapped it on the table. "We're adjourned."

Horton clearly didn't like it, but there was nothing he could do about it. In a surly voice, he said, "I'll pay the fines for disturbing the peace."

"Pay the marshal," Ordway said. "And don't forget McLaren's fine. He was convicted of that charge, too, you know."

Deputy Sutherland unlocked the irons on Perry Severs, Lew Merritt, Larry Dunn, and Vic Russell once Horton had paid the fines to Marshal Dixon. McLaren's irons stayed on him, since he was going back to jail. He shuffled out through a path that cleared in the crowd, followed by the two shotgun-toting deputies.

"Well, that part's done," Dixon said to Ace and Chance as the room began to clear out. "Can I count on you boys to stay around over the weekend so you can testify at the actual trial?"

"We're material witnesses, aren't we?" Ace asked. "You could hold us in custody until then if you wanted to."

"Yeah, but your word's good enough for me." A smile creased the lawman's weathered face. "Although why I ought to trust a couple fiddle-footed drifters, I ain't sure."

"We'll be here," Ace promised.

"You can count on that," Chance added.

Fontana Dupree and Hank Muller came up to them.

Muller said, "Good work, Marshal. It's about time Pete McLaren got what's coming to him."

"Just doing my job," Dixon said. "And a fella might take your words to mean that I ain't been up to it until now."

"Oh, no, I didn't mean that at all," Muller said quickly. "I know you've got to follow the law. It's not your fault McLaren never did anything bad enough and dumb enough to get himself locked up for good until he shot old José."

Fontana said to Ace and Chance, "I guess you two boys will be staying around town for a few days."

"We've already promised the marshal we would," Chance said.

"Good. I wouldn't want to have to threaten you with the law, now would I?"

"Ma'am?" Ace said.

"I can't have you running out on your debt." The smile on her lips and the twinkle in her eyes as she said it took any sting out of the words.

"Ace, we need to figure out a way to earn some money," Chance said with a smile of his own. "I think Miss Dupree is gonna hold us to that deal."

"Of course I am," she said. "Just because I'm a woman doesn't mean I can't be levelheaded about money."

"How are the poker games at the Melodian, Mr. Muller?" Chance asked.

"Honest," Muller declared. "You're welcome to sit in on one anytime you want and see for yourself."

"I may just do that."

They all left the town hall, splitting up to go their separate ways.

Dolly stood a couple doors away, in an alcove where the entrance to a hardware store was located. Her face was scrubbed, she wore a plain gray dress, and her blond curls were tucked up in an old sunbonnet.

The dress and the bonnet were remnants of a life she'd led long in the past. Not so long in years, maybe, but in miles and experience. She'd been fifteen when her folks had started out from Missouri, bound for a new life in California.

The farm back home hadn't been much to speak of, but it had provided them with a meager living. Her pa had the wanderlust, though, and figured he could do better elsewhere so he'd packed up his wife and five kids—two boys and two girls besides Dolly, all of them younger than her—and set off on his grand adventure.

They had made it halfway across Kansas before the whole bunch fell sick with a fever . . . except for Dolly. She had nursed them for nigh on to a week, doing her absolute best to save their lives, but one by one they had died, until she was the only one left.

Some men on horseback came along just as she was patting down the dirt on the last grave. They claimed to be cowboys on their way back to Texas after a drive, but it didn't take Dolly long to figure out they were really rustlers. They offered to take her and her outfit along with them, but they sold the wagon and all the family's possessions in the first town they came to, holed up with Dolly in a hotel where nobody asked any questions, and it was there she found out what men were really like.

She'd gone back to Texas with them. After that, why the hell not?

In the three years since then, she'd worked at a succession of saloons and cathouses, squirreling away what little money she made in each place until she had enough to move on. If she had stopped to think about it, she might have realized she was looking for someplace better, someplace where her life wouldn't be so ugly and hard, but she wasn't given to such turns of mind and somehow things always wound up the same . . . until she'd landed in Lone Pine and met Pete McLaren.

He was just as bad as all the others in most ways—he wanted what he wanted, where and when and how he wanted it—but there were unexpected moments of tenderness, too. Dolly lived for those.

She didn't intend to lose them.

That morning she'd known she had to find out what was going to happen to Pete. She'd washed her face, pulled out the old dress and bonnet, and gone to the town hall. Nobody in the crowd paid any attention to her. Probably nobody even recognized her, dressed like she was.

Her heart had sunk when she'd heard the judge say that Pete had to stand trial. She knew the judge and the marshal and that prosecutor fellow had it in for Pete. They'd makc sure he was convicted and sent to prison, no telling for how long. There was a good chance she'd never see him again.

She couldn't let that happen.

As she stood in front of the hardware store

watching the deputies disappear into the jail with Pete, Dolly knew she would do whatever it took to make sure they weren't parted forever.

Chance took Hank Muller up on his suggestion and spent the afternoon playing poker in the Melodian. He had been raised by one of the best card players west of the Mississippi and had a natural talent for the game, to boot, so it was no surprise he was up a couple hundred dollars by the time dusk began to settle over Lone Pine. His skill at poker was the main way the brothers raised money for supplies as they drifted across the frontier.

Ace watched his brother play for a while, standing at the bar well away from the table and nursing a beer so no one could accuse him of trying to tip Chance off to the other players' cards. Tiring of that, he left Chance to it and walked down to the livery stable to check on their horses. He was confident Crackerjack Sawyer was taking good care of the mounts, but it never hurt to confirm that.

"Hell sure started a-poppin' when you two boys rode into town," the old liveryman commented when Ace was satisfied everything was fine with the horses. "Does that happen regularlike where you fellas go?"

"All too often," Ace said with a sigh.

Crackerjack nodded solemnly "I've seen folks

like that. Trouble seems to follow 'em, when all they was lookin' for was peace and quiet."

"I don't think my brother would like it if things were too quiet. He's got an adventurous streak in him."

"And you don't, huh?"

Ace grinned. "Nope. I'm as placid as a little lamb."

Crackerjack blew out a skeptical breath to show just how much he accepted that assertion.

Ace left the stable and strolled back in the direction of the saloon. Along the way, he passed one of the general stores. The front door opened and a woman stepped out onto the boardwalk, her arms full of a stack of newspapers. Ace recognized her as Meredith Emory and stopped short just before the two of them collided. He touched a finger to the brim of his hat. "Sorry, Miss Emory. I almost didn't see you there in time."

"It's all right, Mr. Jensen," she told him. "The fault would have been equally mine in the event of a collision. It's a bit difficult to see over these papers, especially with the light fading the way it is."

"I reckon that's the new edition?"

"That's right. We normally publish on Friday morning, but Lee and I held up the press run this week so he could report on what happened at the hearing."

"And now you're delivering copies to the places that sell them."

"That's right."

"I can give you a hand with that." Ace reached for the stack of papers, intending to take them from her.

She stepped back. "You shouldn't. They're fresh enough you'd get ink on your hands."

"It'll wash off."

"Actually, no, it doesn't."

"Well, it'll wear off, then."

"Eventually. Maybe. You might get stains on your clothes as well."

"These old duds of mine, it wouldn't matter."

She hesitated, then asked, "You're going to insist, aren't you?"

"I just might."

Meredith smiled then, and Ace thought it made her look prettier than ever as he looked at her in the light that came through the store window.

Chapter Thirteen

Seething with anger, Pete McLaren paced back and forth in his cell like a caged animal. His brain writhed like a basket full of rattlesnakes. He was alone in the cell block and had been all day, except for when Deputy Sutherland had brought him his lunch.

Marshal Dixon had looked through the door between the office and the cell block a couple times but hadn't gone in or said anything to him. That hadn't stopped McLaren from giving voice to his own frustration. He had cursed both lawmen, the judge, the prosecutor, those damned Jensen boys, and everybody else in Lone Pine. He'd cursed his brother Otis for going off to ride the owlhoot trail and leaving him behind. He'd cursed the fates that had conspired to put him behind bars, and he had cursed Severs and the others for abandoning him.

Sol Horton had paid their fines—using money McLaren had given him—and so the four men hadn't returned to the jail after the hearing. That was what McLaren had told the lawyer to do, so he supposed he couldn't hold a grudge against his friends because of it. He thought they would have broken him out already, though.

The jail wasn't going to hold him, McLaren vowed to himself. It couldn't. But knowing he had to have help to get out made him even angrier. He didn't like depending on anybody else.

Most of the light had faded from the small, barred window set high in the cell's side wall when Sutherland stuck his head into the cell block and said, "Your supper ought to be here in a little while, McLaren. Waste o' good grub if you ask me." The deputy chuckled. "But nobody did, did they?"

Thinking that Sutherland was a garrulous, grinning idiot, McLaren made no reply. He didn't want to encourage him to talk even more. He leaned back on the bunk, resting his shoulders against the stone wall, too tired and dispirited to curse any more.

Maybe the boys were just waiting for nightfall to bust him out, he told himself. If that was the case, it wouldn't be long.

He heard the front door of the marshal's office open and close, and then a moment later a voice he hadn't expected. It made him sit up straighter on the bunk in anticipation.

The Dolly Redding she had once been—the immigrant girl in plain dress and bonnet—was gone. The saloon girl with painted face, provocative outfit, and curls spilling freely around her face had replaced her. Dolly had gone to work at the Melodian normally, not wanting anybody to suspect she might be up to something.

As the afternoon waned, she'd gone to Hank Muller and told him she wasn't feeling well. "Female trouble," she'd said with an embarrassed smile.

For a man with a number of women working for him, Muller was surprisingly squeamish about some things. He'd jerked his head toward the stairs and said, "That's fine. Go on and do what you need to do."

She had gone upstairs, but when she'd reached

the second-floor corridor, she'd slipped along it to the rear stairs and descended, stopping at the narrow door that led to a storeroom. Inside, she'd retrieved the items, hoping none of the bartenders would come along and catch her.

Luck was with her. She'd made it out of the saloon with no one seeing her.

The shadows were already thick enough in the alleys that she was able to make it from the Melodian to the edge of town undetected. She took a chance and crossed the road to work her way back to the marshal's office and jail behind the buildings on that side.

Reaching the squat, stone building, she eased along the side of it to the boardwalk. She stepped out into the open again where anybody on the street could see her, but she just had to hope no one would pay much attention. She carried one of the trays she normally used to deliver drinks in the saloon, and on it, covered with a cloth she had pulled up in the center, was a .36 caliber Colt Navy revolver.

She had stolen the gun from one of her customers a couple towns ago. It was loaded when she took it, and she had never disturbed those loads. To be honest, she didn't even know if the gun would fire, but it appeared to be in good shape, and she had kept it clean and dry. There was no reason it shouldn't work.

Of course, she hoped she wouldn't need to

fire it. Just the sight of it ought to be enough.

Even with its grim burden, balancing the tray one-handed was no trouble for her. She used the other hand to open the door of the marshal's office and stepped in confidently, just like she belonged there. A bright smile was on her face.

Deputy Norm Sutherland looked up from the chair behind the desk and frowned in surprise. "Miss Dolly?" He knew her from the Melodian, where she had brought drinks to him many times and even sat at a table and talked with him now and then. "What're you doin' here?"

"I brought the prisoner's supper," she said, lifting the tray a little.

"Why, Marshal Dixon was gonna do that. He left just a little while ago to fetch it."

"I know," Dolly said, thinking rapidly. "I ran into him right outside the café and he asked me if I'd bring the tray over here. He said some other errand had come up he needed to tend to."

"You were walkin' around town in that getup?"

"I just stepped out of the saloon for a few minutes to get a breath of fresh air. It gets awful smoky in there, you know."

"Yeah, I reckon." Sutherland scratched his jaw, still frowning, but then he shrugged.

Dolly knew he had accepted her story. That was why she had picked that time of day. Sutherland was near the end of his shift. He would be heading home as soon as the marshal got back to cover the office until Deputy Soriano took over in a little while. She hadn't wanted to deal with either Dixon or Soriano. They would have been too suspicious, no matter what sort of lie she came up with.

Sutherland got to his feet. "Put the tray on the desk here. I got to take a look, just to make sure. You understand."

"Of course." She placed the tray on the desk, bending over to make sure Sutherland got a good look down the neckline of her dress. The deputy had a wife and five kids, but that didn't mean he was blind. She could feel his eyes on her.

Because he was looking at her, he wasn't watching the tray, so it took him by surprise when she jerked the cloth away from the Colt Navy, snatched up the gun, and stepped back to point it at him, holding it in both hands.

His eyes widened in shock at the sight of the revolver. He started to reach for the gun on his hip but froze when Dolly used her thumbs to ear back the Colt's hammer.

"Don't yell, Deputy. I don't want to shoot you."

His mouth hung open for a couple seconds, then he said, "You fire off that hogleg and folks'll come a-runnin' from all over town."

"They'll come if you start yelling for help, too, so I don't really have anything to lose, do I?"

Sutherland swallowed. "Now, Miss Dolly, you don't want to do this. You know you don't.

You've always been a decent gal, for one who works in a saloon. Tell you what. You put that gun down and get on outta here, and I won't even tell the marshal about this. It'll be our secret, and you won't get in no trouble."

Slowly, Dolly shook her head. "Come out from behind that desk and turn around."

"Miss Dolly—"

"Do it," she grated. "And keep your hands away from your gun."

With a sad sigh, Sutherland moved around the desk and turned so his back was toward her. "You're gonna kill me, ain't you? Son of a bitch. Pardon my language, but I sure would've liked a chance to see my old lady and my younguns again."

"Deputy, do you ever stop talking?"

"Well, yeah, sometimes—"

The sound of his voice had covered up the faint click when Dolly let the revolver's hammer back down. She stepped toward him, reversing the gun as she went, and raised it to bring the butt crashing down on the back of his head.

Nobody had to die.

The unexpected blow made Sutherland fall to his knees. Dolly hit him again, and he pitched forward on his face. With her heart slugging painfully in her chest, she knelt to make sure she hadn't killed him accidentally. Relief went through her when she saw he was still breathing.

McLaren had heard enough of the conversation

to know what was going on. He didn't believe for a second that Dixon had sent Dolly with his supper. She was trying to help him escape. He wouldn't have thought she was that smart . . . or that brave.

He'd heard the exchange about the gun and the dull thuds, and for a moment his nerves were stretched taut, not knowing who was going to appear in the doorway.

It was Dolly, and she had the keys in one hand and a Colt Navy in the other.

"Damn it, girl, you look prettier than I've ever seen you!" he exclaimed. "Get over here with those keys."

Her feet pattered on the stone floor as she came to the cell door. "Do you really think I'm pretty, Pete?" she asked with the desperate need for approval that often got on his nerves.

At that moment, he didn't mind it, that was for sure. "You're downright beautiful. Unlock the door."

She tried but fumbled enough that he grew impatient. Reaching through the bars, he took the keys from her and did it himself. His heart leaped as the door swung open and he stepped out of the cell.

He wasn't free and clear yet, though. He took the gun from her without asking and hefted it. The feel of a weapon in his hand was good. "Did you bring me a horse?"

She shook her head. "No, but there are several

tied up at one of the hitch racks outside, just a few steps away. We can grab a couple, Pete, without any trouble."

"You're coming with me?"

"Well, sure. I-I want us to be together. And I sure can't stay here in Lone Pine, not after helping you escape."

"Did you kill Sutherland?"

"No, I just knocked him out."

"If I kill him, nobody will know it was you—"

"They'll guess," she said, clutching his arm. "Please, Pete. Let's just get out of here! There doesn't have to be any killing."

Grudgingly, he said, "All right." He would have liked to get rid of Sutherland, but a shot would draw attention, and it would take valuable time to hunt up a knife and cut the bastard's throat. Maybe Dolly was right and it was best to light a shuck as quick as they could.

Anyway, having her along for a while might not be too bad. He could always leave her if he got tired of her. Might even be able to *sell* her and raise a little money, he thought.

He caught hold of her hand. "Let's go."

More ideas flashed through his head as they crossed the office to the door. He didn't like the idea of spending the rest of his life as a fugitive, but he supposed it had been inevitable. He never would have been happy, trying to fit in as a law-abiding type.

Maybe he would go find Otis—he had a pretty good idea how to get word to his brother —and together they could return to Lone Pine and tree the town, but good! That thought put a savage grin on his face. He had warned all those sons of bitches that the buzzards were going to roost again, and soon they would see he was right!

With his brain burning from the lust for revenge, he jerked open the office door and stepped out onto the boardwalk.

A dozen feet out in the street, Marshal Hoyt Dixon stopped in his tracks. Both hands were full with the supper tray he'd been bringing from the café, but that didn't stop him from dropping the tray and clawing at the holstered revolver on his hip. The old lawman wasn't the sort to back down, whether he was at a dis-advantage or not.

McLaren didn't stop to think. He brought up the Colt Navy and a split second later it roared and bucked in his hand.

Chapter Fourteen

Dixon cleared leather and even managed to raise his gun and pull the trigger, but he was already reeling to the side as the Colt blasted. The bullet went well wide of McLaren and shattered the window of the marshal's office.

Blood bubbled from the wound in Dixon's chest. His face was washed out, drawn tight from pain and shock. He stayed on his feet, though, and even tried to swing his gun back in line with the escaping prisoner.

McLaren saw the revolver's muzzle angling toward him and fired again before Dixon had a chance to. This slug struck the lawman an inch above his right eyebrow, shattered his skull, and bored on into his brain, killing him almost instantly. He fell loosely to the ground in the street.

The three shots had blasted in as many seconds. People along the boardwalks were taken by surprise and didn't know what was going on, though it wouldn't take them long to look toward the marshal's office and see for themselves.

Meredith gasped and jumped back at the sudden flurry of gunshots, spilling the newspapers to boardwalk.

Ace knew the shots had come from across the street somewhere. He grabbed Meredith's arms and asked, "Are you all right?"

"Yes, I—What in the world?"

Satisfied that she hadn't been hit by a stray bullet, he pushed her toward the door of the store she had just come out of.

McLaren knew he couldn't waste any time getting out of there.

"Hey! You son of a bitch!" The shout came from his left.

He thought it sounded like that night deputy, the greaser. What was his name? Didn't matter. McLaren whirled in that direction, thrust out the Colt Navy as he drew back the hammer, and then pulled the trigger. The gun slammed out another shot.

Too late to stay his finger, he realized Dolly was standing there.

Her mouth opened in a surprised "Oh!" as she staggered back. Crimson welled from the hole in her flesh just above the neckline of the equally red dress she wore. Her eyes were huge. She stood there for a second that seemed longer.

McLaren couldn't see past her, but he heard running footsteps and more shouts.

Then Dolly crumpled to the boardwalk like a wax statue melting, and McLaren could see the night deputy running toward him. The gun in the young lawman's hand spurted flame now that he had a clear shot.

The slug whipped past McLaren's ear. He returned fire automatically. One of the deputy's legs jerked out from under him, spilling him to the boardwalk. The fall made him drop his gun.

Ace whirled toward the sounds of violence and saw Pete McLaren standing on the board-walk in front of the marshal's office, and Miguel

Soriano fall down. Two more people, wounded or maybe dead, sprawled not far from McLaren. Things were moving too fast for Ace to identify them.

McLaren could have put another bullet in the deputy, but he knew it might be his last chance to get away. Without another glance at the fallen lawman—or Dolly, for that matter—he leaped the other way, toward the nearest hitch rack.

He yanked loose the reins of the first of four horses tied there, grabbed the saddle horn, and vaulted into the saddle.

Ace's first instinct was to pull his gun and blaze away at the escaping prisoner, but he realized it might not be a good idea to have even more lead spraying around the street. Quite a few people were out in the open, in danger.

Ace sprinted into the street. He couldn't allow McLaren to get away. The man had just shot down at least three people. No telling how many more he might hurt or kill if he wasn't stopped.

As McLaren wheeled the horse around and kicked it into a run, Ace timed his leap perfectly. He crashed into McLaren, wrapped his arms around the man, and knocked him out of the saddle.

Lucky for him, he hadn't had time to get his feet securely in the stirrups, or the galloping horse might have dragged him down the street to his death.

As it was, McLaren landed on his back in the street with a resounding "Ooofff!"

Ace landed beside him, and the impact was enough to knock the air out of his lungs. Both young men rolled over and lifted their heads to gasp for breath.

Ace recovered first, intending to pull his gun and cover McLaren, but the gunman writhed around, lashed out a leg, and hooked it behind Ace's knees. He swept Ace's legs out from under him and dumped him unceremoniously in the dust.

McLaren got his hands under him and pushed himself upright. A shot blasted somewhere close by and made him duck. Ace looked around and saw Miguel Soriano limping toward them, powder smoke curling from the barrel of the gun in his hand. The deputy might be wounded, but he had a look of fierce determination on his face.

McLaren snapped a shot that came close to Miguel's head and made him dive for cover behind a water trough. The fugitive used that brief respite to grab the reins of another horse.

Ace was about to go after him when another form flashed through the air and tackled McLaren. Chance and McLaren hit the ground and rolled almost underneath the hooves of the horses tied at the hitch rack. As the animals spooked and danced around, their steel-shod hooves slashed through the air around the two fighters.

Chance threw a punch that connected with McLaren's jaw, but the next instant, as Chance tried to follow that up, McLaren planted a foot in his midsection and heaved. Chance sailed backwards, arms flailing.

At least it got him away from the danger of being trampled.

With a speed born of desperation, McLaren sprang up, darted around the horses, and reached for the reins again.

By that time, Ace was on his feet again and met him there. A fast, straight right to the face jolted McLaren's head back. Ace followed that with a left hook to the body, then a right that sunk his fist into McLaren's belly. McLaren doubled over in pain. Ace chopped down with the side of his right fist on the back of McLaren's neck and hammered the escaping prisoner to the ground.

McLaren appeared to be stunned. Wary of a trick, Ace bent, looped his right arm around McLaren's neck, and hauled him upright. McLaren remained limp, so Ace dragged him away from the horses to keep both of them from getting a foot stepped on and busted.

Chance hurried over to join his brother. "You got him?"

"Yeah, I think so."

Deputy Soriano limped up and pointed his

gun at McLaren. The barrel trembled a little, due to the depth of rage showing on his face. "Let go of him and step back," the lawman ordered.

Ace hesitated. "What are you going to do, Deputy?"

"He's an escaping prisoner. Only one way to deal with that."

"*Ley de fuga*, eh?" Chance said. "He's not escaping anymore. In fact, it looks to me like he's out cold. So the *law of flight* doesn't really hold, does it?"

Tired of holding McLaren up, Ace lowered the unconscious man to the ground and moved so he was between Miguel and McLaren. "You can't kill him in cold blood. The marshal wouldn't want that."

"The marshal's dead. What he'd want doesn't matter anymore."

"I reckon it does. Anyway, are you sure he's dead? Hadn't somebody better check on him and whoever else it was McLaren shot?"

That question prompted all three young men to look toward the marshal's office, where they saw Doc Bellem kneeling next to the motionless form of Marshal Hoyt Dixon. As Ace, Chance, and Miguel watched, Bellem lifted a solemn expres-sion toward them and shook his head.

Miguel cursed in Spanish and again swung his gun toward McLaren, who was starting to stir around and moan softly. From the fury in the deputy's eyes, it was obvious that he wanted to pull the trigger and the law be damned, but he controlled his anger and said in a taut voice, "Get him on his feet."

Ace and Chance each took an arm and lifted the groggy McLaren, who shook his head, blinked his eyes, and peered around fuzzily.

"Take him back to the jail," Miguel ordered. "I'll be right behind you."

As they started across the street, Ace glanced back at the limping deputy. "How bad are you hit? You probably need some medical attention, too."

"No, I don't," Miguel said curtly. "McLaren's bullet missed me. He shot the heel off one of my boots, though, and that knocked me down."

Ace was glad to hear that Miguel was all right. It was a shame the same couldn't be said of Marshal Dixon. The front of the marshal's shirt was soaked with blood, and his open eyes stared sightlessly up at the night. Doc Bellem should have at least closed his eyes, Ace thought, but the medico had been in a hurry to check on the other wounded person.

Dolly Redding wasn't moving, either. Bellem stood up after examining her. He hadn't even opened his medical bag. "The young woman is dead, too," he reported to Miguel as the group passed him on the boardwalk.

"I hate to think about what we're gonna find

inside," Miguel muttered. He was talking about the other deputy.

Norm Sutherland was stretched out on the office floor, but at least there wasn't a pool of blood around him.

They took McLaren straight through into the cell block. He had recovered his wits enough to know what was going on and began to struggle as they approached the open cell door.

The Jensen brothers had good grips on his arms, though, so he wasn't able to pull free. They gave him a good hard shove that sent him stumbling through the doorway and toward the bunk. Ace slammed the door closed before McLaren could catch his balance and turn around.

Miguel stood at the door with the gun still in his hand and glared at the prisoner. McLaren seemed to realize just how close to death he really was. He blanched slightly.

Then, with an angry sigh, the deputy holstered his gun.

The law had won out, at least for now.

Doc Bellem appeared in the cell block door and announced, "Deputy Sutherland will be all right. He got walloped a couple times, it looks like, and I'm sure he'll have a devil of a head-ache when he wakes up. His skull is nice and thick, so I don't believe there's any real damage."

"That's good to know, Doc. Thanks." Miguel turned back to the cell to look at the prisoner.

"You're right back where you started, McLaren, only you're not facing prison now."

McLaren gripped the bars. "What the hell are you talking about?"

"I mean you're going to hang for murdering Marshal Dixon and that poor girl. And I'm going to enjoy watching you get your neck stretched, you son of a bitch."

Chapter Fifteen

They left McLaren in the cell and went back into the office. At Doc Bellem's suggestion, Ace and Chance picked up Norm Sutherland and placed the unconscious deputy on an old sofa that sat against the wall.

"Don't try to bring him around. He'll come out of it naturally before too much longer." Bellem looked out the window. "I see Nelson's here with his wagon. I'll go make sure the marshal is tended to properly. And that unfortunate young woman, too, of course."

"Thanks, Doc," Miguel said after he slumped into the swivel chair behind the desk.

Bellem paused in the doorway. "You're the law in Lone Pine now, Miguel. Or should I say Acting Marshal Soriano?"

"It's too damned early to worry about that,"

Miguel snapped. "Marshal Dixon's barely cold. Anyway, I reckon Norm will take over. He's been a deputy longer than I have."

Bellem shook his head. "No, he's going to need to rest up and recover from being hit in the head. Anyway, I'm on the town council, and all of us know Hoyt Dixon had more confidence in you than he did in Norm. That's why he trusted you to watch over the town at night. But, like you said, we can talk about that later. At least McLaren didn't get away, so you don't have to take a posse out after him."

"Yeah," Miguel said with a glum nod. "But that's not much comfort."

The doctor just shrugged and went out.

Miguel looked at the Jensen brothers. "I appreciate your help. If you hadn't stepped in, McLaren might have gotten away."

"We didn't want that to happen," Ace said.

"A varmint like that needs to be locked up," Chance added.

The door opened and Lee Emory came in. "Miguel, I'm sure sorry about what happened," the lanky newspaperman said. "Marshal Dixon was one of the finest men I've ever known."

"Yes, I felt the same way about him," Miguel said with a nod. "He took a chance hiring me, you know. I'd had a few scrapes with the law myself."

"You were just a kid. You needed a reason to

grow up, and the marshal knew that." Emory paused. "Do you know yet exactly what happened?"

"Not really." Miguel nodded toward the sofa. "We're waiting for Norm to wake up and tell us that."

As if he'd been waiting for a cue, Deputy Sutherland let out a little moan and shifted around on the cushions. He blinked his eyes open, tried to lift his head, moaned again, and let it fall back.

Miguel stood up and went to his side. "Take it easy, Norm. The doc says you almost got your head stove in."

"Y-yeah," Sutherland said hoarsely. "Who knew . . . a little gal like that . . . could hit so hard?"

Miguel hunkered next to the sofa. "You mean it was Dolly who knocked you out?"

"Yeah . . . She came in with a tray . . . said the marshal asked her to . . . bring the prisoner his supper. I figured she . . . might be lyin' . . . so I had her set the tray on the desk. I was gonna . . . take a look under the cloth . . . but she had a gun hid under there . . . and got the drop on me." Sutherland groaned, but it didn't seem to be from the pain in his head. "I'm sorry, Miguel. I never shoulda . . . let her fool me like that."

"It sounds like you tried to do the right thing, Norm. She was just too fast and tricky for you."

"Yeah. The marshal's gonna be . . . disappointed in me."

Ace saw the indecision on Miguel's face. He didn't know whether to tell Sutherland about Marshal Dixon or not. After a moment, Miguel made up his mind. "I hate to tell you this, Norm. Pete McLaren shot the marshal while trying to escape. He . . . didn't make it."

Sutherland looked confused. "You mean, McLaren didn't escape, or . . . or . . . Aw, no! Hell, no! You can't mean it!"

"I'm sorry. McLaren was throwing lead around and killed Dolly Redding, too."

"Aw, hell!" Tears rolled down Sutherland's cheek. "The marshal . . . I can't believe he's gone." He started to get up again. "We got to get after McLaren—"

Miguel touched his shoulder. "Take it easy. McLaren didn't get away. He's safely locked up in his cell again."

"You stopped him." Sutherland sighed in relief. "Thank God for that, anyway."

Miguel nodded toward Ace and Chance. "Actually, it was the Jensen boys who pitched in and caught him before he could get away."

Sutherland looked at them. "Thanks, fellas."

"I'm just sorry we weren't able to save the marshal and Miss Redding," Ace said.

"Why in blazes did she help McLaren, anyway?" Sutherland said, his voice rising in anger.

"I know she must've been sweet on him, but hell, he treated her like dirt!"

"Who knows why people feel like they do sometimes?" Chance said. "Life's a mystery, and a damned hard one, at that."

Lee Emory had been standing back, taking notes on a pad of paper with a pencil as Sutherland explained what had happened. He glanced up and asked, "Can I quote you on that, Mr. Jensen?"

"Sure, but I don't know why you'd want to," Chance replied with a shrug. "I didn't really say anything."

"On the contrary, you summed up the random senselessness of life that plagues us all at one time or another. Are you familiar with a man named Nietzsche and his theory of the competing Apollonian and Dionysian drives?"

"We've worked on a couple cattle drives, but I don't recognize the names of those spreads and don't see what it's got to do with this."

"Never mind," Emory said. "I'm not sure philosophy ever really solved anything, anyway."

"It usually takes a bullet or a hang rope to do that," Ace said.

When Sutherland had recovered enough to stand up without being dizzy, Miguel told him to head on home and get some rest.

"Sometimes that ain't easy to do with five

134

younguns in the house, but I'm sure my wife'll try to keep 'em quiet and look after me. I feel bad about leavin' all the responsibility on you, though."

"Don't worry about that," Ace said. "My brother and I will be glad to help out for a while, won't we, Chance?"

With a slight frown, Chance said, "I suppose . . . as long as it doesn't mean pinning badges on us and swearing us in. I never had any hankering to be a lawman, and I reckon the fella who raised us might roll over in his grave if we started packing stars."

"Doc Monday's still alive," Ace reminded him.

"Yeah, but if he was dead, he'd roll over in his grave."

Miguel said, "We'll consider you unofficial deputies, then, if you're sure you want to volunteer."

"We might as well," Ace said. "We have to stay for McLaren's trial, anyway, so we'll be here."

"Did either of you see him shoot the marshal and the girl?"

"No, I was talking to Miss Emory on the boardwalk across the street when I heard the shots. But I looked over there just a second later and saw the bodies, as well as McLaren standing there with a smoking gun in his hand."

"That's more than I saw," Chance said. "I was

in the saloon. But I heard the shots, too. I looked outside to see what was going on, and then dashed into the street to get in on the action."

Miguel nodded. "I saw it happen, but I was too far away to stop it. Quite a few people were on the boardwalks. It won't be hard to round up some other witnesses. It ought to be an open-and-shut case against McLaren for those two murders. He'll swing."

"I hope you're right," Ace said. "You want us to take a shift here at the jail tonight?"

Miguel shook his head. "I'm used to being up all night. I might need you to help out some during the day until I get used to doing things the other way around. Maybe it won't be too long before Norm can start working again, too."

"Are you going to take that acting marshal job the doctor was talking about?" Chance asked.

Miguel sighed. "It looks like I may not have any choice. Somebody's got to do it."

With that settled and with McLaren safely behind bars again, Ace and Chance left the marshal's office. Ace looked along the street and saw lights burning in the newspaper office. Emory and his sister might be putting together an extra. The murders and the attempted escape warranted one, especially in a town like Lone Pine where usually not much happened.

It was a shame that couldn't be said any-more.

"Head for the Melodian and get a drink?" Chance asked.

"You go ahead. I thought I might go across the street and keep an eye on the jail for a while."

"Deputy Soriano said he'd be all right for the rest of the night."

"I know what he said. But I also know McLaren's got at least four friends who aren't accounted for right now."

"And you think they might be planning something?"

Ace gave a short shrug. "I wouldn't put it past them."

José set a jug of tequila on the bar and licked his lips nervously. "You hombres ain't gonna hold any of this against me, are you?"

"I reckon maybe we should," Perry Severs said with a grimace. "If you hadn't been about to give away where Pete was hidin', he wouldn't have shot you, and then he wouldn't have been locked up. The judge would've just fined him and let him go."

Larry Dunn frowned darkly for a moment as if he were thinking so hard it hurt his brain, then his expression cleared. "Yeah, that's right! And if Pete hadn't been in jail, he wouldn't have killed the marshal and that whore, and then they wouldn't be fixin' to hang him."

Lew Merritt and Vic Russell nodded in solemn agreement.

"They're not fixin' to hang him," Severs snapped. "Hell, the trial won't be until next week, and they can't hang him until after the trial." Severs paused. "Who knows? Maybe Pete won't even be convicted."

"I don't see how you figure that," Merritt said. "Had to be a dozen or more people who saw him shoot Dixon and the gal."

Severs poured some tequila in a glass and threw it down his throat. He wiped his mouth with the back of his hand and smiled. "It don't matter what people *saw*. All that matters is what they're willin' to *testify* they saw."

It took longer for understanding to dawn on the faces of his three companions, but finally it did.

Chapter Sixteen

The atmosphere inside the Melodian was subdued when Chance walked in. People were drinking and having low-voiced conversations, but no poker games were going on and the piano was silent. Chance didn't even see Orrie. Fontana Dupree and Hank Muller stood at the end of the bar where they usually were when she wasn't singing.

Chance joined them and saw how red Fontana's eyes were. Streaks from dried tears were evident on her cheeks, too. Muller just looked bleak . . . as if he'd been peering through the gates of hell.

"I suppose that damned murderer is behind bars," he greeted Chance.

"Yeah. He won't be going anywhere."

"That's what we all thought before," Fontana said. "And now Dolly and Marshal Dixon are dead."

"I hear Norm Sutherland is still alive, though," Muller said.

Chance nodded. "Yeah, he was knocked out, but he'll be all right."

"Hoyt Dixon was worth ten of him," Muller snapped. Then he sighed, wearily scrubbed a hand over his face, and shook his head. "I'm sorry. That's not fair. Norm's a family man and a halfway decent deputy, if you don't ask too much of him. I'm thinking Miguel Soriano will take over now, though."

"That's what I hear, too," Chance agreed. "He strikes me as a pretty good lawman."

"Yeah. You wouldn't have thought he'd turn out that way, since he was such a young hellion a few years ago, but I reckon just about everybody around here likes and trusts him now. He's earned it."

Fontana said, "I feel sorry for Dolly. I can't

believe she loved McLaren enough to risk her life for him. What a waste."

Chance couldn't argue with that.

"You want a drink, Jensen?" Muller asked.

"Yeah. Beer would be fine."

Muller signaled to one of the bartenders, who filled a mug and took it down the bar to them.

As Chance took an appreciative sip, Fontana asked, "Where's your brother?"

Chance lowered his voice. "Keeping an eye on the jail. He's worried that McLaren's friends might try something."

"You mean Perry Severs and those other three dullards?" Muller made a face. "Your brother's right. That bunch is liable to do anything."

Despite Ace's concerns and Muller's comment, the rest of the night passed peacefully. When the Jensen brothers went to the jail the next morning, they found Miguel finishing up his breakfast.

"Lars Hilfstrom figured I was shorthanded right now, so he had his daughters bring over food for me as well as for the prisoner," Miguel exclaimed. "If you ask me, Pete McLaren doesn't deserve to be fed that well, but the town's got an arrangement with the café to provide meals for the prisoners."

"No trouble last night?" Ace asked, even though he already had a good idea that was the case.

"Everything was quiet. Even McLaren didn't

carry on much. He seems pretty subdued this morning, too. I guess he's starting to realize just how much trouble he's in. He can't bluster his way out of murdering two people."

"Do you need us to keep an eye on the jail for you?" Chance asked.

Miguel nodded. "That'd be mighty good of you. I want to ask around town and locate some witnesses who saw the shooting. Then I might go back to my room at the boardinghouse and get a little sleep."

"That sounds like a good idea," Ace said. "If there's any trouble in town, one of us can stay here while the other one goes to handle it."

"Sure you don't want some badges?" Miguel asked. "Might make it easier dealing with folks if you had a symbol of authority."

"Badges?" Chance repeated, then shook his head. "No, just tell people when you're talking to them that we're giving you a hand, and if Lone Pine is anything like other settlements where we've been, the word will get around in a hurry."

"I'm sure it will . . . especially if I tell Mr. Sawyer at the livery stable and Colonel Howden at the hotel." Miguel smiled. "Those two old-timers will compete against each other to see who can tell the most folks the fastest."

Ace was glad to see Miguel seemed to have recovered somewhat from the shock and rage that had gripped him immediately following the marshal's death. More than likely, the young deputy would need to be level-headed during the days to come. Ace had a hunch the trouble wasn't over yet.

Miguel got up from behind the desk and lifted a stockinged foot. He had taken his boots off so he could walk without limping because of the shot-off heel. "I have an old pair of boots I can wear while I'm getting mine fixed. I reckon that's the first order of business. If you fellas need me, I'll be around town somewhere. It's not that big a place."

"What about the breakfast trays?" Ace asked.

"One of the Hilfstrom girls will be around to collect them later." With that, Miguel left.

Ace and Chance poured cups of coffee for themselves from the pot staying warm on the stove and settled down to the job of watching the office and jail. Chance sprawled on the sofa with his legs stretched out in front of him while Ace took the swivel chair behind the desk.

"You look natural there," Chance commented. "Maybe Miguel *should* give you a badge."

"I don't think so. Too much responsibility."

Chance laughed. "*Responsibility* is your middle name, brother."

Before Ace could respond to that, Pete McLaren yelled from the cell block, "Hey! Anybody out there? I know you are. I can hear you talking."

Ace stood up and went to the door, stopping

just inside the cell block. "What do you want, McLaren?" He sensed Chance right behind him.

Instead of answering the question, the prisoner stood at the cell door and asked a question of his own. "What are you bastards doing here?"

"Keeping an eye on the jail for Marshal Soriano."

"Marshal Soriano?" McLaren laughed. "It didn't take that greaser long to take over, did it?"

"Well . . . acting marshal. I reckon he'll get the job if he wants it, though."

"No, he won't," McLaren said confidently. "Know how I know that?" Without waiting for either of the Jensen brothers to answer, he went on. "Because he'll be dead! So will the two of you. So will Ordway and Buchanan if they try to put me on trial. When my brother hears what's happened, he'll come back here and kill all of you. People will be lucky if he doesn't burn down the whole town!"

"You're crazy," Chance said. "You don't even know that your brother's still alive."

A smug smile appeared on McLaren's face. "Just keep on thinkin' that, you son of a bitch."

Ace said, "This is a waste of time and breath. You'll get your day in court, McLaren, and then you'll pay for what you've done."

McLaren's grin got even more cocksure and arrogant. "I wouldn't count on that."

• • •

"What's that Mex doin'?" Lew Merritt asked as he and Perry Severs lounged against an empty hitch rail and watched Miguel Soriano go into the saddle maker's shop. In the past hour, Soriano had visited half a dozen businesses along Lone Pine's main street.

"He's looking for people who saw what happened last night. People who are willing to go into court and testify that Pete shot that damn lawman and the whore."

Merritt frowned. "Well, that wouldn't be a good thing, would it?"

"No, it wouldn't," Severs replied, reining in his impatience and frustration at his companion's slowness of thought. Merritt, Dunn, and Russell were all pretty dumb, and denying that wouldn't accomplish a blasted thing.

For that matter, Severs was under no illusions about his own intelligence. He knew he was smarter than his friends, but he still wasn't cut out to be the one who did all the figuring and planning. He'd always been more than happy to leave that to Pete.

But Pete was locked up in jail, and so far Severs hadn't come up with any ideas for getting him out of there. It seemed the best thing to do was make sure Pete didn't get convicted and sent to prison. If the law had to let him go, things could go back to the way they had been . . . before.

Several minutes later, Soriano emerged from the saddle maker's shop and headed on down the street. Severs straightened from his casual pose and said to Merritt, "Come on."

"Come on where?"

"I want to talk to Carhart, too."

The saddle maker's name was Royal Carhart. He was a short, wiry man in late middle age who had been a cowboy until a horse had fallen on him and busted him up that he couldn't handle the work anymore. He'd always been good with leatherwork, so he had gone from sitting all day in a saddle to making them, and he had become quite good at it. He looked up from his workbench as Severs and Merritt came in, ringing the little bell that hung over the door.

Carhart recognized them immediately. A suspicious frown appeared on his face, but he greeted them civilly. "What can I do for you, gents?"

Severs smiled, but he wasn't sure how convincing he was able to make the expression. He jerked a thumb over his shoulder. "We just saw the deputy come out of here. What did he want?"

"You mean Actin' Marshal Soriano?"

Severs grunted. "Yeah, I reckon. Didn't know about that part of it. He come to have a saddle made?"

Carhart set aside the awl he'd been using and

frowned. "I ain't sure it's any of your business what the marshal wanted."

"Hell, no need to get proddy. We were just curious, is all."

"Because you think it might've been about that no-good friend of yours?"

"Hey—" Merritt began.

Severs silenced him with an uplifted hand, then turned to Carhart and went on. "We just want to make sure justice is done."

The saddle maker snorted. "Justice'll be done, all right. It'll be done when Pete McLaren's danglin' from a hang rope!"

Merritt wanted to respond angrily again, but Severs hurried on. "They're trying to railroad him. Pete never did anything to warrant hanging."

"The hell he didn't!" Carhart said with a disgusted snort. "Where have you been? He shot down Marshal Dixon and one of those gals from Muller's saloon in cold blood!"

"That's not possible."

"It sure as hell is," Carhart insisted. "I seen it happen with my own eyes last night, and like I told Miguel, I'll be more 'n happy to stand up in court and say so. I ain't the only one, neither. He's got plenty of witnesses who'll send McLaren right up the steps of the gallows!"

"Like who?"

A canny look appeared in Carhart's rheumy old eyes. "Hold on here. You fellas are McLaren's friends. I shouldn't even be talkin' to you."

Merritt took a step toward him. "Perry asked you a question, you old pelican."

Carhart grabbed the awl again and stood up. He took a quick step back from the bench and held the sharp-pointed tool in front of him in a defensive posture. "Hold on there—"

"Take it easy, Lew." Severs gripped Merritt's arm. "There's no need for things to get nasty here."

"I don't like the way this old man's talkin'," Merritt responded sullenly.

"You see how it is, Carhart," Severs said with a shrug. "We don't like it when people go spreading lies about our partner. If you know anybody who's thinking about doing the same thing, you might want to let them know it's not a good idea."

Carhart swallowed. "You can't come in here and threaten me—"

"I'm not threatening anybody. I'm just saying . . . anybody who goes into court and tells lies after swearing to tell the truth . . . well, they've got to expect some trouble, now don't they?"

"You get outta my shop," Carhart said as he gestured with the awl.

"Sure, we're going. You just remember what I said."

Merritt snarled at Carhart as Severs tugged him toward the door. The little bell jingled above their heads again as they went out, but it didn't sound so merry.

"I don't know why you didn't let me teach that old varmint a lesson," Merritt said. "He's gonna testify against Pete."

"Is he?" Severs chuckled. "He looked a mite spooked to me, Lew. I've got a hunch his memory might get bad over the weekend. He'll warn his friends that they better have memory problems, too. Comes time for the trial . . . if there *is* a trial . . . those fellas trying to hang Pete may discover they don't have anybody on their side after all."

Merritt frowned. "What do you mean, if there is a trial?"

"Just something else I was thinking about. This is just the start of things, Lew . . . and there's no telling what might happen before it's all over."

Chapter Seventeen

Because Marshal Hoyt Dixon's funeral was that afternoon, Chance was at the marshal's office and jail, keeping an eye on things. He'd never cared for funerals and had said he would stand guard. With most of the citizens turning out for the well-liked lawman's funeral, it would be a good time for Pete McLaren's friends to attempt a jailbreak, if they were going to. A couple volunteers were with Chance, including one of the bartenders from the Melodian. All three men had loaded shotguns, making it unlikely anybody could reach McLaren and set him free.

At the cemetery on a windswept hill overlooking the town, Ace stood among the mourners before the service began.

Crackerjack Sawyer pointed to a single pine tree next to the burial ground's entrance and told him, "That's the tree they named the settlement after. If you look around the hills, you can see hundreds of pines, but that's the only one on *this* hill."

"I wondered a little about that. This area isn't exactly short on pine trees." Ace paused. "So it went from being called Buzzard's Roost to being named after a cemetery."

"Does seem to be a little hard to get away from death, don't it? But if you stop and think about it, that's the way it is everywhere you go, no matter what sort of happy names folks like to slap on things."

Ace couldn't argue with that.

A hearse drawn by the customary six black horses creaked through the gates of the cemetery. Miguel Soriano walked along behind it, as did Norm Sutherland. Doc Bellem had advised Sutherland to stay in bed and rest, but he'd refused. He had to pay his last respects to the man who had been his boss and his longtime friend.

Dixon had no family in Lone Pine. He had been a tight-lipped man in some respects, and in fact no one really knew if he had relatives elsewhere. It would come as no surprise if he didn't. Star packers who drifted from town to town bringing law and order to the frontier often never settled down and had families. But he had plenty of friends, as the crowd at the cemetery attested.

The hearse came to a stop next to an open grave. Pallbearers took the simple casket from the vehicle and lowered it into its final resting place. A minister from one of the local churches intoned a short sermon and a long prayer as clouds drifted in front of the sun and then moved on, making the light come and go in irregular patterns.

When the service was over, the crowd broke up quickly and most of the mourners walked out through the cemetery gates to head back down the hill.

Ace stayed where he was, prompting Crackerjack to ask, "Ain't you goin' back to town?"

"There's another funeral," Ace said.

Crackerjack frowned. "You mean for that saloon gal?"

"That's right." Ace looked toward the other side of the cemetery where a plain wagon with an even plainer coffin already in the back of it stood. A mound of dirt marked the location of another grave over there.

"Most folks ain't gonna stand around and offer up prayers for a gal like that."

"She was still a human being," Ace said.

"Yeah, but if she hadn't let McLaren out of jail, Marshal Dixon wouldn't be dead right now. Of course, neither would she, but folks are still gonna hold that against her."

"I suppose they have a right to do that, but I still think the decent thing to do is to see that she's laid to rest properly."

"Oh, well . . . hell. I reckon I can go along with you. Anybody wants their horse from the stable, they can wait a few minutes."

The two of them walked across the cemetery. It appeared the only other mourners who had remained behind after the marshal's funeral was over were Hank Muller, Fontana Dupree, and some of the bartenders and serving girls from the Melodian.

As Ace and Crackerjack stepped up beside the little group, Muller looked over and gave them a curt nod. Fontana smiled slightly, and Ace could tell she was grateful someone else had shown up.

The same preacher performed this service, which was shorter than Dixon's had been. The sky pilot talked about all sins being washed clean and asked the Lord in His infinite wisdom to have mercy on the soul of Dorothy Redding. A few of the saloon girls sniffled. Not many people had shown them mercy in their lives, and they prob-ably didn't hold out much hope of receiving any from the Good Lord, either.

While the service was going on, the grave diggers had already gone to work on the other side of the cemetery. The regular thuds of dirt falling on Dixon's coffin made a grim counter-point to the preacher's words.

When the service was over, Fontana went over to Ace and asked, "Where's your brother, Mr. Jensen?"

"He stayed at the jail to make sure nobody tried anything else," Ace explained. "We're helping out Marshal Soriano. Sort of unofficial deputies, I guess you'd say."

Hank Muller overheard that. "You and your brother have been in the thick of things ever since you rode into town, haven't you?"

"Yeah. Somehow it usually seems to work out that way," Ace said with a rueful smile. "I'm not sure why, since really we're the peaceable sort."

"Well, I'm glad you've been around," Fontana said. "Otherwise the trouble might have been even worse."

"Stop by the Melodian anytime you get a chance," Muller added. "I'll buy you a beer. You and your brother both."

"We'll be there," Ace said. "I know Chance

is eager to hear you sing again, Miss Dupree."

"It's hard to think about singing in a place like this," Fontana said with a glance over her shoulder as they walked out of the cemetery. "But I guess death is a reminder that life goes on for those left behind, isn't it?"

Ace gave a grim smile. "You could look at it that way."

Miguel Soriano went back to his rented room after the funeral, pulled off his boots, and stretched out on the bed. Normally he would have undressed, but he was too tired. Everything that had happened, culminating with the emotional ordeal of Marshal Hoyt Dixon's funeral, had sapped Miguel's strength and left him exhausted. When he closed his eyes, he felt like he could sleep for a week.

He fell asleep right away, but a little more than four hours later, he was wide awake again.

The human body—and mind—were creatures of habit. As the night deputy, Miguel was always up and around at that time, getting a good start on what was for him, his day's work.

Sleeping at that time of day just seemed wrong. He stayed on the bed for a while, trying to doze off again, but eventually he gave up.

His mind was just too full to let him relax. Memories cascaded through his head like a waterfall.

A carefree vaquero, Miguel rode with the wrong crowd. He never rustled any stock himself but was pretty sure some of his friends did. Sooner or later, on some moonless night, he would probably find himself riding toward the border, driving cattle that didn't belong to him.

Hoyt Dixon stepped in, offering Miguel the job of night deputy when old Cyrus Trammell handed in his badge and moved to El Paso to live out his remaining years with his daughter and her family.

Miguel asked the marshal, "Why in the world would you extend such an offer?"

Dixon grinned.

"I figure I can either hire you now or hang you or shoot you in a couple of years. I'd rather hire you."

Happy for the opportunity, Miguel took the job and started by making the evening rounds of the town, checking in with the proprietors of the businesses that were still open, making sure the doors were locked at the ones that were closed. Marshal Dixon had taught him it was important for the law to have a visible presence around the settlement.

Miguel's thoughts returned to the current time. Since that day, he had done his best not to let Dixon down, but the marshal was dead, and

Miguel wasn't the night deputy anymore. He was the acting marshal. All the members of the town council were in agreement on that. They were counting on him to maintain law and order in Lone Pine. It was the biggest responsibility he had ever had.

Even though he didn't blame himself for what had happened—he'd been doing his job when Pete McLaren escaped—the whole thing still gnawed at his guts like a hungry coyote.

Donald Barr ran one of the general mercantiles in Lone Pine and lived with his wife Eunice and two daughters, Millie and Deborah in a pleasant but not too fancy house on the edge of the settlement. He was in his forties and was regarded as a decent, unassuming man who conducted his business fairly and could be found every Sunday morning in one of the pews of the Methodist Church, singing hymns along with his family.

Before Sunday morning came Saturday night, and that was when Donald and Eunice got up to *mischief,* as Eunice liked to call it. None of her friends in town knew that she had a bit of an adventurous streak when it came to certain matters, but Donald was well aware of it and was very appreciative of it.

However, that mischief had barely gotten under way when a hard metal ring pressed against the back of Donald's head and a voice whispered hoarsely, "Don't move."

Donald had been moving quite energetically, but he froze. Even though he'd never had a gun barrel shoved against his head, he realized that was what he felt. He choked out, "Oh, God. Please don't kill me."

"Donald?" Eunice said, her voice somewhat muffled by her position. "What is—"

"Be quiet, lady," the intruder rasped, a little louder.

Eunice let out a startled cry.

"Don't you move, either."

She started to jerk away from Donald, but he grabbed her and held her tightly. If she spooked the man with the gun, the weapon's hammer might fall and then Donald's brains would be splattered all over the wall above the headboard.

"Eunice, be still." Donald's pulse had been racing before the interruption, but now his heart was pounding so much it felt like it was about to burst out of his chest.

"You're a smart man, Barr," the unseen man said. "I reckon this is as embarrassing as all get-out, but it's better to be embarrassed than to be dead, right?" The gun barrel prodded hard. "I said, right?"

"R-right," Donald managed to get out.

"You're smart enough to know when to listen to good advice, aren't you?"

"I . . . I hope so."

"I do, too, for your sake, and for the sake of your wife and those little girls of yours."

Eunice couldn't restrain herself. She cried, "You leave my daughters alone, you monster!"

"I'm not gonna bother them. I give you my word on that. My friend, though, who's right down the hall outside the door of their room . . . well, I can't speak for him."

"What . . . what do you want?" Donald asked.

Instead of answering the question directly, the intruder said, "Your friend Royal Carhart came to see you today, didn't he? Came to talk about Pete McLaren?"

"I—I—."

"The way I hear it, you and Carhart and some others have been spreading lies about McLaren, telling that Mex deputy you saw him shoot Marshal Dixon and that gal from the Melodian, and that's just not true. McLaren was out on the boardwalk when it happened, but there's no telling exactly where the shots came from, is there? Somebody else could've killed those folks. And you ought to know that better than anybody else, because your store is right across the street from the marshal's office and you were still open last night when it happened. I hear tell you were looking out the window when the shooting started, and even you couldn't tell where the bullets came from that killed Dixon and the girl. Isn't that right?"

Before the storekeeper could respond, his wife

exclaimed, "For God's sake, Donald, *agree with him!*"

"But—but—"

"How old are those gals of yours?" the intruder whispered. "Fourteen and twelve, right? Something like that?"

Donald Barr felt sick with fear, but at the same time he was angry. "If you touch them, I'll—"

The gun barrel was pulled away from his head, but an instant later something slammed into his skull with enough force to stun him and knock him forward onto his wife. Eunice let out a muffled scream and tried to writhe out from under him.

She stopped as a dark figure loomed over her and a hand caught hold of her long brown hair, which she had taken down from its braids before she and Donald went to bed. A gasp of pain escaped from her lips as the man pulled her head back and nudged the gun barrel under her chin.

"Your husband's not hurt bad," the man said. "He'll come to in a few minutes. When he does, you tell him he'd better do the smart thing or we'll be back. And we won't treat you . . . or your girls . . . so gentle next time. The same thing'll happen if you go running to that greaser deputy, too." The man let go of Eunice's hair and ran his hand along her body, causing her to shudder.

She closed her eyes and clutched at her

husband's senseless form. Donald was breathing, so she knew he was still alive.

Footsteps sounded quietly on the floor. The bedroom door closed behind the intruder as he left. Eunice stayed where she was for several long moments before her concern for her children made her get up and reach for a robe.

There would be no more mischief tonight.

Not the enjoyable kind, anyway.

In the thickest, most impenetrable shadows under the trees about a hundred yards away from the Barr house, Severs and Merritt paused and pulled down the bandannas that had covered the lower halves of their faces. They hadn't said anything after leaving the house.

Finally, Merritt asked, "You reckon they understood?"

"The woman did," Severs said. "I'm not so sure about Barr, but hell, it's better that she got the message. She'll make sure her husband does what he's told."

"You threatened to hurt the girls?"

"Yeah. I had to."

Merritt took a deep breath, then said, "I don't like it."

"Neither do I." Severs knew out on the frontier, only the lowest of the low would molest a respectable woman or even threaten to do such a thing. "But I don't want to see Pete hang, either."

"No, I reckon not. We gonna pay a visit to any of the others?"

After leaving Royal Carhart's saddle shop, Severs and Merritt had kept an eye on the place. Just as Severs expected, Carhart had closed up the business and hurried around town for a while, stopping to talk to Donald Barr and several other merchants whose stores would have been open at the time of the shootings. Severs had figured those were the men Miguel Soriano was lining up to testify against McLaren.

"That probably won't be necessary," Severs said in answer to Merritt's question. "Barr will spread the word. The rest of them will know they're taking a big chance if they testify against Pete."

"Soriano saw the shooting, too, you know."

"Yeah, but the girl was standing between him and Pete. He can't swear a hundred percent that he saw Pete shoot the marshal. That lawyer Horton will trip him up, you mark my words. Horton's slick that way."

"Yeah, I guess." Merritt sighed. "I'm glad you're around to figure out what to do, Perry. Tryin' to figure it all out would make my head hurt."

"I'm not that fond of it, either. I'll be glad when Pete's loose again and can take care of all that."

They started walking away from the Barr house. After a few steps, Merritt said, "Perry . . .

what if Barr or his missus says it was us who got into their house?"

"They can't prove a damn thing," Severs said. "They never saw our faces, and I whispered so they couldn't tell for sure whose voice it was. The girls slept through the whole thing, right?"

"Not a peep out of 'em," Merritt assured him. "I sure hope this works."

"So do I, but if it doesn't, we'll try something else. We'll do whatever it takes. They'll never hang Pete."

Chapter Eighteen

Ace took over watching the jail Saturday night. He had a couple unexpected volunteer helpers— Crackerjack Sawyer and Colonel Charles Howden. Howden showed up first to offer his services as a guard, but Crackerjack knocked on the office door—which Ace had locked when the sun went down—less than five minutes later.

When Ace let him in, the liveryman glared at Howden. "What's that damn Yankee doin' here?"

"I could ask the same thing about you, you unreconstructed Rebel," Howden snapped.

"I come to help this young fella keep an eye on the prisoner," Crackerjack replied as he waved a hand at Ace.

"Well, so did I," Howden said. "And since I was

here first, I don't think we need any help from the likes of you."

Ace tried not to sigh. "Take it easy, both of you."

"You should respect your elders," the old-timers said in unison. Then they glowered at each other.

"The war was a long time ago, and to be honest, I don't even remember much about it," Ace said. "I was too young. I recall hearing people talking about Appomattox, but that's all."

"A mighty sad day," Crackerjack said.

"We're in agreement on that," Howden said. "It's sad it took four long, bloody years to bring you rebels to heel."

"Damn you—" Crackerjack took a step toward the colonel.

Ace got between them. "That's enough," he said firmly. "I've got a hunch you two have a lot more in common than you realize. Neither of you want Pete McLaren's friends busting him out of jail, do you?"

"Durn right I don't," Crackerjack said. "That varmint's finally behind bars where he belongs, and I want to help keep him there."

"I feel the same way." Howden frowned. "I suppose we might be able to put aside our differences if it's for the good of the town."

"And to see that justice is done," Crackerjack added.

"That's what I thought." Ace nodded toward

the rack on the wall where rifles and shotguns were kept. "Grab a couple Greeners and get a pocketful of shells from the box on the desk. If McLaren's pards show up and try anything, we'll give them a buckshot welcome."

"That's somethin' we can agree on for sure!" Crackerjack said.

While they were arming themselves, Colonel Howden asked, "Where's Marshal Soriano tonight, Ace?"

"Getting some rest, I hope. He spent most of the day talking to folks around town, finding out who saw the shooting last night."

"What about that brother o' yours?" Crackerjack asked.

That question made Ace smile. "I don't know for sure, but I'd bet a brand-new hat he's probably over at the Melodian."

With the town's marshal and the young saloon girl laid to rest only a few hours earlier, a solemn air hung over the Melodian. As Fontana had told Ace earlier, though, life had to go on.

After a while she drifted toward the piano and motioned to Orrie for him to join her.

"What do you want me to play, Fontana?" he asked as he sat down on the bench in front of the keys.

She thought for a moment, then said, "How about 'Farther Along We'll Know More About It'?"

Orrie frowned. "A hymn? In this place?"

"Do you know it?"

His narrow shoulders rose and fell in a shrug. "Sure. I've played it before, and once I play a song, I never forget it. My mind's funny that way."

"That's one reason I love having you play the piano for me. Go ahead."

He nodded. "Sure, if that's what you want."

His fingers moved over the keys with easy assurance and coaxed out the notes of the hymn. Fontana began to sing.

The conversations in the room died away as her clear, pure voice filled the air. Men lifted their heads from their drinks and looked at her. The serving girls stopped in their rounds and did likewise. The hymn's sad but hopeful words touched everyone, and so did the sweet voice that sang them.

Chance stepped into the saloon to find everyone watching and listening to Fontana. He didn't blame them. She was a beautiful sight, standing beside the piano in a dark blue gown, and the song that came from her lips was compelling. Not wanting to break the spell, he sat down at the nearest empty table, took off his hat, and placed it in front of him.

When the song was over, one of the cowboys in the room called softly, "Now sing 'Amazin' Grace.'" Several other men murmured agreement.

Fontana looked at Orrie, who said, "Of course I know it."

He played the introduction, then Fontana sang,

"Amazing grace, how sweet the sound . . .
that saved a wretch like me . . .
I once was lost, but now am found . . .
was blind but now I see."

She continued with the rest of the hymn, and when she was finished, the room was so hushed Chance could hear people breathing. Even though the Melodian was by no means a dive, it was still a frontier saloon, and its patrons were a rough crowd with plenty of sins among them. The same was true of the people who worked there.

But at that moment, all of them were as visibly moved as if they had been devout churchgoers. Some of them probably were, Chance mused, since plenty of frontier folks, like those elsewhere, subscribed to the doctrine of sin on Saturday night and salvation on Sunday morning. He didn't doubt that they were sincere in what they were feeling right now, though.

The cowboy who had requested the hymn broke the silence by saying, "I ain't heard that song since I left home. Thank you, Miss Fontana."

She smiled at him. "You're welcome, Curly."

"You done a beautiful job of singin' it, too. I never heard better."

Another man said, "Do you know 'The Old Rugged Cross'?"

Fontana kept smiling, but Chance thought she looked a little surprised.

She said, "I think so . . ." She looked over at the bar where Hank Muller stood.

The saloonkeeper's forehead creased slightly in a frown. Clearly, neither he nor Fontana had expected a church service to break out on a Saturday night. And when people were sitting around listening to hymns, they weren't drinking much, which meant the profits went down. But after a moment, Muller nodded.

Fontana looked at Orrie, who gave a little shake of his head in disbelief and started playing.

Chance sat there, watching and listening, as Fontana went through several more hymns requested by the Melodian's patrons. Growing up as they had, with a professional gambler as their guardian and the closest thing to a father they were ever likely to have, they hadn't spent much time in church as youngsters.

Doc Monday hadn't completely neglected their spiritual growth, however. They had attended a few Christmas Eve and Easter services, when all the saloons had closed down. So Chance had heard all those hymns before, even though he wasn't familiar enough with them that he could have sung along. Fontana's voice was so beautiful he figured the time was well spent, no matter what she was singing.

Finally she smiled and told the customers, "That's all for now, boys."

The men went back to drinking and talking, although the atmosphere in the saloon was still very subdued.

Chance was glad to see Fontana come across the room toward him, instead of returning to the bar where Muller was. He got to his feet as she came up to the table. "Good evening, Miss Dupree. Would you care to join me?"

"That's what I had in mind. Where's your brother tonight?"

Chance held a chair for her and waited until she was seated before he answered her question. "Ace is standing guard over at the jail."

"That's right. The two of you are lending a hand to Miguel Soriano, aren't you?"

"Yep. But we're not deputies. Not officially."

"It wouldn't matter to me if you were."

Chance shook his head. "We're not the sort to pack a star. Spent too much time in places like this while we were growing up, I suppose."

Fontana's eyebrows rose. "You were raised in saloons?"

"Well, more or less."

"That sounds interesting. Tell me about it."

Chance explained how he and Ace had never known their mother or their father. Their mother had died when the boys were born and their father's identity was still a mystery. All they really knew was their mother's name was Lettie Jensen, and she had been good friends with Doc Monday, who had taken the little ones to raise.

"It sounds to me like *he* is probably your father," Fontana commented.

Chance shook his head. "He never let us call him Pa or Father or anything like that when we were kids, and when we were old enough to understand things, he swore up and down he wasn't. He told us our mother was, uh, already in the family way when he met her. Her husband had gone off to war and gotten himself killed in the very first battle."

"Do you think it really happened that way?"

Chance shrugged. "It could have, I suppose. Lots of fellas went to fight and never came back. After a while, it seemed to Ace and me like it didn't really matter. Doc took good care of us." He grinned. "Better than anybody would think a shiftless scoundrel like him ever could."

"Where is he now? Is he still alive?"

"Yeah. He got sick a while back and had to go to one of those sanitariums for what he called a rest cure. I wouldn't be surprised if he's running an endless poker game for the other patients. We stop by and see him every now and then. We would have stayed there in the same town to make sure he was all right, but Doc wouldn't hear of it. He said for us to get out and enjoy our lives while we're young."

Fontana put an elbow on the table, rested her chin on her hand, and smiled. "And have you been? Enjoying your lives, that is?"

"I reckon we have. Except for the parts where people start shooting at us."

"I think you probably even enjoy that in a way. You strike me as boys who have a thirst for adventure."

"We're not really boys, you know. In fact, we're probably older than you."

"I'm twenty-two," Fontana said without hesitation.

"See? We've got you beat by a few years."

"Sometimes it's not the years that matter. It's the sort of life you've led."

Chance knew that was true. He didn't want to pry too much into the life Fontana had led, though. After all, she sang in a saloon for a living, even though she dressed more decorously than the other girls who worked in the Melodian.

Before the moment of silence between them could become awkward, Chance broke it by asking, "Can I buy you a drink?"

"No, but thanks. I have to protect my vocal cords, you know."

"Will you be singing more tonight?"

"In a little while," she said. "I'll try to pick something more cheerful."

Chapter Nineteen

José kept casting nervous glances toward the table where Perry Severs, Larry Dunn, Vic Russell, and Lew Merritt were playing penny-ante poker and drinking tequila. Dunn and Russell had been there all evening. Severs and Merritt had joined them a short time earlier, and a few minutes of intense, low-voiced conversation had occurred before the men relaxed and began passing the time with cards and liquor.

A few more men were in the cantina, but they stayed as far away from that table as they could. José wasn't the only one Pete McLaren's friends made nervous.

The jug of tequila was pretty much empty. Severs shook the last few drops into his glass, then stood up, carried the jug to the bar, and set it on the planks. "Reckon we'd better have another, José."

"*Sí, señor.*" José took another jug from a shelf. His left shoulder was bandaged and his arm was in a sling, but he could manage all right with one arm. He didn't have much choice in the matter, since he had nobody else to run the cantina and he depended on it for his livelihood.

Severs smiled at him. "You seem a mite jumpy tonight, amigo."

"Me? Jumpy?" José shook his head, making his chins wobble. "No, señor, I am fine."

"Bet that shoulder hurts, though."

Out of habit, José started to shrug, then winced in pain as he realized that was a bad idea. "All of life hurts at one time or another. That is how we know we are still alive."

"Yeah, I reckon the dead don't feel a thing, do they? I just thought you might be worried about what happened at that hearing the other day. You know, how you testified against Pete, and now here we are, his best pards, drinking in your cantina."

"It . . . it did not matter what I said." José swallowed. "Marshal Dixon and the young Señor Jensen saw the whole thing. To have told a different story would have done no good."

"Are you absolutely sure about that?" Severs drawled, still smiling. "Certain enough to bet your life on it? You'll have another chance to tell your story, you know . . . if the whole thing comes to trial."

"*If* it comes to trial?" José repeated. He caught the veiled threat Severs had just made without any trouble, but he was puzzled by the man's other comment. "Why would it not?"

"You never know about these things. How much do I owe you for the tequila?"

"It . . . it is on the house, señor."

Severs chuckled. "Just like the last jug, eh?" He picked it up and turned away from the bar.

Giving up on sleep, Miguel sat up, swung his legs off the bed, and reached for his boots.

A few minutes later, he was moving along the street, going about his job the way he usually did. One or both of the Jensen brothers would be at the office, and he instinctively trusted them to look after things. Marshal Dixon had taught him how to be a good judge of character. He would check in at the office later.

A moment later, furtive movement across the street caught his eye and he stopped where he was on the boardwalk. Frowning, he looked closer and saw a man walking through the shadows carrying a long object that looked like it might be a gun.

As Miguel watched, a stray beam of light from a window illuminated the person for a second. He recognized Royal Carhart, the old cowhand who had a saddle shop in Lone Pine.

The thing Carhart was carrying was a double-barreled shotgun.

Miguel couldn't think of any reason the shop owner ought to be toting a shotgun in town. That, combined with Carhart's surreptitious attitude, made him suspicious. Staying on the opposite side of the street, he turned around and went back the way he had come, staying across from and just behind Carhart. The saddle maker didn't appear to have noticed that someone was following him.

For a minute, Miguel thought Carhart was going to walk clean out of town and into the hills.

On the outskirts of the settlement, though, the old-timer veered toward a squat adobe building all too familiar to Miguel. Before he had become a lawman, he had spent too much time in José's cantina, drinking and listening to the stories of the men he admired, men who had been little better than bandits.

The door of the cantina stood open to let in the night air. Carhart stalked into the place with the Greener's twin barrels shoved in front of him.

Severs stopped short before he took a step back toward the table where his friends sat.

Royal Carhart stood just inside the cantina's entrance.

The scrawny little saddle maker had a double-barreled shotgun pointed at Severs.

José muttered a prayer in Spanish under his breath and started to edge away from Severs, out of the line of fire.

Over at the table, the conversation had stopped. Dunn shifted slightly in his chair as his hand dropped toward the gun on his hip.

"Larry, stay still." Sever's heart had slugged heavily in his chest as soon as he found himself staring down the twin barrels of that Greener, but he kept his wits about him. More than likely, panic would get him killed—whether it was his panic or that of his friends. None of them were fast enough to put Carhart down before he could jerk the shotgun's triggers.

Severs forced himself to take a deep breath. "What's this all about, Carhart? I don't cotton to having a gun pointed at me."

"You know good and well what it's about," Carhart replied as his leathery face twisted in a snarl. "I been thinkin' all day about what you said this mornin', and I'm mad as hell. You figure you can come into my shop—*my shop!*—and threaten me and get away with it?"

Severs shook his head. "I don't know what in blazes you're talking about."

"The hell you don't! You warned me I'd better change my story if I knew what was good for me. You want me to get up in court and say I never saw Pete McLaren shoot Marshal Dixon and that saloon gal!"

It was a struggle to keep his nerves under control, but Severs managed. "Well, if that's the truth, that's what you need to tell the judge and jury."

"But it ain't the truth and you know it!" Carhart took a step forward. The shotgun barrels shook a little, making Severs's nerves draw even tighter. "I've fought rustlers and Injuns in my time. I've been caught out on the range in a blizzard that damn near froze the life outta me. You really think I'm afraid o' gutter trash like you and your friends?"

"I wish you'd put that shotgun down. There's no need for anybody to get hurt here—"

"You threatened to kill me!" Carhart interrupted.

"If I pull the trigger on you right here and now, it ain't nothin' but self-defense. And that's just what I'm gonna do!"

Severs saw the old-timer's finger whiten on the first trigger. He dived to the floor, knowing it probably wouldn't save him, but it was all he could do.

Miguel hurried across the street.

As he came closer, he heard the angry voices inside. The rising pitch of Carhart's voice told Miguel the saddle maker was about to do something desperate. Miguel could think of only one thing that could be.

He lunged through the doorway, reached over Carhart's shoulder, grabbed the shotgun's barrels, and yanked them up toward the ceiling just as the old-timer pulled one of the triggers.

The report slammed against Miguel's ears like fists. The shotgun's recoil almost wrenched it out of his grip, but he held on pulling the weapon away from Carhart at the same time his shoulder rammed into the old man's back and knocked him off his feet.

As Carhart fell to the floor, Miguel caught a flicker of movement from the corner of his right eye and wheeled in that direction. Three of Pete

McLaren's friends coming up from chairs at a table.

All of them were trying to draw their guns.

Sitting across from Fontana in the Melodian, Chance was enjoying their conversation and wanted to reassure her. "Nobody minded the hymns, you know. In fact, they probably provided some comfort for folks."

"Well, I hope so. I know everybody's upset—" She stopped short and lifted her head as a dull boom came from somewhere in town.

Everybody else in the saloon heard it, too, and once again conversations lurched to a halt. Chance was already on his feet.

"Was that—?"

"Sounded like a shotgun." He hurried to the batwings, slapped them aside, and disappeared into the night.

With one hand wrapped around the shotgun's barrels, Miguel slapped his other hand on the breech and found the triggers. "Hold it!" he called, leveling the scattergun at the three men who stood close together. If he fired the other barrel, the buckshot would blow all three of them to hell.

"Don't shoot, Deputy!" another voice said urgently from under a table.

Miguel flicked a glance toward it, saw Perry Severs lying on the floor.

"We didn't do anything wrong," Severs went on. "That loco old man tried to kill me!"

Miguel's nerves crawled. With Severs in front of him and the other three off to the side, they sort of had him whipsawed. He couldn't point the shotgun in two directions at once. The remaining barrel was enough to dispose of one threat, but could he drop the empty shotgun and haul out his revolver before whoever was left got lead in him?

Of course, the one who'd been about to do the shooting was Royal Carhart, Miguel reminded himself, not any of McLaren's friends. None of the men at the table had cleared leather, and their guns were all back in their holsters. They stood with their hands held clear of the weapons. Severs wasn't trying to draw, either.

Miguel told him, "Get up. And then somebody tell me what's going on here."

Severs climbed to his feet and dusted himself off. "I already told you. Carhart tried to kill me."

Holding the shotgun in his right hand, Miguel reached down with his left, closed it around Carhart's stringy upper right arm, and pulled the saddle maker up. "What were you doing, Mr. Carhart?"

Severs sneered. "Him, you talk to with respect."

"He's earned the benefit of the doubt," Miguel snapped. He turned his attention back to Carhart. "I want to know what this is about."

Seeming a little dazed by the collision and the fall, Carhart pointed a trembling finger at Severs. "Him! He come in my shop and threatened me! Said if I didn't change my story about McLaren shootin' Marshal Dixon and the girl, somethin' bad 'd happen to me."

"That's a damned lie!" Severs said.

Miguel didn't doubt for a second that Severs was capable of such a thing. All of McLaren's friends were.

Anger burned inside Miguel. "Did you go to Mr. Carhart's shop today?"

"Yeah, Lew and me stopped in there. I was thinking about buying a new saddle."

"He never said nothin' about that!" Carhart put in.

"While we were there, I asked the old man if he was sure about what he saw. You know, he might have bad eyes at his age."

"He wasn't askin'!" Carhart raged. "He was threatenin' me, I tell you!"

Severs shook his head. "I never did any such thing. He must've misunderstood what I was saying. You know . . ." He tapped a forefinger against the side of his head.

Carhart would have charged the younger man if Miguel hadn't had a good grip on his arm.

As he held Carhart back, he asked, "Was anybody else in there at the time?"

Carhart scowled and licked his lips. "No, I don't reckon there was."

"Then it's just your word against his, Mr. Carhart. You can't prove Severs threatened you."

"You don't believe me?"

"It's not a matter of believing you. It's a matter of proof."

Carhart stared at Miguel in disbelief. "You ain't gonna arrest him?"

Severs said, "If anybody's arrested, it ought to be that crazy old-timer. In fact, I think I'll charge him with attempted murder."

Miguel jerked his head at the hole in the ceiling where the load of buckshot had gone. "He didn't shoot at you."

"Only because you grabbed his gun!"

"Then I prevented an attempted murder," Miguel said coolly. "I'm not arresting Mr. Carhart, and I doubt if you can talk Judge Ordway into signing a warrant against him, either."

"That's the kind of crooked law we've got in this town," Severs grumbled.

"You anxious to pay another fine for disturbing the peace? If you are, just keep running your mouth, Severs." Miguel turned to the old saddle maker. "You go on back home, Mr. Carhart."

"But don't you understand?" Carhart pleaded. "If he done that to me, there's no tellin' how he might threaten the other folks who saw McLaren kill the marshal!"

179

From behind Miguel, Chance Jensen asked, "Everything all right here?"

Miguel glanced around and saw the young man standing in the doorway, gun in hand.

"Fine. Nobody hurt. Chance, do you think you could take Mr. Carhart on back to his house?"

"Sure, but I don't know where it is."

"He'll tell you." Miguel urged Carhart toward Chance, who put a hand on the old-timer's shoulder to steer him out of the cantina.

Miguel turned back toward Severs, who had drifted back over to the table to join his friends. "I'm going to talk to the other witnesses, Severs. If I find out you've been trying to intimidate them, I'll be looking for you."

"You won't have any trouble finding me," Severs replied with a sneer. "I've got nothing to hide."

"We'll see about that." Miguel kept the shotgun cradled in his hands as he backed out of the cantina, rather than giving Severs and the others too tempting a target.

Chapter Twenty

Ace, Chance, and Miguel sat in the marshal's office the next morning, along with Judge Alfred Ordway and the local prosecutor, Timothy Buchanan. Earlier, the bells in the steeples of the town's four churches had rung, calling the faithful to worship. Normally, Ordway and Buchanan would have been at the Baptist and Methodist churches, respectively, and Miguel would have attended mass at the Catholic church.

On that Sunday morning, however, they had pressing matters to discuss.

"Royal Carhart's not going to change his testimony," Miguel reported to Ordway and Buchanan, "but I'm not sure about some of the others. There's no telling how many of them McLaren's friends threatened, or how they'll react to those threats."

"You believe Mr. Carhart's story, then?" Buchanan asked.

"About Perry Severs and Lew Merritt trying to intimidate him?" Miguel nodded. "I sure do. He wouldn't have any reason to lie about it, and I don't believe he just made a mistake like Severs tried to claim. Mr. Carhart's too sharp for that."

Judge Ordway nodded. "Yes, I've known the man for years. I agree with you, Marshal."

Ace saw the look in Miguel's eyes at the judge's statement and figured he still wasn't used to being called *Marshal.* That would take some getting used to, all right.

"If all the witnesses change their story, or even if most of them do, it could ruin our case," Buchanan fretted.

Ordway got to his feet. "I should leave. I'm supposed to be impartial, so I shouldn't be privy to this discussion."

"I'm sorry, Your Honor," Miguel said. "I shouldn't have asked you to stop by this morning. I see that now. I just value your advice."

"And I appreciate that, my boy. But things should be done properly if they're to be done at all. We're not Texans, you know. We still have some respect for the rule of law here in New Mexico Territory."

Ace wasn't sure what the judge meant by that, unless he was referring to the fact that the Texans Ace had met in the past had a tendency to bend the rules if necessary to get the right things done. It wasn't necessarily a bad quality.

Ordway put his hat on and left the marshal's office.

Buchanan said, "Marshal, I want you to speak to everyone who saw Pete McLaren commit those murders and make sure they're still prepared to swear to the truth in court."

Miguel nodded. "I'll do that after church is over. I reckon that'll ruin a nice Sunday afternoon for some of them, but it can't be helped. We have to know what sort of problems we're facing."

"That's absolutely right." Buchanan picked up his hat from the desk. "Keep me informed." He left the office, too.

Miguel sighed and sank down in the swivel chair behind the desk.

Ace picked up one of the ladder-back chairs, turned it around, and straddled it. "Chance and I can continue guarding the place. You don't have to worry about that."

"I appreciate it. It's a good thing you fellas came along when you did."

Chance said, "I'm not so sure about that. This whole thing sort of started with the ruckus in the saloon between us and McLaren's bunch. If that hadn't happened, McLaren and his friends wouldn't have jumped us later, José wouldn't have gotten shot, and McLaren wouldn't have been locked up so he could try to escape."

Miguel looked at him for a moment and then shook his head. "We don't know how it would have worked out. You can't tell about things like that. But I know one thing. Sooner or later there was going to be a showdown with McLaren. He's been spoiling for it for a long time. I suppose he wants to get out of that long, ugly shadow his brother cast around here and be notorious in his own right."

"I'd say he made it," Ace said. "He'll be remembered for a long time."

"Especially if he hangs," Chance added.

By that evening, Miguel had talked to all the witnesses again. Ace and Chance had taken turns

183

getting some sleep, but they were both in the marshal's office when Miguel came in to relieve them for supper.

"What did you find out?" Ace asked. "Do you still have plenty of testimony against McLaren lined up?"

"Seems like it, but I wish I knew for sure." Miguel sighed. "People have heard about what happened at José's last night. There's a feeling of nervousness all around town. Nobody knows what Severs and the others are capable of, but they're afraid it's not good. The witnesses themselves all told me nothing has changed, but some of them were jumpy as cats. I don't reckon we can be absolutely sure what they're going to testify to until the time comes."

"But *you* saw McLaren shoot Marshal Dixon and the Redding girl," Chance pointed out. "By itself, that ought to be enough to convict him, even if everybody else backs out."

"I hope so. Solomon Horton's a mighty tricky lawyer, though. No telling what he might have up his sleeve."

Ace said, "One of us will stay here with you while the other goes and gets something to eat."

"That's not necessary," Miguel said with a shake of his head. "I'll be all right."

Ace frowned. "We've had at least two men here and sometimes three the whole time."

"No, go ahead, both of you," Miguel insisted.

Ace looked over at his brother. Chance shrugged. They could see that arguing wasn't going to do any good.

"The café's not far off," Ace said. "If there's any trouble, we can be back here in a hurry."

Miguel smiled faintly. "If you hear any guns going off, you'll know to come a-runnin'."

The Jensen brothers left the office. Ace heard Miguel bar the door behind them. More than likely, he would be fine while they were gone. The building was quite sturdy, and McLaren's four friends weren't really a big enough force to break him out by assaulting the place.

A lynch mob might have been more of a threat, but there had been no talk about that. The citizens of Lone Pine wanted Pete McLaren to hang, but they wanted the sentence to be carried out legally.

Ace and Chance were crossing the street toward the café when Ace spotted Lee and Meredith Emory approaching along the opposite boardwalk. The brother and sister newspaper publishers paused just outside the café door and waited for Ace and Chance to join them.

"Good evening, Jensens," Emory greeted them. "We saw you leave the marshal's office just now. Is everything still all right over there?"

"It's fine." Ace pinched the brim of his hat as he nodded to Meredith. "Evening, Miss Emory."

"Mr. Jensen." Her voice was bland and non-

185

committal, but Ace saw a friendly light shining in her eyes.

"If you're going into the café, why don't you join us?" Emory suggested. "Having Mrs. Hilfstrom's pot roast for Sunday supper is sort of a tradition for us."

"Sounds good," Chance said. "Based on what we've had so far, she's a fine cook."

"You'll find the pot roast equally delicious," Meredith said.

The four of them went inside and took seats at one of the tables covered with a blue-checked cloth.

As one of the Hilfstrom girls brought coffee for everyone, Emory told her, "We'll all have the pot roast and fixin's."

When the waitress was gone, Emory said to Ace and Chance, "I've heard rumors Marshal Soriano is concerned about the testimony in the trial tomorrow. Is that true?"

"Are you asking as a newspaperman or a concerned citizen?" Ace said.

Emory smiled. "Can't I be both?"

Ace didn't know how much Miguel would want him to reveal, so he said, "As far as I know, everything's still the same as it was yesterday."

"Sol Horton asked Judge Ordway for a delay, you know. He said since it was a murder trial instead of attempted murder, he needed more time. The judge denied the request. Trial is set for tomorrow morning at nine o'clock, just like it was before."

Ace and Chance already knew that, having been told as much by Timothy Buchanan earlier in the day.

Ace said, "Better to go ahead and get it over with, I suppose."

"But is that fair to McLaren?"

Meredith said, "It wasn't exactly fair that McLaren shot down the marshal and that poor girl, was it?" Her tone was rather crisp and cool.

Emory chuckled. "I'm merely playing the devil's advocate, dear. Sometimes as a journalist, you have to do that."

"I was raised with the smell of printer's ink, too, you know."

"Of course. I'd stack up your journalistic skills against anyone's, my own included. For what it's worth, I think McLaren is guilty as sin and ought to hang, but I won't print that in the newspaper."

"Not even as an editorial?" Ace asked.

"I don't think it's necessary," Emory said. "The trial will be open and shut, and the verdict is a foregone conclusion."

Ace hoped the newspaperman was right. If anything happened that allowed Pete McLaren to escape justice . . . well, that might be enough to make Lone Pine explode.

Chapter Twenty-one

Even though Ace wouldn't have been surprised to see something happen overnight, things remained quiet. The next morning, when he took Pete McLaren's breakfast into the cell block, he saw the worry on the prisoner's face.

McLaren expected that his friends would have tried to get him out of there already. He tried to put up a brave front, but Ace saw the fear lurking in his eyes. It was the fear of a hang rope. Considering what McLaren had done, he was perfectly justified in feeling that way.

Ace passed the tray through the slot. "We'll be taking you to court in a little while, but you'll have plenty of time to eat your breakfast."

"You're making a big mistake," McLaren said.

"No, it's only a little after eight o'clock—"

"I mean about putting me on trial." McLaren's mouth twisted in a snarl as he interrupted. "You and that greaser deputy and that addlepated old judge and everybody else who thinks they can get away with doing this. All you're gonna accomplish is to bring hell rainin' down on Lone Pine."

"Because of your brother," Ace said.

"You'll see," McLaren said in a surly voice.

"When Otis comes back, you'll all see." He retreated to the bunk with the tray.

Ace went back into the office. As he closed the cell block door, Chance and Miguel Soriano came in the front.

"I just took the prisoner's breakfast in to him," Ace reported as he pointed a thumb at the cell block. Then he nodded toward the tray with its empty plates and coffee cup that sat on the desk and added, "I already had mine."

"Everything's set up over in the courtroom," Miguel said. "We brought in some extra chairs, but I don't reckon they'll be enough. This trial is the biggest thing that's happened in Lone Pine for a long time. Maybe ever."

"There's a lot of talk around town this morning," Chance said. "Folks are nervous. Some of them are afraid of McLaren's friends, and others are worried that Otis McLaren will show up."

"Best way to deal with that is to have a nice, quick trial and get it over with," Miguel said. "Then people will see that justice is done."

"Is there any chance that Otis McLaren might interrupt the trial?" Ace asked. "Pete just threatened me with that again when I took in his breakfast."

Miguel shook his head. "Nobody's seen hide nor hair of Otis McLaren in these parts for a long time. Given the violent sort of life he led, there's a good chance he's dead by now." He grunted. "I suppose it wouldn't be a very Christian thing to say I hope so."

"Nothing wrong with hoping there's no trouble," Ace said. "Whatever it takes."

Miguel sat down behind the desk. Time passed slowly as Ace and Chance cleaned the shotguns they would be carrying as they escorted the prisoner to the town hall.

Finally Miguel took a turnip watch from his pocket, opened the case, checked the hour, and snapped it shut. "Time to go." He took a shotgun down from the rack, broke it open, and thumbed shells into the two chambers. He went into the cell block, followed by Ace, while Chance remained in the office just outside the cell block door.

Miguel twisted the key in the lock and said, "Let's go, McLaren."

McLaren stood beside the bunk. He swallowed hard and didn't move.

"We can come in there and drag you out," Miguel said.

With a resigned sigh, McLaren put his hat on and moved slowly toward the door. Ace and Miguel moved apart, so when the prisoner stepped out they were covering him from different angles without being in the line of fire themselves.

"Put your hands behind your back," Miguel ordered.

"You're gonna make me walk over there with my hands cuffed?"

"I damn sure am. Now do what I told you."

McLaren put his hands behind his back.

Miguel moved in and swiftly and surely fastened the metal cuffs around McLaren's wrists then put a hand in the middle of his back and gave him a little shove. "Let's go."

Chance opened the office door and checked the street. "Lots of folks around, but I don't see any of McLaren's friends this morning. They must be lying low."

"I checked around earlier," Miguel said. "José said they rode out after last night's business with Royal Carhart at the cantina, and nobody's seen them since. Hear that, McLaren? Looks like your pards have lit a shuck. They don't want any part of what's going to happen to you."

McLaren muttered a curse but didn't say anything else.

The buzz of conversation in the street stopped abruptly as Ace, Chance, and Miguel escorted McLaren out of the building. Miguel led the way toward the town hall while Ace and Chance followed with the prisoner, flanking McLaren and staying a little behind him as he trudged through the dusty street.

The crowd on the porch of the town hall parted as the little procession approached. Ace, Chance, and Miguel took McLaren through the gap, through the open double doors, and into the courtroom.

Once again every spectator chair in the place was occupied, and people stood along the walls, even more than during the hearing several days earlier. They watched in silence as the three men took McLaren up to the defense table where Solomon Horton sat, scowling.

"I demand that you take those handcuffs off my client, Marshal," Horton said as the group reached the table. "This is a disgrace! An outrage!"

Miguel took the handcuff key from his watch pocket. "He can have his hands cuffed in front of him so it'll be easier for him to sit, but he'll still have to wear them. He's charged with two counts of murder, you know, not getting drunk and starting a ruckus."

"Such treatment is prejudicial—"

"That's something you'll have to take up with the judge." Miguel unlocked the cuffs and transferred them to the front when McLaren brought his arms back around. He put a hand on McLaren's shoulder and pushed him down into the empty chair at the defense table.

As McLaren and Horton started talking together in low voices, Miguel stepped back and said to Ace and Chance, "Keep an eye on him. I'll go see if the judge is about ready to get started." He went to the door that led into the judge's "chambers"—just a small office at one side of the main room.

A few minutes later, Miguel stepped back out and called, "All rise."

Ace and Chance were already on their feet. Everyone else stood up. Judge Ordway came in wearing a sober black suit and went to the heavier, raised table that served as his bench. He sat down, and Miguel told everybody else to do likewise.

Ordway rapped his gavel. "Court is now in session in the matter of the Territory of New Mexico versus Peter McLaren, a citizen of said territory. The charge is two counts of murder, as well as lesser charges of attempted murder and unlawful flight from custody. How does the defendant plead?"

Horton nodded to McLaren, and both of them stood up.

"Solomon Horton for the defense, Your Honor. My client pleads guilty—"

An abrupt stir filled the room. Ordway glared and gaveled the interruption to silence.

Horton resumed. "Guilty to the charge of unlawful flight. He pleads *not guilty* of all other charges."

Ace and Chance had withdrawn to the back of the aisle between the two sections of spectators' chairs, where they stood with the shotguns cradled in their arms. Ace was a little surprised McLaren had pled guilty to anything, even the charge of busting out of jail, but he figured

193

Horton had talked McLaren into that. The charge wasn't worth defending, Ace supposed. It would carry a relatively short prison sentence. The attempted murder charge would land McLaren behind bars for a considerably longer time.

But none of that would matter if McLaren was convicted of the two murder charges. Those were the ones he had to fight. He would never serve any time for the other crimes if he wound up on the gallows for the killings.

"Very well," Judge Ordway said when the pleas had been entered by the court clerk, who sat off to the side at a little desk. "Is the prosecution ready?"

Timothy Buchanan stood up. "It is, Your Honor."

"And the defense?"

"Ready and eager to have justice done on behalf of my client, Your Honor," Horton said. "And to that end, I make a motion for a change of venue."

Chance looked over at Ace and frowned. Ace gave a little shake of his head. He didn't believe the judge would grant Horton's motion.

"A change of venue, Counselor?" Ordway said.

"That's right, Your Honor. Due to the unreasonable level of hostility toward my client in this town, I believe it's impossible for him to get a fair trial in Lone Pine."

"The attitude of the town's citizens toward your client is a direct result of his actions, Mr. Horton. He can't use past misdeeds to his advantage now.

Besides, only the facts of this case are relevant to these proceedings. Your motion is denied."

"I want to object for the record, Your Honor."

"Go right ahead," Ordway said. "It's duly noted. Now, then. The defendant has a right to a trial by a jury of his peers. Do you wish to waive that right, Mr. McLaren?"

"My client does not, Your Honor. We request a trial by jury."

"I haven't heard a word from your client yet, Counselor. Mr. McLaren, do you waive your right to a trial by jury?"

"No sir, Your Honor." McLaren turned his head and cast a look over the spectators. "Let 'em stand in judgment of me, if that's what they're bound and determined to do."

Chapter Twenty-two

Ace thought the cold-eyed, vicious expression on McLaren's face was intended as a warning, and judging by the nervous murmur that ran through the crowd, so did many of the spectators.

Ordway smacked his gavel on the table and snapped, "I didn't ask for a comment, Mr. McLaren. Just an answer. A trial by jury it is. You can sit down. Mr. Buchanan, I believe you keep a list of eligible jurors on hand?"

"Yes, Your Honor," the prosecutor said as he got to his feet. He picked up several sheets of paper from the table in front of him. "I'll read off the first twelve names on the list."

The names of the dozen townsmen from Lone Pine meant nothing to Ace. He didn't recognize any of them.

When Buchanan was finished, Judge Ordway said, "If those men are in attendance, step forward."

Nobody budged.

Ordway leaned forward and peered through slitted eyes at the crowd. "I know some of you are out there. I see a couple of you. Now come forward, or you'll be fined for contempt of court."

A man got to his feet. "You go ahead and fine me, Judge, but I got a family dependin' on me. I'd rather pay a fine than have Pete McLaren holdin' a grudge against me!"

That brought muttered agreements from several others in the crowd.

Ordway rapped the gavel. "You can't refuse to serve on a jury without a good reason!"

The man who had stood up coughed. "I got a good reason. I'm sick."

Ordway's face darkened in anger.

Buchanan looked mad, too, but he said, "There are other names on the list, Your Honor. Perhaps those men will be willing to perform their civic duty. I suggest in the interests of simplicity, we move on."

Ordway jerked his head in a nod. "Proceed, Counselor."

Buchanan opened his mouth, but before he could say a word, a veritable stampede occurred as men got to their feet and headed for the doors. Everybody had been anxious to attend the trial and see Pete McLaren get what he had coming to him, but clearly it hadn't occurred to them that they might have to play a part in it.

Ace and Chance could have blocked the exit, but as they glanced at Miguel Soriano to see what he wanted them to do, the acting marshal spread his hands and shrugged. Nobody could be legally forced to attend a trial.

The Jensen brothers stood aside and allowed the unexpected exodus to proceed.

The effort to intimidate the witnesses against McLaren had had an unexpected side effect, Ace realized. Rumors had spread through the town and fueled fears. Coupled with McLaren's reputation, that made folks afraid to serve as jurors. From the slight smirk that had appeared on McLaren's lips, Ace figured the prisoner had been hoping something like that would happen.

The defendant had a right to a trial by jury. If the court couldn't seat a jury . . .

Ace didn't know enough about the law to know what Judge Ordway would do in a situation like that. He couldn't just drop the charges and set McLaren free, although Ace was sure that's what Solomon Horton would press for.

The longer things remained unresolved, the greater the chance something else would happen.

Ordway waited a minute or so for the hubbub to die down then banged his gavel on the table until the room was quiet again. Snarling out the words in barely suppressed fury, he said, "The court will take a short recess. Marshal, take the prisoner back to jail. I'll send for him when we're ready to resume." With that, the judge smacked the gavel down again, stood up, and stalked out of the courtroom into the office at the side. The door slammed behind him.

"You heard the judge," Miguel told McLaren. "On your feet."

Horton said, "Surely you're not going to cuff my client's hands behind his back again just to take him down the street."

Miguel hesitated. "All right, he can keep his hands in front of him. But if he tries anything, he'll get six loads of buckshot for his trouble."

"He'll cooperate fully," Horton said.

And why wouldn't he? Ace thought. To the surprise of just about everybody in the court-room, things were going McLaren's way.

Judging by the smirk on McLaren's lips, he knew it, too.

McLaren still looked cocksure and arrogant when Ace slammed the cell door a few minutes later. He took off his hat, tossed it on the bunk, and grinned through the iron bars. "That didn't go the way you expected, did it?"

"If you're counting on going free, don't bet on it," Chance said as he continued to cover McLaren with a shotgun.

"Can't have a trial without jurors," McLaren taunted.

"You didn't expect that to happen," Ace said. "You were just as surprised as the rest of us when it did. But you'll take advantage of it if you can, I know that."

The Jensen brothers went out into the office where Miguel was talking with Timothy Buchanan. Ace closed the cell block door.

"Mr. Buchanan and I are going to talk to some folks," Miguel said. "We need to impress on them just how important it is that they do what the law calls for."

Holding the list of potential jurors, Buchanan said, "I saw a lot of men going into the Melodian just a few minutes ago. I'm sure at least a dozen of them are on this list. Why don't we start there, Marshal?"

"Sounds like a good idea to me," Miguel said with a nod. "Maybe we can get enough of them to agree and won't have to go all over town rounding up more. Ace, come along with us. People need to see a show of force from the law, and right now that's what you fellas represent, whether you're wearing badges or not."

"You want me to stay here and hold down the fort?" Chance asked.

"If you don't mind."

Ace said, "There ought to be someone else on guard with Chance."

"No, I'll be fine," his brother assured him. "I'll line up three Greeners on the desk and have them ready. That'll be enough to stop a small army. Anyway, McLaren's friends lit a shuck, remember?"

"They could come back," Miguel warned. "Stay alert."

"Don't worry. I will."

Ace, Miguel, and Buchanan left the office and headed for the Melodian. It was a little early in the day for drinking, but after what had happened at the town hall, folks weren't too concerned about that.

The saloon was busy, just as they expected. Men lined the bar and sat at the tables. The bartenders and the serving girls went about their work with swift efficiency. Hank Muller should have been happy with the profits he was making, but a grim expression filled his bulldog-like face as he surveyed the room from the end of the bar.

The talk in the room carried an uneasy tone. Nobody was telling bawdy jokes or laughing at them. They were discussing the trial and the way it had been interrupted.

The conversations came to a halt as men noticed that Ace, Miguel, and Buchanan had come in.

The man who had spoken up in the courtroom threw back the whiskey in the glass he clutched. "You can't force us to serve on a jury. There's gotta be a law against that!"

"Actually, Mr. Riley, there's a law saying that the court *can* compel you to serve. You'll be found guilty of contempt if you don't," Buchanan responded.

"Well, then, find me guilty and fine me! Like I said, I'd rather pay up than have Pete McLaren's friends paying a visit to me and my family some dark night!"

"I'll pay the fine, too," another man said. "What if we hang Pete and then his brother shows up looking for revenge? I don't want anybody blaming me, and sure as hell not Otis McLaren!"

"Otis McLaren's not going to come back," Buchanan insisted. "Even if he's still alive, he doesn't give a damn about his brother. If he did, he wouldn't have abandoned Pete here."

One man at the bar rubbed his chin. "What happens if the judge fines a man and he can't pay?"

"He'd have to serve a jail sentence," Buchanan said.

The man nodded. "But he'd still be alive at the end of it."

"He sure would," another man said. "That might not be true if he served on a jury."

Miguel's face was flushed with anger, though he tried to control it. "Wait just a minute. That's what the law's here for, to protect folks so they can do what they're supposed to without being afraid."

"That badge don't mean much when it's bein' used as a target, Deputy."

"It's Marshal," Miguel snapped.

"Yeah, because Hoyt Dixon's dead. McLaren shot him down like a dog."

"And he ought to hang for that!"

A man at the bar said solemnly, "Maybe if we tell McLaren we'll let him go, he'll agree to leave town and never come back. That would be a pretty good deal for him, wouldn't it?"

Several others nodded as they considered the suggestion.

One of them said, "He'd be so grateful he wouldn't bother us no more."

Buchanan burst out, "Are you people crazy? McLaren's a mad dog! You could never trust his word, and even if you could, what about Marshal Dixon? What about Dolly Redding? Don't they deserve justice?"

"The marshal didn't have no family around here. Hangin' McLaren wouldn't bring him back to life. As for the girl, she was just—"

"Shut up!" The furious roar came from Hank

Muller. He grabbed the man by the collar, lifted him from the floor, and started shaking him. "Shut your damn filthy mouth!"

"Hank . . ." Buchanan said.

With a disgusted snort, Muller shoved the man away from him. His scathing gaze swung over the entire crowd. "All of you make me sick! Dolly might not have been the sort of girl you'd take home for Sunday dinner, but she was a human being, damn it! She had hopes and dreams just like the rest of us, and McLaren killed her! I thought I served men in this saloon, but you're all squeaking and scurrying around like a bunch of mice!"

Men hurriedly got out of his way as he stomped over to Buchanan. "I'll serve on that jury. I've got as much right as anybody. Who else is with me?"

Silence hung over the saloon in the wake of Muller's shouted question.

Chapter Twenty-three

"I'll do it," a voice said from the saloon's entrance. "I'll serve."

Ace looked around to see Lee Emory standing there, holding the batwings open. The newspaperman came on into the Melodian.

"That gives you two members of your jury,

Mr. Buchanan," Emory said. "Surely there are ten more men here who aren't afraid."

"You don't know what McLaren's bunch is capable of, Lee," a man called from the bar.

"I know what good Americans are capable of," Emory said. "I know they're capable of standing up to evil and tyranny wherever they find it, like the men who stood in the road at Lexington and Concord with muskets in their hands and watched the British troops marching toward them. Or the men who rallied behind Andrew Jackson at New Orleans and pushed the redcoats back into the sea, or those who crossed the line Colonel Travis drew in the sand with his sword at the Alamo. I know there are some Texans here. Some of you probably have relatives old enough to remember *that* revolution."

"That was war," a man objected. "The whole country was at stake."

Emory hooked his thumbs in his vest, and Ace thought how much newspapermen were like politicians, even though they probably would never admit that. They all liked the sound of their own voices, although usually those words were in print, not spoken from some platform.

"You think nothing's at stake here?" Emory asked. "I'd say the whole country is very much at stake! If you start letting lawbreakers go simply because you're afraid to see justice done, how long will it be before the entire nation is overrun with criminals? If a dog comes at you, snarling and snapping, do you throw it a chunk of meat and hope it'll go away? No! You stand up to it and let it know you're not afraid of it! It's the same way with two-bit bullies and bravos like King George and Santa Anna and, yes, like Pete McLaren! You can stand up to him and do the right thing now . . . or you can live the rest of your lives in fear." Emory drew in a deep breath and blew it back out. "It's as simple as that."

Silence reigned again following the impassioned speech.

Finally, with a scrape of chair legs on the floor, Colonel Charles Howden stood up from the table where he'd been sitting. "Lee is right. If we let McLaren get away with what he's done, it's only a matter of time until Lone Pine isn't a fit place to live. I'll serve."

Sitting at a table as far across the room as he could get from Colonel Howden was Crackerjack Sawyer. The words were barely out of Howden's mouth, before he was on his feet, too. "If a damn Yankee can do the right thing, then by God, a good Confederate can go him one better. Mr. Buchanan, a jury needs a foreman, don't it?"

"That's accepted procedure, yes," Buchanan agreed.

"Then I'll volunteer for the job!"

"Wait just a minute," Howden said. "We don't want to let a Rebel be in charge—"

"You two old pelicans hush your squawking," Muller said. "We're not gonna fight the whole blasted war over again."

"Hank's right," Emory said. "Besides, the foreman is usually elected by the members of the jury. So we need to find eight more men." He looked around the room. "Surely there are eight men here with the courage to see that justice is done."

Slowly, one by one, more men rose to their feet. Ace counted them as they stood up.

Six. That made ten, but a jury had to have twelve members.

Emory said, "Someone else? Anyone?"

Most of the men who hadn't volunteered looked down at the floor, or at the drinks on the table in front of them. Most looked ashamed, too, but that wasn't enough to prod them to action.

Without stopping to think it over too much, Ace said, "My brother and I can do it."

Buchanan turned to look at him. "You're deputies. You wouldn't be eligible—"

"You don't see a badge pinned to my shirt, do you?" Ace asked. "We haven't taken any wages. Chance and I are just volunteers. We can quit being volunteers any time we like."

Emory said, "But you don't live here in Lone Pine."

A frown had appeared on Buchanan's face as he thought about Ace's suggestion. "Wait a

206

minute. Do you have a permanent residence, Mr. Jensen?"

"Not to speak of," Ace said. "When we were little, we lived in Denver, but as soon as we were old enough, Doc Monday started drifting around again. We traveled with him, and for the past few years, we've still been drifting, just on our own."

"So you're citizens of the world, you might say."

Ace couldn't help but smile. "I sort of like that."

"Which means you're citizens of Lone Pine as much as anywhere else." Buchanan nodded. "I think I can persuade Judge Ordway of the legality of this move. And that would give us twelve jurors."

Emory said, "But shouldn't we allow the other Mr. Jensen to speak for himself?"

"Hell, yes," Chance said. "Sign me up." He was standing in the marshal's office along with Ace, Miguel, Buchanan, and Lee Emory.

"You're aware that it might be dangerous," Buchanan said.

"So's getting up in the morning. So is being born!" Chance put the shotgun he was holding back on the wall rack. "Let's go get that trial started again."

"I can't guarantee that Judge Ordway will go

along with seating the two of you as jurors, but I think he will. You'll have to be impartial and decide the case strictly on the evidence. Can you do that?"

"As much as anyone else in Lone Pine can," Ace said. "Maybe even more so, since we haven't had to put up with McLaren for as long as everybody else."

"That's a good point. I'll use it in trying to convince the judge, if I have to."

Ace turned to Miguel. "Sorry to leave you without any volunteers."

"I'll do without sleep until the trial's over if I have to," Miguel said. "As long as McLaren winds up getting what's coming to him."

"That'll be up to the jury to decide," Buchanan said. "I'll go let Judge Ordway know we're ready for court to reconvene."

A few minutes later, he returned to the marshal's office and told them to take the prisoner back to the town hall.

Ace said, "I reckon that'll be our last act as unofficial deputies."

"All the other men who have agreed to serve as jurors will be there," Buchanan said. "This shouldn't take long. I hope the trial will be over by the end of the day."

They entered the courtroom and delivered McLaren to the defense table. Solomon Horton glared at them, but Ace saw worry lurking in the lawyer's eyes, too. More than likely, Horton had been hoping for a mistrial when it looked like the court wouldn't be able to seat a jury. He couldn't be sure what was going to happen, but odds were it wouldn't be good for his client.

Judge Ordway came in, everyone stood up, and then sat down again. The judge rapped his gavel on the table and said, "Court is in session. We'll resume with the selection of a jury, if there's no objection from either counsel."

Horton was on his feet right away. "I object, Your Honor. My client has a right to a speedy trial by a jury of his peers—"

"Then let us get to it, Counselor." Ordway nodded at the prosecutor. "Proceed, Mr. Buchanan."

Buchanan stood up. "I'll read off the names of the first twelve men on my list, and they'll come forward. Hank Muller—"

"Objection!" Horton yelled as he shot up again. "That man was the employer of one of the victims in the case. How can we expect him to be impartial?"

"So you'd like to challenge this juror for cause?"

"Yes, Your Honor, I would."

"Duly noted," Ordway said. "Challenge is denied."

"But Your Honor—"

"I've known Hank Muller for a good long time. If he swears to deliver an honest, impartial verdict, I'm going to believe him. Would you like to peremptorily challenge the juror, Counselor?"

Horton hesitated. He didn't know who the other jurors were going to be, and he had only a limited number of challenges. The prosecution could be trying some sort of trick to tie his hands. After a moment he said, "Not at this time, Your Honor."

Ordway nodded to Buchanan. "Go on."

"Lee Emory," the prosecutor said.

Ace could tell that Horton didn't like that, either, but the lawyer didn't say anything.

Chance leaned over and whispered into his brother's ear, however. "If we were on the other side in this case, we'd say the defendant was getting railroaded."

"You're right," Ace whispered back. "But we all know McLaren really is guilty."

Judge Ordway frowned in their direction, so both brothers fell silent.

Emory joined Muller in front of the chairs where the jury would sit.

Buchanan said, "Clarence Sawyer."

Crackerjack went to take his place.

Colonel Howden was next, followed by the other men from Lone Pine who had volunteered in the Melodian. Solomon Horton didn't object to any of them.

But when Buchanan called Ace, the defense attorney shot to his feet again. "Your Honor, does the prosecution intend to seat the other Jensen brother on the jury as well?"

"Chance Jensen's name is the last on the list," Buchanan said.

Horton shook his head. "I most strenuously object. These two young men aren't even citizens of Lone Pine."

"How are they not?" Buchanan responded. "They've been here for several days and display no signs of leaving anytime soon. Ever since they rode in, they've done nothing but help our people and lend assistance to our duly appointed lawmen."

"They're deputies!" Horton insisted. "They're not eligible jurors."

"They merely helped Acting Marshal Soriano as friends and volunteers. All *citizens* are expected to lend assistance to the law when necessary."

Seething inside, Horton's face turned even darker. He turned to the judge. "I challenge Ace and Chance Jensen for cause."

"Those challenges are denied," Ordway said. "I find Mr. Buchanan's argument that they can indeed be considered citizens compelling."

Buchanan motioned to the Jensen brothers, who went forward and positioned themselves at the end of the line of jurors.

"Do you wish to make any peremptory challenges, Mr. Horton?" Ordway asked.

Horton was mulling it over. He glanced at Buchanan, who merely smiled confidently and looked down at the sheet of paper in his hand, trying to make Horton think that if any jurors were removed, he would just call replacements for them and not worry about it. It was a masterful stroke.

After a few moments Horton muttered, "I have no further challenges, Your Honor."

"Very well," Ordway said. "Marshal Soriano, if you would, swear in the members of the jury, and let's get these proceedings started."

Chapter Twenty-four

Ace had attended a few trials before but had never served as a member of a jury. Despite being convinced of Pete McLaren's guilt, he reminded himself that he had to keep an open mind, listen to all the evidence, and then vote according to whether or not the prosecution had proven its case. It was a weighty responsibility.

The smile Chance wore as the trial got under way told Ace that his brother wasn't taking things quite as seriously as he was . . . but nothing unusual about that. Chance didn't take much seriously except poker games and pretty girls.

Timothy Buchanan laid out the prosecution's

case in an opening statement that took quite a while. Solomon Horton followed with a passionate opening statement of his own that didn't really say much but he said it at great length. Ace figured lawyers could be added to the list of those fellows in love with whatever they had to say, along with politicians and journalists.

Both opening statements went on so long that, coupled with the earlier delay, it was the middle of the day before the court was ready to begin hearing testimony.

Judge Ordway picked up his gavel and said, "We'll reconvene at one o'clock. Court is adjourned." The bang of the gavel signaled the beginning of the break for the midday meal.

Miguel had found a couple men willing to help him escort McLaren to and from the jail. Ace, Chance, and Lee Emory watched as the little group headed for the sturdy stone building. Most of the people on the street—and there were quite a few of them—were equally interested.

After a moment, Meredith came up to join them. She had a worried frown on her face as she took hold of her brother's arm. "Lee, I'm not sure this is wise. You should be reporting the news, not . . . not taking part in it. And it's dangerous besides. You'll be making enemies by doing this."

"A newspaperman can't worry too much about

the enemies he makes," Emory said. "If he does, he can't do his job properly."

"Like I just said, your job isn't to be in the middle of things."

"Let's go get something to eat, and we can talk about it. I can't very well back out now, though."

"I just wish you'd talked to me before you volunteered."

Emory didn't respond to that, but turned to Ace and Chance. "Why don't you join us?"

"Sounds like a good idea," Ace said.

They went over to the café and got the last empty table. Lars Hilfstrom and his wife and daughters were doing a booming business because of the trial.

"You're not going to be too angry with me, are you?" Emory asked his sister while they were waiting for their food.

Meredith managed to smile. "I don't suppose it would do any good if I was. The trial has started, so it's too late now to do anything about it."

"That's right. Don't worry. It won't last long, and then this will all be over."

"I hope so," Meredith said.

So did Ace, but an uneasy feeling had started to creep in on him. Solomon Horton had a reputation as a slick, smart lawyer, even though he hadn't yet displayed much evidence of it. He might still have some tricks up his sleeve, however. Besides that, Ace just had a hunch things weren't going to go as smoothly as everyone on the prosecution's side hoped.

Mrs. Hilfstrom was working hard in the kitchen to make sure everyone got fed before the trial started again, but it was a near thing. The hour was almost one o'clock by the time Ace, Chance, and the Emorys returned to the town hall, joining the rest of the crowd gathering there. The three men took their seats on the jury while Meredith snagged a chair in the second row of the spectators' section.

It was a few minutes after one o'clock by the time Judge Ordway gaveled the court into session. "Call your first witness, Mr. Buchanan."

The prosecutor got to his feet. "I call Acting Marshal Miguel Soriano."

Miguel went forward, was sworn in, and took the witness chair. At Buchanan's request, he restated his name and position for the record.

Then Buchanan said, "In your own words, Marshal Soriano, tell us what you witnessed in front of the marshal's office and jail two nights ago."

"Well, I'd been making my evening rounds, the way I usually did before I took over at the jail. I was the night deputy under Marshal Hoyt Dixon. I was on the boardwalk on the same side of the street, heading toward the jail, when I saw some people—a man and a woman—run out of the building. Marshal Dixon was in the street, approaching the jail with a dinner tray in his hands for the prisoner we had locked up in there. I recognized the man who had just come out of the jail as that prisoner, Pete McLaren."

"And is that man in court today?" Buchanan asked.

"Yes, sir, he is." Miguel nodded toward the defense table. "That's him right there, the defendant."

Buchanan said, "Go on. What happened then?"

Miguel said, "McLaren shot the marshal, and then he shot the woman with him . . . Dolly Redding, one of the saloon girls who worked at the Melodian. I was running toward McLaren by then, and he tried to shoot me. His bullet hit one of my boot heels and knocked it off, causing me to fall down. McLaren grabbed a horse at the hitch rack and tried to get away, but a couple citizens stopped him and I took him into custody and returned him to the jail."

Ace watch Solomon Horton while Miguel was testifying. The lawyer fidgeted a little, wanting his shot at the witness. He would get it soon enough.

Buchanan said, "Marshal Dixon and Miss Redding suffered fatal injuries at the defendant's hands?"

Miguel nodded. "Yes, McLaren shot and killed both of them."

"Can you tell us why the defendant was being held in jail prior to this incident?"

Horton stood up. "Objection. Irrelevant."

"The defendant is also on trial for those charges, Your Honor," Buchanan argued.

"I'll allow it," Ordway ruled. "Answer the question."

Miguel said, "The defendant was being held on charges of attempted murder and disturbing the peace."

"So the marshal and Miss Redding weren't the first people the defendant tried to gun down." Buchanan pointed out.

Horton was up again. "Objection! That's not a question, Your Honor."

"No, it's not," Ordway said. "I'll sustain that objection, Counselor. Mr. Buchanan, you've already made your opening statement."

"Sorry, Your Honor," Buchanan murmured.

"Do you have anything more for this witness?"

"No, Your Honor."

"Cross-examination?"

"Certainly, Your Honor." Horton stalked out from behind the defense table, approached Miguel, and clasped his hands together behind his back. "Acting Marshal Soriano, I'd like to know exactly where you were when you allegedly witnessed the incident in front of the jail."

"Like I said," Miguel replied with a trace of impatience in his voice, "I was on the boardwalk headed toward the jail, on the same side of the street."

"But where *exactly?* How far away from the jail were you?"

"I was . . ." Miguel frowned. "I'm pretty sure I had just passed Miss O'Mara's dress shop."

"Pretty sure?" Horton repeated as he cocked an eyebrow.

"I'm certain. I, uh, I remember looking in the window as I passed and thinking that was, uh, a pretty dress she had on display there."

A few of the spectators chuckled. Judge Ordway frowned but didn't reach for his gavel.

"And how far is that from the jail?"

"I never measured it, but I'd say it's about fifty yards."

"So you were fifty yards away, at night, in poor light—"

"There's nothing wrong with my eyes, mister, and there was plenty of light in front of the jail because McLaren and the girl left the door open behind them, and light was coming through the window, too."

Horton looked over at Ordway "Your Honor, please instruct the witness not to interrupt and to confine his responses to answering questions."

"You heard the man, Marshal," the judge said.

Miguel looked like he wanted to say something, but he settled for a curt nod.

"Now," Horton went on, "where were Marshal

Dixon, Miss Redding, and the defendant—*exactly.*"

"The marshal was right in front of the office in the street. I'd say fifteen or twenty feet from the boardwalk. McLaren and the girl had just come out the door."

"But how were they standing when you first saw them?"

"McLaren was facing out into the street. Miss Redding was looking at him and had her back to me."

"So you didn't know her identity at the time?"

"No, not really, but I don't see what that matters."

"You say she was looking at the defendant and had her back to you. If I'm visualizing the scene correctly, that means she was standing *between* you and the defendant."

"Yeah, that's right, I guess," Miguel said.

"So that means your view was blocked and you didn't actually *see* Pete McLaren shoot Marshal Dixon."

That made talk break out all over the room. Judge Ordway grabbed his gavel and smacked it on the table.

When things quieted down, Horton smiled at Miguel. "You didn't answer my question, Acting Marshal Soriano."

"You didn't ask one," Miguel snapped.

"Then let me rephrase it. Did you actually *see* my client shoot Marshal Dixon? You saw the gun in his hand, saw the flame from its barrel when he pulled the trigger?"

"No, the girl was in the way—"

"And when Miss Redding was shot, you didn't see *that,* either, did you?"

"She was between me and McLaren. But the marshal went down, and then the girl collapsed, and McLaren was standing there with a gun in his hand, a gun that had been fired several times—"

"So what you're saying is that it's possible someone fired from ambush and killed Marshal Dixon and Miss Redding, and Mr. McLaren merely returned that fire in self-defense—"

"You know good and well that's not what happened!" Miguel shouted as he started to stand up.

"Marshal Soriano!" Judge Ordway's voice lashed out. "Sit down and control yourself!"

Miguel sank back into the witness chair, but his chest rose and fell as he breathed heavily in anger.

"Go on, Counselor," Ordway told Horton.

"Let me be sure I phrase this properly, Your Honor . . . Acting Marshal Soriano, in your professional opinion as a peace officer, is it possible someone else fired the shots that killed Marshal Dixon and Miss Redding?"

"No, it's not," Miguel answered in a flat, hard voice.

"I'd advise you to reconsider that response. As you know, perjury is a crime, and you swore to tell the truth, the whole truth, and nothing but—"

"All right, blast it! I didn't *see* the gun in McLaren's hand when it went off until he was shooting at me. But he *did* shoot at me."

"Perhaps he was startled by the ambush that took the lives of Marshal Dixon and Miss Redding and believed you were attacking him. In that case, he would have fired in defense of his own life." Before Miguel could say anything about how ridiculous that was, Horton said, "No further questions at this time, Your Honor," and turned away.

"Redirect, Mr. Buchanan?" Ordway asked.

The prosecutor shook his head. Buchanan looked grimmer than he had earlier.

Ace could see why Solomon Horton had a reputation for being slick. He watched Miguel leave the witness chair looking angry and a little confused.

"That didn't go as well as we figured it would," Chance whispered.

"No," Ace agreed, "it didn't."

Chapter Twenty-five

As soon as Miguel had vacated the witness chair, Timothy Buchanan stood up. "The prosecution calls Donald Barr, Your Honor."

A middle-aged, medium-sized man with thinning brown hair stood up from his chair in the spectators' section and moved forward, but not before glancing down at the pale-faced woman in the next chair.

He tried to smile at her, but it was a pretty feeble attempt, Ace thought.

When the clerk swore him in, Barr had to clear his throat a couple times before he was able to get out the words he was supposed to say. He sat down, and his fingers knotted together as he held his hands in his lap.

Ace saw that, too, and thought that Barr was nervous about something. Actually, *nervous* might not be a strong enough word. In Ace's opinion, the witness was downright scared.

Buchanan approached Barr. "For the record, please state your name and occupation."

Barr cleared his throat again. "Donald Barr. I own the Apex Mercantile Store here in Lone Pine."

"How long have you been in business here, Mr. Barr?"

Horton said, "I fail to see what significance that question has, Your Honor."

Buchanan turned his head to look at the defense attorney. "I'm establishing the witness's credentials as a longtime member of the community."

Judge Ordway said, "That seems reasonable enough to me, but don't belabor the point, Counselor."

"Of course, Your Honor." Buchanan turned back to Barr and waited.

"I've, uh, lived in Lone Pine and operated the store here for eight years," Barr said.

"What are your business hours, specifically on Friday?"

"I open at eight in the morning, and I stay as late as folks need me to. I usually close down around eight in the evening."

"So this past Friday, three nights ago, your store was still open at the time of the incident in front of the jail."

Barr swallowed and nodded. "Yes, sir."

"Where is your store located in relation to the jail?"

"It's across the street and, uh, one door east, I guess you'd say. Although the buildings don't line up quite that exact. Almost, though."

"So you have a good view of the jail from your store."

"Yes, sir, I suppose. If you were on the porch or at the front window."

"Where were you at the time of the incident?"

"I was . . . standing at the window." Barr sounded like he had to force the words out, but he went on. "There was only one customer in the store . . . Mrs. Gertrude Stevens . . . and she was looking through some bolts of cloth. I was looking out the window to see if anybody else seemed to be on their way to the store because I was thinking about closing up as soon as Mrs. Stevens was done."

"So you were watching the street."

"Well . . . I was just sort of looking around all over, you know."

"Did you see Marshal Hoyt Dixon?" Buchanan asked.

"Yes, sir. He was walking toward the jail, carrying a tray from the café."

"And what happened then?"

Ace glanced at the woman who'd been sitting next to Barr, who he assumed to be the storekeeper's wife. She had her lower lip caught between her teeth and was leaning forward slightly in her chair, ramrod stiff with tension.

"I, uh"—Barr cleared his throat again—"I don't rightly know. I was looking off down the street when I heard some shots, and when I looked around again, Marshal Dixon was lying in the street and there was a girl lying on the board-walk in front of the jail, and a man was standing there beside her shooting at Deputy Soriano."

Buchanan seemed to be taken aback. He stared at the witness for a couple seconds before saying, "Wait just a minute, Mr. Barr. Are you saying that you weren't looking at the area directly in front of the jail when the shooting started?"

"That's right. I was looking down the street."

Buchanan's face began to turn red with anger. He opened his mouth as if to ask another question, then seemed to think better of it. His jaw snapped shut. Another tense moment went by before he said, "No further questions."

"Mr. Horton?" Judge Ordway said.

"Certainly, Your Honor," Horton said. "I have questions for the witness." He walked toward Barr. "Do I understand you to be saying that you actually didn't witness Marshal Dixon and Miss Redding being shot?"

Barr's face was as pale as milk, but he nodded. "That's right. I didn't see them get shot."

"So you can't testify as to who shot them, can you?"

"No, I . . . I suppose I can't."

"That's all." Horton smiled and swung around toward the defense table.

Buchanan stood up. "Your Honor, may I approach the bench?"

"Of course," Ordway said. "Mr. Horton, please join us."

The two lawyers bent over to the table to talk to the judge. Their voices were pitched low enough that no one else in the room could understand what they were saying. However, the vehemence with which Buchanan spoke made it clear he was angry. Horton just looked smug.

Chance leaned over and whispered to Ace, "What do you reckon this is about? That witness lied, didn't he?"

"That's the way it looked to me." Ace had seen the relief on the woman's face when Barr said that he hadn't seen the actual shooting.

It was pretty clear what had happened. Somebody—most likely Pete McLaren's friends—had paid a visit to Barr and warned him to change his testimony. They must have threatened the storekeeper's family. Buchanan was complaining about that to the judge, but Ordway could do nothing about it. Barr either told the truth or he didn't, and under the circumstances there was no way to prove he was lying.

Barr was just one witness, Ace reminded himself. Miguel had talked to several more who had witnessed the shooting.

Unfortunately, all of them were in the room at the moment. They had all seen an obviously frightened Barr change his testimony.

Ace gave thought to what had just happened. If the prospect of telling the truth made Barr that afraid, they would be asking themselves what might happen to *them* if they told the truth. They probably had families, too, he mused, and would do almost anything to protect them.

Buchanan and Horton straightened up from their discussion with Judge Ordway. Buchanan still looked furious.

Ordway said, "The prosecution has requested a delay. In accordance with that, I'm going to adjourn for the day. The trial will resume at nine o'clock tomorrow morning."

The bang of the gavel punctuated that declaration.

Mutters of disappointment came from the crowd. They had come expecting to see a speedy trial that ended with Pete McLaren being found guilty and sentenced to hang. Instead, the trial was going to take longer, and its outcome wasn't a sure thing anymore.

The members of the jury started to stand up, but Miguel motioned them back into their chairs. "Stay there until the place clears out." Then he and a couple volunteers marched McLaren out of the town hall at gunpoint to take him back to the jail and lock him up.

"What in blazes happened?" Chance said.

"McLaren's bunch got to that witness," Ace said. "That may be enough to scare the other witnesses into changing their testimony. And with what Horton was able to do when Miguel testified, there may not be anybody to come right out and say they saw McLaren shoot Marshal Dixon and the girl."

"But that's crazy! Everybody in town knows he did it. What's to stop us from voting to convict him even if nobody's willing to tell the truth?"

Ace frowned. "Our votes are supposed to be based on the evidence presented by both sides. If there's no real evidence—"

"Now *you're* talking crazy. You can't tell me you'd really vote to set McLaren free."

"I sure don't want to," Ace said.

"Then don't." When Ace didn't say anything, Chance blew out an exasperated breath and went on. "You've got to be stubborn about everything, don't you? How is it you were raised by a professional gambler and turned out so blasted honest?"

"Doc's a square dealer and always has been," Ace protested.

"Yeah, but he knows sometimes you've got to bend the rules a little when the deck's stacked unfairly against you."

"We can argue about this later." Ace shrugged. "Maybe it won't even come to that. Maybe the rest of the witnesses will tell the truth."

"After what we just saw, you really think so?"

Ace didn't have an answer for that.

Chapter Twenty-six

The four men reined to a halt. The lights of Lone Pine lay in front of them, less than a mile away.

Stocky Vic Russell leaned forward in his saddle and frowned. "I still ain't sure why we came back here tonight, Perry. That camp up in the hills was plenty good. We could've laid low there until the trial was over."

"Yeah, we could have," Severs answered, "but what if things don't work out right for Pete? We don't want the next thing we hear to be that they've stretched his neck, do we?"

"José said things were goin' just fine for Pete," Larry Dunn said. "That's what you told us, anyway."

Severs suppressed the impatience he felt. Sol Horton had made a fool of that greaser deputy. Horton might be a weasel, but he was a damn good lawyer, Severs thought.

To top things off, Donald Barr had done the smart thing and testified that he hadn't seen Pete shoot the marshal and the whore. With any luck, the other witnesses were smart enough to catch on and realize they'd better do the same thing.

After everything that had happened, José was desperate to regain favor with the McLaren bunch. He was more than happy to serve as a spy and his report had been a good one, telling Severs everything that had happened at the trial when he had slipped into town earlier. He didn't doubt the fat cantina owner was telling the truth.

But there was never anything wrong with a little insurance.

Knowing that, after his surreptitious conference with José in the cantina's back room, Severs had returned to the camp. Along the way he pondered everything José had told him, and by the time he got there, he had reached a decision.

They would go back to Lone Pine after dark.

As they regarded the settlement's lights ahead of them, Severs said, "Even if some of those witnesses don't get the message, all it takes is one juror to upset the applecart. We need to throw a scare into them, just like we did with the witnesses."

"How do you figure on doing that?" Lew Merritt asked. "The ones who'd scare off easy never volunteered to be on the jury in the first place."

"Most of 'em are just townies," Severs said with scorn in his voice. "Nothing special or tough about them. We're going after the ones who have caused us the most trouble—those damn Jensen boys. If we beat the hell out of them, the others will get the idea they'd better deliver the right verdict."

"Why not just kill 'em?" Merritt suggested.

Severs shook his head. "What we've wanted all along is for Pete to be found not guilty. Otherwise those charges will be hanging over his head from now on."

"What about him shootin' José?"

Severs scoffed. "José's never going to testify against Pete. Dixon's dead, and Ace Jensen is the only other one who saw what happened in the cantina. When we get through with Jensen, he'll know he'd better toe the line if he knows what's good for him."

Severs could sense that the others were dubious of his reasoning. He went on angrily, "Well? Do any of you have any better ideas?"

"No, I reckon not, Perry," Russell admitted. "And I got to admit, whalin' the tar outta them Jensens sounds pretty good."

"Where do we find 'em?" Merritt asked.

"Lone Pine's not that big a place," Severs said. "We'll find them . . . and they'll be mighty sorry when we do."

Ace and Chance went into the marshal's office.

Miguel Soriano looked up from the chair behind the desk and scowled. "Mr. Buchanan told me I shouldn't be talking to you fellas, now that you're jurors. I know Judge Ordway likes to keep things informal, but some things just wouldn't be proper, according to Mr. Buchanan."

"Couldn't agree more," Ace said with a smile as

he set the tray he was carrying onto the desk. "We didn't come to talk about the trial. We just brought you a bowl of Mrs. Hilfstrom's stew and a cup of Lars's coffee."

A grin replaced Miguel's frown. "I can use both of those."

Chance thumbed his hat back. "We won't ask you any questions about what you've been doing since Judge Ordway adjourned the court for the day. We know that if you've got any sense, you and Buchanan have been talking to the rest of the witnesses you lined up and making sure they're not going to change their story like Barr did."

Miguel sighed. "You're ruining my appetite here, Chance."

"So you've run into trouble with them," Ace said, nodding slowly. "Not that you said that, of course. We're just assuming here."

"Yeah, just an assumption," Chance agreed. "But not a particularly pretty one."

"Yeah, if it's like you think, it would be a pretty ugly situation," Miguel said. "And when people get scared, they get stubborn. They don't want to believe you when you tell them they'll be safe . . . that the law will protect them."

Ace said, "I reckon they've seen too many times when that didn't happen. You can't blame people for being cautious, especially family men."

"There are quite a few of those on the jury, aren't there?" Chance asked.

"Half a dozen. More than enough." Miguel didn't have to explain what he meant by that.

It only took one vote to deadlock a jury. If enough witnesses changed their stories and the case against Pete McLaren ended in a mistrial, it might be well nigh impossible to ever seat a jury in Lone Pine for a retrial. Eventually, the law would have to let McLaren go.

He would either light a shuck out of that part of the country . . . or he would go on a rampage of revenge against the settlement that had locked him up.

"Well, we didn't mean to ruin your supper," Ace said. "You go ahead and eat. Lars said whichever of his daughters brings your breakfast in the morning can pick up the tray and the bowl and the cup."

Miguel nodded. "Thanks, fellas. For bringing this over . . . and for everything else you've done to help so far."

"It may not be enough," Ace warned.

"Nobody can do more than their best. That seems to be what you boys are cut out to do."

"We try," Chance said with a grin.

They left the marshal's office and paused outside in the street.

"What do you want to do now?" Chance asked.

Ace was looking down the street toward the office of the *Lone Pine Sentinel*, where a light was burning in the front window. "Looks like

Lee and his sister are working on the paper," he mused instead of answering Chance's question.

That brought a chuckle from Chance. "And you want to go give 'em a hand, don't you? Even though you don't know the first blasted thing about newspapers except how to read them?"

"So what was your idea?" Ace said. "Go down to the Melodian and engage in some music appreciation?"

"Hey, I appreciate music."

"You appreciate Miss Fontana Dupree."

"I won't deny that. And your interest in journalism has dark hair and a nice shape."

"How about I see you later at the hotel?" Ace suggested.

"Sure. But I'll walk with you down to the newspaper office and say hello to the Emorys before I go on to the Melodian. Don't worry. I won't try to beat your time with Meredith. She's a little too reserved for my taste, anyway. Blood runs a little cool, if you know what I mean."

"Keep a respectful tongue in your head," Ace warned him.

"Hey, I'm always respectful to them that deserve it," Chance said. "I'd say Meredith and her brother do. Fine folks, if you ask me."

Ace couldn't have agreed more with that.

Side by side, they ambled toward the newspaper office.

● ● ●

Cloaked in the thick shadows of a nearby alley, Severs, Dunn, Merritt, and Russell watched the Jensen brothers walk toward them. All four men had tugged their hat brims low over their eyes and tied their bandannas over the lower halves of their faces. As disguises went, those weren't that effective, but they were better than nothing.

"We gonna jump 'em when they go by?" Merritt whispered.

That had been Severs's plan, but he was able to think on his feet and saw there might be a better idea. "It looks like they're headed for the newspaper office. Let's wait and see. If they go in there, we can give Emory a beating as well and bust the place up. He's a juror, too, so that'll be even more of a lesson to the others."

"Emory's sister is pretty easy on the eyes," Dunn said. "We might have a little fun with her, too."

"Don't let it go too far," Severs warned. "There are some things folks won't stand for."

Out on the street, the Jensen brothers walked on past.

Severs edged forward to watch as they knocked on the front door of the newspaper office and went inside. He said to his companions, "Come on. Let's slip around to the back and give those sons of bitches a surprise."

• • •

"Ace! This is a nice surprise," Meredith said as the Jensens stepped inside. "And it's good to see you, too, of course, Chance."

"I'm not staying, but my brother here has a sudden hankering to learn the newspaper business."

Ace cast a warning glance at Chance. "That's not it, exactly. We just saw the light burning down here and figured it wouldn't hurt to make sure you and your brother are doing all right."

"We're fine," Lee Emory said as he came out of the back room where the press was. He held one of the metal composing sticks used to assemble type for printing. "We were just setting some type for tomorrow's extra."

"You're putting out another paper?" Ace asked.

"Just one sheet that will come out tomorrow afternoon, after the trial is over and Pete McLaren is found guilty. The story I'm setting up now is about what happened today in court."

"You're pretty optimistic, thinking that McLaren's going to be convicted," Chance commented.

Emory smiled thinly. "I have to believe that justice will triumph—" He stopped short as a noise came from the other room. "That sounded like something fell over. What in the world!" He turned and disappeared into the back room.

Meredith started after him, saying, "Lee, do you need some—"

Suddenly, Emory reeled back through the doorway, one hand clutching his head. Crimson welled between his fingers. He lost his balance and sprawled on the floor at Meredith's feet as she cried out in alarm. The composing stick Emory had been carrying clattered as he dropped it.

A masked man with cold eyes peering out from under a pulled-down hat brim stepped through the doorway and leveled a gun at Meredith, Ace, and Chance. Three more men, similarly masked, crowded through the doorway behind him.

"Nobody move! Or there'll be plenty of ink spilled in here. Red ink—like blood!"

Chapter Twenty-seven

Defying the command not to move, Meredith dropped to her knees next to her brother and clutched at him. "Lee! Oh, my God, Lee!"

Emory groaned and stirred slightly, but obviously the blow that had opened up a cut on his forehead had also stunned him.

"Take it easy, little sis," said the spokesman for the intruders. "He'll be all right. You all will, if you listen to reason and do what we tell you."

Ace's first impulse had been to slap leather as

soon as he saw the masked, gun-wielding men. A glance at his brother told him Chance felt the same way, but both restrained the impulse. In the close quarters, especially with Meredith in the room, they had to avoid lead flying around.

"What is it you want, Severs?" Ace asked, his voice taut with anger.

Under the pulled-down hat brim, the man's eyes widened in surprise.

Chance said, "You didn't think those pathetic excuses for disguises were going to fool anybody, did you? Even if your faces were completely covered up, there are four of you, and three of us are on Pete McLaren's jury. It's a pretty easy deduction to make."

"Shut up," Severs snarled. "You sons of bitches think you're so damn smart! Well, we're here to teach you better!"

Meredith looked up from where she knelt beside Emory. "My brother is hurt. He needs the doctor."

"You can get him when we're done. Now stand up and back away from him, girl."

Meredith clutched Emory's shoulders. "I won't! I won't let you hurt him any more, either."

Severs ignored her for the moment and gestured with his gun at Ace and Chance. "Shuck those irons, you two," he ordered.

"So you can gun us down without us even putting up a fight?" Chance said. "I don't think so."

Noticing Emory's hand stealing toward the composing stick on the floor, Ace said, "You've overplayed your hand, Severs. You should have stopped with intimidating the witnesses and not gone after the jurors. Now you're going to wind up behind bars with your friend McLaren."

Lee Emory still acted groggy, but Ace suspected the newspaperman had regained his senses enough to want to fight back. The printing tool was fairly lightweight, but it was a better weapon than nothing. Lying practically at Severs's feet he stealthily closed his hand around the composing stick.

Severs thrust his gun forward "Maybe it would be better if we *did* kill the three of you. The trial couldn't go on with only nine jurors, now could it?" His eyes flicked toward Meredith. "It'd be a shame, though."

Ace knew perfectly well what the hardcase meant. They couldn't murder the Jensen brothers and Emory without killing Meredith, too, to keep her from identifying them. Emory understood the implication as well. He acted then, lunging up from the floor and slashing at Severs's wrist with the composing stick.

The blow packed enough force to knock the gun toward the ceiling. Severs jerked the trigger and the revolver roared, but the bullet went high over the heads of Ace and Chance.

Ace drove forward, lowering his shoulder and

going under the gun to ram Severs backwards. They crashed into the other three men, who held their fire because Severs was in the way. A couple lost their balance, stumbling as they tried to stay on their feet.

Chance was right behind Ace, charging into battle. He knocked aside the Colt in one gunman's hand and slammed a fist into the hombre's masked face. As that man wilted, Chance pivoted and lifted a foot into the belly of another man. When he doubled over in pain, Chance brought the edge of a hand down sharply on his neck, knocking him to the floor.

Holding on to Severs's gun wrist, Ace struggled to keep the Colt's muzzle away from him. From the corner of his eye, he saw Emory grab hold of Meredith's hand and tug her after him as he hustled out the front door of the newspaper office. Ace figured Emory was going for help, not running away, but the important thing was getting Meredith out of the line of fire.

Now that she was safe, the Jensen brothers could really cut loose.

Severs's gun blasted again, and the bullet ripped through the calf of one of his companions. The man toppled, howling in pain. Ace dug a knee into Severs's belly and pinned him to the floor. He slammed his fist into the man's face, once and then again. Severs went limp and the gun slid from his fingers.

Three of the hardcases were down, but one—the man Chance had punched first—was still on his feet and had recovered enough to lunge at Chance and try to pistol-whip him. Chance got his head out of the way of the descending gun in time, but the blow caught him on the left shoulder. Grimacing, he staggered back, his left arm hanging at his side, numb from the impact.

With a little space between them, the man brought the gun up again and fired. Chance dived aside just in time. The slug whipped through the space he had occupied a split second earlier and shattered the office's front window.

Chance reached out with his right leg, hooked the toe of his boot behind the man's calf, and jerked. With the startled yelp, the hardcase went over backwards.

Having scrambled to his feet after knocking out Perry Severs, Ace kicked the gun out of the last man's hand, then reached down, caught hold of the man's shirt, and dragged him to his feet. Ace's left fist sunk into the man's gut, and his right looped around to crash into his jaw. The man's head slewed to the side, his eyes rolled up in their sockets, and his knees buckled.

Ace stepped back and let him fall.

Three of the intruders were unconscious, and the fourth man lay on the floor whimpering as he clutched the leg Severs's wild shot had ventilated. His gun laid on the floor beside him.

Ace scooped it up, just to make sure the varmint didn't get any ideas.

Chance flexed the fingers of his left hand, swung that arm back and forth as he tried to get some feeling back into it, then bent over and jerked down the masks on the men who were out cold—Perry Severs, Vic Russell, and Lew Merritt, just as he and Ace expected. Larry Dunn was the one who'd been shot in the calf. Ace covered all of them with Dunn's revolver.

Rapid footsteps pounded on the boardwalk outside. Miguel Soriano burst through the doorway, carrying a shotgun. He stopped short, looked around the room, and then grunted. "Lee said there was bad trouble in here, but it looks like you boys have already taken care of it."

Already collecting the guns of the other men, Chance glanced up. "Looks like you're gonna have some more customers for your jail, Marshal."

"What are the charges?"

"Assault, for one," Ace said. "I don't know which of the varmints walloped Lee Emory in the head, but since they broke in here together, it seems like all of them ought to have to answer for it."

"And they all pointed guns at us and threatened us," Chance added. "That's a crime, isn't it?"

"It's plenty to lock them up for." A smile tugged at Miguel's mouth. "And since Judge Ordway is busy with McLaren's trial, he won't be able to hold a hearing for them until that's over."

"Meaning that the witnesses they threatened will be safe," Ace said.

Lee Emory stepped into the office, followed by his sister, who wore an anxious frown.

Emory held a bloodstained rag to the cut on his head. "The witnesses and the jurors will only be safe as long as this bunch is behind bars."

Miguel said, "But if McLaren is convicted by the time they get out, they won't have any reason to threaten anybody. It'll be too late for that to work."

Emory shrugged. "If we rule out simple revenge on their part, I suppose that's true."

Doc Bellem bustled into the office carrying his medical bag. "A fella came to fetch me, said there was an injured man down here."

"I sent for you, Doctor," Meredith said. "You can see, Lee has a bad cut on his head."

"Let me take a look there." Considerably shorter than Emory, Bellem went up on his toes to peer owlishly at the wound when the newspaperman took the cloth away. "Not too bad, I don't think, once we get all that gore cleaned away. Might take two or three stitches to close it up. Come along with me, my boy."

"I need to work on the paper—"

"I'll handle that," Meredith said briskly. "You get that head tended to."

Her tone left no room for argument, but Emory

said, "I hate to leave you here by yourself . . ."

"Nonsense. With these vermin locked up, no one else in Lone Pine has any reason to wish me harm."

Ace said, "And I can stay and help Miss Emory with the paper, if she'd like, as well as keeping an eye on the place."

Chance laughed. "Somehow, I'm not surprised to hear you volunteering for that job, Ace."

Ace glared at him for a second, while a pink tinge appeared on Meredith's cheeks.

"I'll give you a hand getting these men locked up, Marshal," Chance went on. "A juror can do that without acting improperly, can't he?"

"I don't see why not. You're a juror in a totally different case."

Perry Severs had started making noises and moving around a little. Chance nudged him in the side with a boot toe. "On your feet, Severs. You're so fond of Pete McLaren, you're gonna get to go pay him a visit."

On by one, Miguel and the Jensen brothers got the hardcases awake enough to stand up. They stumbled out of the newspaper office with Miguel and Chance following them. Miguel kept the shotgun pointed at the prisoners while Chance carried two revolvers in his hands.

That left Ace and Meredith in the office with Emory and Doc Bellem. The medico took Emory's arm and led him toward the door.

"Don't worry about your brother, my dear," he said over his shoulder. "He'll be fine."

Once the two men were gone, Meredith looked at Ace. "I'm sure I'll be fine here if there's something else you'd rather be doing."

"There isn't. Anyway, I'm glad to pitch in and help."

"With the newspaper, you mean?"

"Sure. I've read plenty of them, but I don't really know much about how they're printed."

"Well, I can show you," Meredith said. "But I warn you . . . you're liable to get your fingers dirty."

He smiled. "I reckon I'll risk it."

Chapter Twenty-eight

Already asleep when Chance got back to the hotel, Ace didn't see his brother until the next morning. He sat up in bed yawning. "You're up bright and early."

Standing in front of the mirror shaving, Chance looked over his shoulder with lather still on his face and grinned. "How do you know I'm not *still* up?"

"Well, I don't, I reckon. But I'm too much of a gentleman to speculate on such things when there's a lady involved."

"Fontana is some lady, all right," Chance said

as he resumed scraping stubble off his cheeks. "And for your information, I actually did come back to the hotel and get a few hours sleep. But then I woke up earlier than usual. I suppose I'm just anxious for that blasted trial to be over with. Pete McLaren's been nothing but a thorn in our sides ever since we rode into Lone Pine."

"That's true enough." Ace swung his legs out of bed. He stood up, stretched, and yawned again.

"Tired out from your night?" Chance asked with a chuckle.

"Nothing improper happened." Ace held up his hands with the fingers spread to display the dark stains on them and his palms. "I learned how to set type."

"A skill that might come in handy in your old age . . . assuming either of us live that long. How's Lee?"

"He came back to the newspaper office a while after you left. He had a bandage on his head and orders from Doc Bellem to take it easy for a few days. I suspect he won't follow those orders very well, though. He's like you and me . . . he's got a trial to go to today."

A short time later, the Jensen brothers went downstairs. As they passed through the hotel lobby, they said hello to Colonel Howden.

He stopped them with a wave to come closer. "The town's excited this morning, boys. People have heard about what happened last night."

"I'm not surprised, what with guns going off and all," Chance said.

"Folks know that McLaren's cronies are locked up. They're excited because they think justice might actually be done in this trial after all. It was looking pretty unlikely there for a while."

Ace nodded in agreement. As he had told Severs, McLaren's pards had overplayed their hand. They should have been satisfied with what they had done already to influence the trial's outcome. They'd ended up behind bars and were no threat to anyone.

"Maybe it'll be over today," Ace said.

"We're all hoping so," Howden said.

The people in the café expressed similar sentiments to Ace and Chance while they ate breakfast. Folks acted like they were local heroes, something that had always bothered Ace. The way he saw it, he and his brother just tried to do the right thing.

He gave a brief thought to the way the world was and decided maybe that made them heroes. He preferred not to ponder on that too much.

The street in front of the town hall was already crowded when they got there. At least folks didn't cheer at the sight of him and Chance, Ace thought. That really would have made him uncomfortable. Chance, on the other hand, probably would have enjoyed it.

The crowd had swelled even more by the time

the trial was ready to get under way. The court-room was full, and more than a hundred people waited outside the building, obviously eager to hear a verdict. It looked like most, if not all, of the population of Lone Pine was there today, along with plenty of other folks from the ranches and mines in the area. Pete McLaren's brutal, arrogant personality had made him plenty of enemies in that corner of New Mexico Territory.

Accompanied by his sister, Lee Emory looked a little weak and washed out when he showed up. The newspaperman had a fresh bandage on his head. As he took his seat among the jurors, Ace asked him how he was feeling.

"Like somebody cracked a gun barrel over my head," Emory replied with a faint smile. "But I'll be all right. Say, I'm not sure I thanked you last night, Ace. I'm sure Meredith felt better having you around while the doctor was tending to me. She said you turned out to be a pretty fair type-setter, too."

"I don't reckon newspaper blood is in my veins," Ace said, "but I enjoyed helping out."

Hank Muller and Fontana Dupree came in, Muller taking one of the empty jurors' chairs while Fontana took a seat in the front row of the spectators' section when a man stood up and offered her his chair. She smiled her thanks at him, then turned to look at the jury, specifically Chance. He smiled back at her.

"This isn't a Sunday picnic, you know," Ace said quietly.

"No, but a picnic isn't a bad idea. I'll have to suggest that to Fontana." Chance paused. "Maybe you and Meredith would like to come along, too."

Ace just cleared his throat and tried to look serious. At the same time, the thought of spending some time out in the country with Meredith Emory held a definite appeal.

He didn't have time to ponder that because Miguel and his new volunteer deputies brought in the prisoner. McLaren's hands were cuffed behind his back again, although Miguel switched the cuffs around to the front once McLaren was sitting at the defense table next to Solomon Horton.

Ace would have liked to check with Miguel and make sure everything had gone peacefully the night before after Severs and the other hardcases were locked up, but he supposed they had or he would have heard about it.

Miguel ducked into the office that served as the judge's chambers, then came back out a few moments later and announced, "All rise."

When everyone, including Judge Ordway, was settled again, he smacked his gavel on the table. "This court is now in session once more. Mr. Buchanan, I believe you were about to call the second witness for the prosecution."

"That's right, Your Honor," Buchanan said as he got to his feet. "I call Dooley Finn."

Sitting next to Ace, Emory leaned over and whispered, "Dooley's a boot maker. Often works late at his shop."

Buchanan's line of questioning came as no surprise. He established that Dooley Finn's business had a good view of the front of the marshal's office and jail and that Finn had been there on the previous Friday evening. "Tell the court what you observed that evening, please, Mr. Finn."

The stocky Irishman, who had graying red hair and a permanent squint in one eye, pointed at McLaren. "I saw that no-good spalpeen shoot Marshal Dixon and that poor curly-headed gal from the Melodian."

"Objection, Your Honor!" Horton practically bellowed as he shot to his feet. "Such a characterization is prejudicial to my client."

"This isn't a music hall, Dooley," Ordway told the witness. "Just answer the questions as plain as you can."

"Be sure and I will, Your Honor," Finn said.

Buchanan said, "Just to be absolutely clear, Mr. Finn, it's your testimony that you saw the defendant, Pete McLaren, shoot and kill Marshal Hoyt Dixon and Miss Dorothy Redding."

"That is absolutely what I saw. Never a doubt in me mind."

"Thank you. No further questions."

Horton got up to cross-examine, but no matter how hard he tried to rattle Finn, the boot maker stood firm in his testimony. No one had been in his way to obscure his view, and despite the squint, his eyesight was perfect as he offered to demonstrate with any test the defense cared to propose.

"That won't necessary," Ordway said. "We know you can see just fine, Dooley."

Horton gave up on the cross-examination, and Buchanan called his next witness, one of the men who worked for the local undertaker. He had been crossing the street about a block away from the jail when the shooting erupted. The story he told was the same as Dooley Finn's.

"I knew right away the marshal and Miss Redding were dead," the man added. "If there's one thing I know when I see it, it's a dead body."

That brought some nervous laughter from the spectators and a warning glare from the judge.

Three more witnesses testified in fairly short order, and all of them corroborated the testimony that had come before them. Horton was unable to shake them on cross-examination. When Buchanan was finished with those witnesses, he rested the prosecution's case.

Solomon Horton looked a little sick as he got to his feet, Ace thought. Pete McLaren looked furious, but there was nothing he could do except sit there and wait, hoping that his lawyer could do some-thing to save him.

"I call my client, Pete McLaren, to the stand, Your Honor," Horton said.

The spectators were quiet as McLaren scraped his chair back, stood up, and went to the witness chair. Ace saw hatred on the face of a lot of them. McLaren had lorded it over the people of Lone Pine for quite a while, using fear, intimidation, and brutality to get his way. It had all caught up to him, and there wasn't a sympathetic eye in the place.

In a way, McLaren was lucky he hadn't been taken out of the jail and lynched. Only the fundamentally decent nature of the citizens had saved him from such a fate.

When McLaren had been sworn in, Horton took a deep breath. "You've heard all of these accusations against you, Mr. McLaren. How do you answer them?"

McLaren sat there breathing heavily. He pushed his lips in and out and frowned. Finally, he said, "I didn't shoot Dolly and the marshal. I don't know who did. I don't deny bustin' out of jail. I didn't want to go to prison for shootin' that fat greas—I mean, for shootin' José. But I didn't shoot anybody else. The bullets just came outta nowhere. Musta been somebody lurkin' in an alley, and when they saw their chance, they opened fire."

"Then you didn't murder anyone, did you, Mr. McLaren?"

"No, sir, I sure—" McLaren stopped short. He was breathing even harder, almost panting. His face had slowly turned a darker and darker red.

"Mr. McLaren?" Horton prodded. "You were testifying that you're innocent of these crimes—"

"Shut up!" McLaren roared as he surged up out of the witness chair. His cuffed hands shot out and grabbed the front of Horton's vest. As he started shaking the lawyer, he shouted, "Shut up, you damned oily shyster! You're no better 'n the rest of these pissant townies! All of you scurryin' around in your useless little lives! Yeah, I shot that damn badge-toter! He had it comin' for lockin' me up! *Me! Pete McLaren! Otis McLaren's brother!* He deserved to die for that."

McLaren gave Horton a hard shove. Horton stumbled backwards and fell in front of the defense table.

An uproar of shouts filled the room, but McLaren bellowed over it. "Go to hell, all of you! Hang me and be damned to you! See what it gets you! Lone Pine will *burn!*"

McLaren turned and acted like he was going to leap at Judge Ordway, but Miguel laid him out with a stroke from the butt of the shotgun he carried. McLaren sprawled on the floor, senseless from the blow.

"Shackle that man!" Ordway said. "I want him in irons!"

Miguel sent one of the deputies running to the jail for shackles. While the commotion in the courtroom gradually quieted down, they secured McLaren and dragged him back to the defense table, where they propped him up in his chair as he began to come around.

Ordway hammered the gavel on the table until the room quieted down, then he asked, "Do you have any further questions for your witness, Mr. Horton?"

The lawyer, who had gotten up, straightened his clothes, and tried to restore some of his lost dignity, shook his head. "No further questions, Your Honor."

"I'll waive cross-examination, Your Honor," Buchanan said, not too successful at not sounding smug about it.

"We'll hear closing statements, then."

Buchanan stood. "I can think of no closing statement more eloquent or convincing than the defendant's own words, Your Honor."

Ordway blew out an exasperated breath, then looked at Horton. "Counselor?"

Horton just waved a hand weakly and shook his head.

"Very well, then." Ordway turned to the jurors. "Members of the jury, you may withdraw to elect a foreman and deliberate your verdict."

Colonel Howden said, "I don't think we need to do that, Your Honor."

"For once I agree with the damn Yankee," Crackerjack Sawyer added. "I reckon we all know how we're gonna vote."

"In that case, I'll have to poll the jury." Ordway frowned. "And you'd better be right, Crackerjack."

"I'll get it started," the liveryman said. "I vote guilty!"

"As do I," Colonel Howden said. "Guilty."

"Guilty as charged," Hank Muller rumbled.

One by one, the jurors spoke up, and each of them said in a clear voice, "Guilty."

Lee Emory's turn came, and the newspaperman said, "I take no real pleasure in this, but . . . guilty."

"Guilty," Ace said, and Chance finished it off by saying the same.

Ordway nodded slowly. "The verdict is unanimous, as it must be for conviction. Mr. Horton, you and your client will stand while I render the verdict and pass sentence."

"Not my client any longer, Your Honor," Horton said, still appearing shaken. "I've resigned."

"Not until this trial is over, you haven't," Ordway snapped. "Marshal, get the defendant on his feet."

Miguel took one of McLaren's arms, and a deputy took the other. They lifted him. McLaren stood there, looking slowly around the room, his eyes burning hate toward everyone.

"Peter McLaren," Judge Ordway said, "you have been found guilty of murder by a jury of your peers. It is the sentence of this court that you be hanged by the neck until dead, two mornings hence. May God have mercy on your soul. Do you have anything to say?"

"All of you can go to hell," McLaren snarled.

"You'll be there to meet us if we do." The gavel slammed down on the table. "Court's adjourned!"

Chapter Twenty-nine

McLaren sank back down into his chair, a numb look stealing over his face as he realized the weighty implication of what had just happened. Solomon Horton began gathering up the few papers he had on the table. It was over and done with as far as he was concerned and he wanted nothing more to do with it.

Ace watched from the chairs along the wall where the jurors still sat.

The crowd began leaving the courtroom. They took a lot of excited talk with them, and the uproar grew even louder as word of the verdict and the sentence reached the greater number of people waiting outside.

Not all the spectators left, however. Meredith

Emory and Fontana Dupree came over to the jurors, who were getting to their feet since their job was finished.

"Thank God that's over," Meredith said. "Maybe now we can put all this behind us."

"Not until McLaren's stretching hemp," Fontana said. "Then it'll be done."

"That's the blasted truth," Muller said.

Feeling eyes on him, Ace looked over at the defense table. McLaren sat there alone now that Horton had left. Miguel and his new deputies were moving in to take charge of the prisoner and return him to the jail.

McLaren's head had swiveled toward the jurors, and the hate Ace saw in his eyes had achieved new levels of virulence. If that old saying about how looks could kill had been true, twelve dead men would be in the courtroom.

Miguel took hold of McLaren's arm and pulled him to his feet. "Come on. We're done here."

"It ain't done," McLaren said coldly, echoing what Fontana had said. "It won't be done until all you bastards have paid."

"And who's going to collect?" Miguel said. "Let's go."

With the shackles on his ankles, the prisoner could only shuffle along, so it took a moment for the little group to leave the courtroom. They took him out the back way to avoid the crowd in the street.

"You know," Chance mused, "I thought I'd feel more relieved when the trial was over, but I really don't."

"A good man and an innocent woman are still dead," Ace said. "No verdict can ever change that."

"I appreciate you calling Dolly an innocent woman," Fontana said. "She really did have a good heart. She just never could see McLaren for what he really is."

Muller raised his voice and addressed the other jurors. "All of you fellas come on over to the Melodian later. Drinks are on the house for you today."

Lee Emory said, "I'm not sure I want to celebrate a man being sentenced to hang, even though it was a necessity."

"Well, I don't mind wettin' my whistle," Crackerjack said. "I'll see you later, Hank, and much obliged to you."

Judge Ordway had gone to his chambers after adjourning the court. He returned to the room, the hat on his head making it obvious he was ready to leave.

"You men don't have to stay here," he told the jurors. "Your work is done."

"We know that, Your Honor," Emory said. "Just letting the crowd clear out a little."

Ace said, "I was wondering, Your Honor . . . what about McLaren's friends?"

"The four who are locked up for assaulting

Mr. Emory here and attacking you boys? I intend to send them to prison for a couple years. By the time they get out, McLaren will be moldering in his grave and I doubt any of them will ever return to Lone Pine. That's what I hope happens, anyway."

"Then we should have peace and quiet around here from now on," Colonel Howden said.

That comment stirred some uneasiness inside Ace. In his experience, it was all right to hope for peace and quiet . . .

But assuming you were going to get it was usually a mistake.

By the next morning, the settlement was still buzzing about Pete McLaren being convicted and sentenced to hang. Not many people noticed the little procession headed from the town hall toward the jail.

Perry Severs, Larry Dunn, Lew Merritt, and Vic Russell were facing their trial. Lee Emory had worked in a mention of it in the *Lone Pine Sentinel* extra at the last minute, after McLaren's trial but before cranking up the printing press.

Miguel had informed Ace and Chance they would have to attend the trial and be available as witnesses, along with Emory and Meredith. They were the only ones in the courtroom other than the prisoners, the marshal and his deputies, Timothy Buchanan, Judge Ordway . . . and

259

Solomon Horton, who had evidently been prevailed upon to represent the four hardcases, despite his lack of success with McLaren's case.

As soon as the judge gaveled court into session, Horton got to his feet before Buchanan could say anything and announced, "Your Honor, my clients would like to enter guilty pleas."

Ordway frowned. "What's that, Counselor? You're not going to present a defense?"

"No, Your Honor. Perry Severs, Lewis Merritt, and Victor Russell all plead guilty to the charge of disturbing the peace."

"They're charged with assault," Buchanan pointed out. "And what about Dunn?"

"Laurence Dunn pleads guilty to the charge of assault, Your Honor. With this plea on the record, I move that the assault charges against my other clients be dropped. It's only fair, since only Mr. Dunn struck the blow resulting in the charges."

"Wait just a blasted minute," Ordway said. "Lee, did you see which one of these men actually pistol-whipped you?"

"Your Honor, I object!" Horton said. "It's very irregular for you to question a witness directly, and he hasn't even been sworn in!"

The judge glared at Horton "Do really want to tell me how to run my court, Counselor?"

"I just want things done according to the law, Your Honor."

"And I don't want to waste any more of the

court's time than I have to." Ordway turned his attention back to the newspaperman. "How about it, Lee? Can you testify as to which one walloped you?"

Emory got to his feet, looking uneasy "As a matter of fact, Your Honor . . . I can't. They were all masked, and it happened so fast. I was taken by surprise, and all I really know for sure is that one of them hit me with his gun." He gestured toward the bandage on his head. "I've got proof of that, right enough."

"Humph. Yes, I'd say you do." Ordway took a deep breath. "Very well. Under the circumstances, I have no choice but to accept the guilty pleas. The charges of assault against the other three defendants will be dropped. I fine them one hundred dollars each for disturbing the peace. On the charge of assault against Laurence Dunn, I sentence the defendant to eighteen months in the territorial prison in Santa Fe."

Dunn winced at that, but he didn't say anything to Horton or the judge.

"Mr. Dunn will be returned to the jail to await transport to prison," Ordway went on. "The other three defendants will be released as soon as they pay their fines."

"I'll take care of that right now, Your Honor," Horton said.

"See that you do." Ordway reached for his gavel to signal the end of the proceedings.

"Your Honor, a moment," Buchanan said. "I would ask that in addition to the fines you've levied, you also sentence these three men to one week in jail. Given the way they terrorized two of our finest citizens, it only seems fitting that they serve some time behind bars."

"I agree with you in principle, Counselor," Ordway said, "but I've already passed sentence. The guiding principle of this court has always been not only a strict interpretation of the law but fairness as well. I've already levied fines that are four times the usual amount. I can't in good conscience add jail time to that." Ordway didn't look happy about what he was saying.

Ace figured the judge was annoyed with himself for not realizing in time it would be better to keep McLaren's friends safely behind bars until after the hanging. Ordway had approached the case in his typical fashion . . . but the circumstances weren't really typical.

As the judge had said, it was too late. If he tried to change the sentence, Horton would set up a howl. Also, Ordway's own stubborn pride entered into the matter as well.

That didn't stop Miguel from speaking up. "Your Honor—"

Ordway lifted a hand to stop him. "Before you go on, Marshal, be advised that I won't change my sentence."

Horton moved out from behind the defense

table and handed some greenbacks to Miguel, who took them reluctantly.

"I believe that satisfies the terms of your sentence, Your Honor." Horton was back to being his smug, oily self after his defeat the day before.

"Indeed it does. Your clients are free to go. Except for Mr. Dunn, of course."

"I'll have to send word to the prison at Santa Fe," Miguel said. "They'll have to send a deputy U.S. marshal to pick up Dunn and take him there."

"I'm sure I can trust you to tend to that, Marshal." Ordway smacked the gavel down. "Court's adjourned."

A few minutes later, Ace and Chance stood on the front porch of the town hall with Emory and Meredith and watched Miguel lead Larry Dunn back toward the jail. Dunn went along meekly. That by itself was enough to bother Ace, but he didn't like the way the whole thing had played out.

Severs, Merritt, and Russell had disappeared quickly as soon as they were freed. Horton and Buchanan were gone as well.

"I don't like this," Lee Emory said. "I suppose having three of McLaren's friends loose is better than four, but—"

"Surely they won't try anything else," Meredith said. "Nothing they've done to help McLaren has worked so far. In fact, you could say it's backfired on them."

Ace nodded slowly. "The smartest thing for them to do would be to light a shuck out of these parts and never come back. Problem is . . . those fellas have never struck me as being all that smart."

Chance said, "No, but they're plenty mean, and that varmint Severs is the cunning sort. Could be he's got some sort of trick up his sleeve."

"If he does, we'll be ready for it," Ace said.

"You fellows aren't leaving town now that the trial's over?" Lee Emory asked.

"No, I reckon we'll be around here for a while yet, just to see how things play out," Ace said.

His brother nodded in unhesitating agreement.

Chapter Thirty

Ace and Chance spent most of the day at the Melodian, Ace nursing a beer at one of the tables, Chance partaking of a poker game with an assortment of players, most of them ranchers or mine owners from the area. The pots were fairly large, but Ace watched enough of the game to know that Chance was holding his own. It was unlikely he would lose their stake. In fact, he would probably come out of the game a good deal ahead.

That would allow them to move on whenever

they were ready, but Ace wasn't sure when that was going to be. Lone Pine was a pleasant place, or at least he thought it would be once Pete McLaren ascended the gallows and dropped through the trap the next morning. Ace knew he wouldn't mind having the opportunity to get to know Meredith Emory better, and he was sure his brother felt the same way about Fontana Dupree.

They weren't going to put down roots or anything, Ace was certain of that, but at the same time, he didn't think they were in any hurry to leave, either.

At suppertime, they headed for the Lone Pine Café and more of that good cooking from Mrs. Hilfstrom.

Perry Severs frowned into the glass of tequila in his hand. Outside the cantina, the last light of day was fading. He had been drinking all day, since leaving the town hall, but it hadn't helped. His mind was still wracked with indecision.

"It's gonna be dark soon, Perry," Lew Merritt said. "If we're gonna do something—"

"If we're going to do anything, it'll be better to wait until later," Severs said, his voice sharp with irritation. "You fellas said you'd let me do the thinking."

"Well, sure," Vic Russell agreed. "We know you're better suited to that than we are."

That was part of the problem, Severs mused.

If he and his companions got their horses and rode away from Lone Pine, never to come back, he would be the leader of the group, no doubt about that. Pete had been the boss, taking charge by the sheer force of his arrogant self-confidence and hair-trigger temper. Severs had never been convinced that Pete was smarter than he was . . . but he had never cared to buck the other man's command.

Now, things could be different.

Merritt wouldn't let it go. "Last night in the jail, we said—"

"I know what we said," Severs interrupted again.

Actually, it was a pretty good plan. Not foolproof, by any means, but at least it gave them a chance to help McLaren. And it had worked. Although Dunn had pled guilty to the assault change, it had been Severs who had walloped Lee Emory, but the judge didn't have to know that.

Dunn was willing to risk a prison sentence to please his friends, and Severs, Merritt, and Russell were free to help their friends who were still locked up.

Or not, Severs mused. Merritt and Russell wouldn't like it if they abandoned McLaren and Dunn to their fates, but he could talk them into it. He was sure of that. The question was whether or not he really wanted to.

José came over to the table where the three men sat, carrying a tray with tortillas, beans, beef, and chili peppers on it. "Some supper for you." The cantina owner was still trying to make amends for his part in the debacle that ultimately had doomed McLaren to the gallows. "With my compliments, of course."

Merritt grinned. "José, if you ain't careful you're gonna wind up feedin' us from now on."

"It is the least I can do, señor," José assured him. "A moment of weakness on my part, and a lifetime of regret. I fear this is my fate."

"That's the way life is," Severs said. "Folks never know what they're getting into, but it's usually bad." He tossed back the rest of the tequila and reached for the jug.

For a few minutes, the men contented themselves with eating the food José had provided.

Then Merritt said, "So what's the plan, Perry? How're we gonna get Pete and Larry outta that jail?"

"Yeah," Russell said around a mouthful of beans and tortilla. "We got to figure it out. They're gonna be hangin' Pete in the mornin'!"

The hell with it, Severs decided. If he let McLaren hang, he would have to continue doing the thinking for those two, and they were dumb as stumps. Severs didn't want that responsibility. He would rather go back to the way things used to be, just drifting along and letting McLaren do the thinking for *him,* too.

"The whole thing comes down to those new

deputies the greaser's taken on," Severs said in a low, confidential tone as he leaned forward. "Before now they were just layabouts. They've let themselves get all puffed up since the pinned on badges, but they're really not much count and everybody knows it. Soriano can't stay at the jail all the time. He's got to leave the others there sooner or later . . . and that's when we'll make our move."

"How are we gonna know when that is?" Merritt asked.

"That's where you come in, Lew. You go and keep an eye on the jail. When you see Soriano leave, you hurry back here and fetch Vic and me. We'll go in, get the drop on those deputies, and let Pete and Larry out. We'll have horses saddled and ready to go for all of us. Before anybody knows what's happening, we'll put Lone Pine a long way behind us."

Russell frowned. "I don't know if Pete will go along with that. He's plenty mad about the whole deal. He's liable to want to shoot the town up first, before we light a shuck."

"He's not that big a fool," Severs said. "First we get away. Then, when the time is right . . . we come back here and raise hell."

The other two men began to grin at that prospect. Lone Pine was in for all kinds of trouble . . . and the poor fools who lived there didn't even know it yet.

• • •

As Ace and Chance left the café pleasantly full, they saw Miguel coming toward them along the boardwalk.

"Evening," he greeted them as he stopped on the boardwalk.

"And good evening to you, Acting Marshal Soriano," Chance said with a smile.

With a bit of a sheepish smile himself, Miguel said, "Actually, it's not acting marshal anymore. The town council offered me the job full-time and permanentlike this afternoon, and I accepted."

"Congratulations," Ace said. "I don't reckon it'll come as a surprise to anybody. You're the most qualified candidate for the job."

"Norm Sutherland has more experience"— Miguel shrugged—"but he would be the first to admit that he'd run screaming from that much responsibility. With that big family of his, he's got enough to take care of at home. I'm on my own and can devote all my time to keeping law and order around here."

"I'm sure you'll do a fine job," Ace told him.

"Well, I'd like for my first official act to be hiring you two fellas as real deputies. Ed Boulden and Matt Farmer have been helping me out, but I'd rather have the Jensen brothers backing me up."

"We've talked about this," Chance said. "Ace

and I have no interest in settling down and becoming real lawmen."

"That's true," Ace agreed. "I expect we'll be around here for a while, but one of these days we'll get the urge to move on again."

"I'd be glad to hire you until that day comes," Miguel said.

Chance shook his head. "Sorry. I intend to spend my days playing poker and watching and listening to Miss Dupree sing." He grinned. "There was some talk about a picnic, too, as I recall."

Miguel sighed and nodded. "Well, I tried. Can't blame me for that."

"Are those other fellas you mentioned watching the jail?" Ace asked.

"That's right. I'm still in the habit of making evening rounds."

"McLaren and Dunn haven't given you any trouble?"

"They've both been meek as lambs. McLaren's pretty quiet. I imagine he's thinking about what's going to happen in the morning. I told him he could talk to the priest if he wanted to, or the Baptist or Methodist preacher, but he just shook his head."

"He'll probably change his mind, come the dawn tomorrow."

"I wouldn't be surprised. It must be a terrible thing to know the hour of your death. I reckon most folks would rather just be surprised. I know I would be." Miguel moved on to continue his rounds. Night had fallen, although many of the businesses in Lone Pine were just now closing up for the night. That didn't include the Melodian or the other saloons, which would be going strong for hours yet.

"Coming with me to listen to Fontana?" Chance asked.

"No, I reckon I might turn in early," Ace said. "Anyway, you don't need me around."

"You wouldn't be figuring on moseying down to the newspaper office, would you?" Chance squinted in that direction. "Place looks dark to me."

"Yes, I'm sure Lee and Meredith have gone home for the day."

"Too bad. You might have a future as a newspaper reporter, the way you're going."

Ace snorted. "Not hardly." He lifted a hand in farewell. "I'll see you later."

The Jensen brothers parted company. Chance headed for the saloon while Ace drifted toward the hotel. He had been telling the truth about intending to turn in early. A lot had happened since he and Chance had ridden into Lone Pine several days earlier, and none of it had been particularly restful.

But that old saying about good intentions and the road to hell leaped into his mind as he caught a glimpse of movement in the shadows near the marshal's office and jail. That didn't have to be anything suspicious, but it was too soon for Miguel to be winding up his rounds. Ace frowned as he saw a man glide along the boardwalk and pause just long enough to blow out the flame in the lantern hanging near the marshal's door.

Ace veered from his course and headed for the jail. Maybe what he had seen was nothing . . . but maybe it wasn't. Either way, he intended to find out.

Chapter Thirty-one

Severs didn't trust either of his companions to take the lead. Merritt and Russell were followers, at best . . . although Merritt had carried out his job assignment just fine. He had hurried back to the cantina and let the other two know just as soon as Miguel Soriano set out on his evening rounds.

It was just a matter of going in, throwing down on the two new deputies, and forcing them to unlock the cells. As soon as McLaren and Dunn were free, Severs intended to cut the deputies' throats to ensure there wouldn't be any outcry until the fugitives were long gone. Five fast horses, saddled and ready to go, waited in an alley less than fifty feet away.

Severs's right hand was wrapped tightly around the butt of his gun as he gripped the doorknob with his left. The knob turned and he thrust the door back as he stepped through the opening.

From the desk, Ed Boulden asked, "What can I do for—," then stopped short as he looked up and saw the gun in the newcomer's fist.

Severs's face was bare under his hat brim. No point in masks as everybody would know who had busted the prisoners out of jail. He pointed his Colt at Boulden and snapped, "Don't reach for your gun, Deputy. I can find the keys and open those doors just as good as you can, so I don't need you alive."

What the escape needed was silence. Gunshots would draw the attention of the townspeople right away. Severs didn't explain that to Boulden. Let the deputy think he was on the verge of being shot.

He was going to wind up dead before the night was over, anyway.

"Don't shoot, mister," the balding Boulden said as beads of sweat appeared on his forehead. He kept his hands in plain sight on the desk.

Merritt and Russell came into the office behind Severs. Russell eased the door closed behind them.

"Where's the other one?" Severs wanted to know. "Where's Farmer?"

"He . . . he ain't here. He went home to eat supper."

"Soriano left you here to watch the jail by yourself?"

"That's right." Boulden swallowed. "He said you fellas would be fools to try anything so soon after you dodged prison."

"He's the fool," Severs said as his upper lip curled. "Get the keys. We're going in the cell block."

"You're gonna let McLaren and Dunn loose, aren't you?"

Severs grinned. "You're not as dumb as you look, Deputy."

Boulden opened a drawer in the desk, took out a ring of keys, and stood up. Almost too scared to move, he forced his muscles to work and walked toward the cell block door, which was closed and locked. He fumbled some with the lock but got it open and swung the door back.

In cells across the aisle from each other, McLaren and Dunn hurried to the cell doors and gripped the bars as Boulden came in with Severs right behind him, prodding him in the back with a gun barrel.

Dunn grinned hugely. "You came back for me, just like you promised you would!"

"Did you think I'd go back on my word, Larry?" Without waiting for an answer, Severs stared at the deputy. "Unlock those doors, pronto."

If it had been up to Severs, he would have freed McLaren first, but Boulden turned first toward the cell where Dunn was. Again, Boulden fumbled with the keys, and the delay chafed at Severs. He was thinking about knocking the stupid deputy on the head and taking over himself when he heard Merritt exclaim, "What the hell!"

That was all the warning Severs had before the air was filled with the roar of guns going off.

Matt Farmer had worked as a hostler at Crackerjack Sawyer's stable, a freight wagon driver, and a cowhand, and he hadn't been particularly good at any of those jobs. He'd hoped he had finally found something that suited him, when he'd volunteered to help out as a temporary deputy.

Then Marshal Soriano had asked him to stay on, at least for the time being, and Matt's heart had swelled with pride, even though he'd be working for a Mex. They had themselves a Mex lawman over in Socorro County, that fella Elfego Baca, and he seemed to be doing pretty well in the job . . . so Matt was pretty content for a change.

He opened the back door of the marshal's office, went through the storeroom, and strolled into the office itself, carrying the partially used mail order catalog he had taken to the outhouse with him. He stopped short as he saw two men with drawn guns standing just outside the cell block door.

They saw him at the same time and one of them cried out profanity. They swung their guns toward him and flames spouted from the muzzles as he clawed at the weapon on his hip.

He never got his gun drawn before hammer blows smashed into his chest and knocked him backwards into oblivion.

The shots erupted just as Deputy Boulden clicked the lock over on the cell block door and pulled the key out. He tried to turn and draw his gun, hoping that Severs would be distracted by the unexpected commotion, but the gunman acted instinctively. His taut-drawn nerves made him pull the trigger, slamming a shot into Boulden's back and driving the deputy against the door, which flew open and narrowly missed Larry Dunn, who jumped back out of its way.

Boulden stumbled forward, blood welling from the wound where the bullet had torn through his gut and burst out the front of his belly. With the last of his strength, something possessed him to flick the ring of keys toward the cell's lone window. They missed the bars and flew through one of the narrow openings, disappearing into the darkness outside the jail.

Boulden pitched forward on his face to die a miserable death.

Severs's heart hammered in his chest and

thoughts whirled madly inside his brain. The keys were gone, and by the time he could get outside and find them in the dark, Marshal Soriano would be hurrying back to the jail in response to the shots. Other townspeople would show up, and the inevitable result would be a gun battle that might cost him and his friends their lives.

Fate had turned against them.

With nothing they could do about it except get out of there while they still had the chance, Severs yelled at his friends as he grabbed Dunn's arm and practically threw the man out of the cell. "Go! Get to the horses!"

Across the aisle, Pete McLaren gripped the bars of his cell and stared in wide-eyed disbelief. "Perry!" he cried. "You gotta get me out of here!"

"Sorry, Pete. We tried, but it's all shot to hell." Severs pounded after the others already fleeing from the building.

"Damn you!" McLaren screamed after them. "You can't leave me here to hang! *Damn you!*"

None of the others even slowed down.

Ace was still about twenty feet from the door of the marshal's office when the shooting started. He knew that if he rushed in blindly, he might not accomplish anything except to get himself killed.

As the Colt seemed to leap into his hand with blinding speed, he darted to his right, toward a water barrel at the corner of a nearby building. He had just dropped to one knee behind it when the door of the marshal's office flew open and several men rushed out.

As they turned toward Ace, he heard horses stamping somewhere close by and realized it was an escape attempt. The fleeing men were heading for saddled mounts they had ready.

"Hold it!" he shouted.

The fugitives slowed down, but only for a split second, then Colt flame bloomed in the shadows and Ace heard the wind-rip of bullets as they passed by his head. He leveled his revolver and triggered three swift rounds toward the gunmen.

One of the men staggered and fell. Another stumbled but stayed on his feet, evidently hit but not bad enough to put him down. The others kept shooting. Bullets plunked into the water barrel but didn't penetrate to the other side. A few of the slugs struck the top of the barrel and chewed splinters from it that showered down on Ace's hat. He leaned out and pumped two more shots at the fugitives. A second man spun off his feet.

Shots blasted from out in the street. Ace glanced in that direction and saw Miguel Soriano angling toward the jail. Orange flame geysered from the gun in his fist. A third man went down.

But the fourth one had disappeared. Ace knelt behind the barrel and thumbed fresh rounds into his Colt as he listened for the telltale sounds of flight. As he snapped the revolver's loading gate shut, he heard a swift rataplan of hoof-beats. The fourth man had reached the horses and was getting away.

So the marshal wouldn't shoot him, Ace sprang to his feet and called, "Miguel, it's me!" then dashed into the mouth of an alley. A dark shape bulked against the starlight at the far end of the passage. Ace recognized it as a man mounted on horseback and smoothly brought up his gun. The weapon roared as he squeezed off three rounds.

The shape broke into two as the fleeing man tumbled out of his saddle.

Miguel ran up beside Ace. "Did you get him?"

"I think so. We'll have to check to be sure."

"Careful. We don't want to waltz right into a bullet."

Ace couldn't have agreed more with that sentiment. He and Miguel moved along the alley, staying on opposite sides of the passage until they reached the far end. Their eyes had adjusted to the darkness for them to make out the sprawled figure on the ground. The man groaned but didn't move.

Miguel moved forward and kept his gun trained on the fallen man until he hooked a toe under his shoulder and rolled him onto his back. By then, Ace had fished a lucifer from his shirt pocket. He snapped it to life with his thumbnail, squinting against the glare. The flame's garish light fell across the pain-wracked face of Perry Severs.

The front of Severs's shirt was sodden with blood where Ace's bullets had ripped all the way through his body. He coughed, and more crimson welled from his mouth. Clearly, he had only moments to live.

Severs blinked his eyes open, looked up at Ace and Miguel, and rasped, "I . . . I never wanted . . . to be in charge . . . anyway."

The grotesque rattle in his throat that followed the words testified that he was gone.

"We'd better see about the others," Miguel said. "Severs isn't going anywhere until the undertaker gets here."

Neither were the other three, as it turned out. Chance, Hank Muller, Crackerjack Sawyer, and several other men armed with rifles or shotguns were standing over the bodies, but they didn't need any guarding. Dunn, Merritt, and Russell were every bit as dead as Severs.

Chance shook his head disgustedly. "I sit down for a nice friendly game of poker and all hell breaks loose. What happened here?"

"These bastards must've tried to break McLaren out of jail," Miguel said.

"Where *is* McLaren?" Chance asked.

Without answering, Miguel hurried toward the open office door with Ace and Chance right behind him.

Miguel stopped short and cursed bitterly at the sight of one of his new deputies crumpled in a bloody heap in a corner. They went into the cell block and found the other deputy lying facedown in the cell where Larry Dunn had been held until his escape.

Pete McLaren was still in his cell, holding on to the bars as he looked out bleakly.

Miguel turned toward him, the gun in his hand coming up. McLaren didn't move, just stared defiantly as Miguel lined the muzzle between his eyes.

"Miguel . . ." Ace said quietly.

Miguel ignored him and addressed McLaren. "You son of a bitch. This is all your fault. Three good men are dead because of you, and all four of your friends. They're no great loss, but Ed and Matt are."

"Why don't you go ahead and shoot me, then?" McLaren said, his voice as tight with strain as Miguel's. "Pull the trigger, greaser."

"Miguel, don't listen to him," Chance said. "You know if McLaren wants you to do it, it's not the right thing."

"He deserves to die! He's brought nothing but trouble to this town!"

"He'll die," Ace said. "He'll be executed for his crimes less than twelve hours from now. There's nobody and nothing left to save him."

McLaren started to laugh. Miguel's face twisted

even more at that, and the gun in his hand trembled from the depth of the rage he was feeling.

"You just go on believing that, you stupid sons of bitches," McLaren said as he paused in his laughter. "You just keep thinkin' you're really gonna hang me." He turned his back on Miguel in contemptuous dismissal.

Slowly, Miguel lowered the gun and drew in a deep breath. He let down the hammer, slipped the gun back into its holster, and turned to Ace and Chance. "You're right. He'll hang in the morning, and justice will be done."

Somehow, the words sounded hollow in the death-haunted cell block.

Chapter Thirty-two

After the carnage of the night before, morning dawned gloomy and overcast with thunder rumbling in the distance over the mountains. Those peaks loomed darkly, like humpbacked monsters surrounding the town.

Ace and Chance had spent the night in the marshal's office with Miguel. They'd taken turns dozing on the old sofa. It seemed like the threat was over, with all four of McLaren's friends being dead, but after everything that had happened, no one wanted to take a chance.

McLaren's arrogant insistence that he would

never hang was disconcerting, too. Ace marked it up to sheer bravado, but just in case he was wrong, he'd thought he and Chance ought to be on hand to help out.

For his part, McLaren seemed to sleep peacefully. Ace didn't see how that was possible unless McLaren really was confident that he was safe from execution.

As the sky lightened from black to gray, Lars Hilfstrom and one of his daughters brought four breakfast trays to the marshal's office. Ace carried one of the trays into the cell block while Chance followed with a shotgun tucked under his arm.

"Time for breakfast, McLaren," Ace said.

McLaren sat up and looked confused, as if he were surprised to find himself still locked up. He shook his head and then swung his legs off the bunk. "It's morning?"

"Yeah. Thursday morning." Ace's voice held a tone of grim finality.

McLaren stood up, stumbled over to the cell door, and took the tray Ace passed through the slot. He looked down at it for a moment, then abruptly twisted around and threw the tray against the wall, shattering crockery and splattering food and coffee over the stone. He lurched against the bars, gripped them with maniacal strength, and howled, "Lemme outta here! Damn you, lemme out!"

"You're not going anywhere until it's time,

McLaren." Chance raised his eyebrows at the mess. "And I don't reckon there's any law that says you have to have a last meal."

McLaren started tugging frantically at the bars as if he were trying to shake the door down, but of course it didn't budge. A stream of profanities and threats spewed from his mouth. He was still ranting when the Jensen brothers left the cell block.

"The prisoner doesn't sound happy," Miguel commented when they returned to the office.

"He's starting to figure out that nobody's going to save him after all," Ace said.

Miguel rubbed his chin and then said with a worried frown, "I hope you're right."

"Who's left to help him?" Chance asked.

"We don't *know* that his brother hasn't found out about it somehow."

"The dreaded Otis McLaren?" Chance said. "Wouldn't he have been here by now if he was coming?"

Ace said, "That depends on where he was when he heard about Pete being locked up. Without knowing that, we don't know how long it would take him to get here."

Miguel nodded. "That's just what I was thinking. I passed the word to some of the men in town and asked them to be armed when they come to the hanging, just in case someone tries to interrupt it."

That air of tension hung over the office as the three men ate their breakfast. They had just finished when a knock sounded on the barred front door.

Miguel opened one of the shutters over the window just enough see who was there then he opened the door to admit Timothy Buchanan and Judge Alfred Ordway. Buchanan was carrying a Winchester.

"It's almost time," Ordway said as he looked at a big turnip watch he pulled from his pocket. "A crowd's gathering already. I must say, it always puts a bit of a bad taste in my mouth when people act like an execution is an excuse for a holiday."

"You can't blame them for feeling that way, especially this execution," Buchanan said. "There's probably not a person in this town who hasn't been afraid of Pete McLaren at one time or another. Having him in our midst has been like living with a rabid dog. You never knew who or when he was going to attack."

"That's true." Ordway took a thin black cigar from his vest pocket and clamped one end of it between his teeth, leaving it unlit. "I still find this simply a necessity, not a cause for celebration."

"I just want to get it over with," Miguel said.

"Then get your hat and let's get on with it. The hour is at hand."

McLaren's tirade had run out of steam by the

time Ace, Chance, and Miguel entered the cell block. The prisoner was slumped on the bunk, head down, breathing heavily.

"Come on, McLaren," Miguel said. "It's time."

McLaren slowly shook his head, but other than that, he didn't budge.

"You might as well cooperate. You know we'll just come in there and drag you out if you don't."

"You can't do this," McLaren mumbled. "You just can't."

"The law says we can. The law that you flouted for years. It's caught up to you at last."

A shudder went through McLaren. He covered his face with his hands for a moment. When he lowered them and looked up at the three men outside the cell, his features were hard as stone. He stood up and walked to the door. "Do it and be damned to you," he said in a voice like ice.

Pete McLaren might be an utterly sorry human being, Ace thought, but he had a thread of steel inside him, and he had found it at the moment of impending death. Whether it would last all the way to the top of the gallows, only the next few minutes would tell.

While Ace and Chance covered the prisoner, Miguel unlocked the door, swung it open, and stepped back. He drew his revolver as McLaren emerged from the cell.

"I'd be obliged if you didn't shackle my legs," the condemned man said. "I'd rather walk free."

"You know we'll cut you down if you try to run."

"I know." A faint smile touched McLaren's face. "You don't think I'd deprive the town of its show, do you?"

"Put your hands behind your back." Miguel cuffed him, and they went out into the office.

Buchanan and Ordway were waiting with solemn expressions on their faces. The group moved out to the street, where the overcast morning perfectly suited the mood.

As the procession started toward the gallows, a few cheers went up from the assembled crowd, but they died out quickly and a hush fell over Lone Pine. More thunder, like the sound of distant drums, disturbed the silence. Fingers of lightning clawed at the sky over the mountains, and the air was still and heavy. It was dry country for the most part, but a storm was building.

Miguel led the way. McLaren was behind him with Ace and Chance on either side, and Buchanan and Ordway brought up the rear. McLaren's steps didn't falter as they walked along.

Closer to the gallows, Ace saw Colonel Howden, Crackerjack Sawyer, Hank Muller, and several other men among the crowd, all of them holding either rifles or shotguns. Lee Emory was there, too, but apparently not armed. Neither were his sister or Fontana Dupree. Meredith looked pale and drawn. Fontana appeared to be more accepting of what was about to happen. Of course, Dolly had been her friend, and she knew justice was being done.

The undertaker's wagon was parked near the gallows, with its owner waiting on the seat along with Doc Bellem. The padre from the local mission stood on the platform. The town had no official hangman, so Miguel would perform that duty. Reaching the steps leading up, he stood aside so McLaren could go first.

For the first time since leaving the jail, McLaren hesitated. He shuddered again then mounted the first step. Then another and another until all thirteen were behind him and he was at the top. Miguel followed, then Ace, then Chance.

Ace's guts tightened as he climbed the steps. He had never participated in an execution . . . and he hoped he never had to again.

"It's funny," Chance murmured quietly that only Ace could hear. "I always figured it would be one of us getting a rope necktie."

Ace didn't respond, but the same thought had occurred to him.

They moved to either side of the platform to flank the trapdoor. Miguel took hold of McLaren's arm and steered the prisoner into position. The padre move up and started to mumble the last rites.

McLaren said, "I ain't a Catholic."

"You never said one way or the other," Miguel told him. "I didn't know."

"No need for a sky pilot of any sort to waste his breath prayin' over me. It wouldn't take."

"That's your decision, I reckon." Miguel nodded to the priest, signifying that it was all right for him to step back and went on to McLaren. "If you'd like to say anything . . ."

"Last words, you mean?" McLaren's mouth quirked bitterly. He looked out over the crowd. "You're all a bunch of damned sheep. If I've got to be hanged for bein' a wolf, then so be it. I reckon it's my nature. But when I'm dead and gone, don't start feelin' like you're safe. You'll still be a bunch of damn sheep . . . and there'll always be more wolves in the world." His jaw tightened and he looked over at Miguel. "Get it over with."

Miguel picked up the black hood draped over the railing and placed it over McLaren's head, shutting off the killer's view and hiding his face from the crowd. Miguel took hold of the rope and put it over McLaren's head, as well. Never having done it before the marshal was nervous. He wanted to get it right. Nothing was more gruesome or grotesque than a botched hanging.

Ace knew Miguel had tested the rope with a bag of sand and the trapdoor the day before, just to make sure everything worked properly.

It was different, now that a man stood there

waiting to meet his end. That made it all real in ways a bag of sand never could.

Satisfied with the rope, Miguel stepped back and nodded to Judge Ordway, who stood at the bottom of the steps.

The judge cleared his throat. "Peter McLaren, you have been convicted of the crime of murder and duly sentenced to death under the laws of this territory. That sentence will now be carried out. May God have mercy on your soul." Ordway jerked his head in a curt nod to Miguel, who had wrapped both hands around the lever attached to the trapdoor.

Miguel took a deep breath and shoved the lever across.

Ace caught his breath as he watched McLaren's hooded figure drop through the opening. The crowd gasped at the sharp crack of McLaren's neck breaking. The man's feet kicked spasmodically, but only once, and then he hung there limp and still except for a slight swaying back and forth that soon came to an end.

It was over. No one had intervened on McLaren's behalf.

As he dangled at the end of the hang rope, thunder boomed louder than ever before, and a flash of lightning lit up the settlement. The crowd began to scatter before the storm broke.

Because they all knew it was coming.

Chapter Thirty-three

It took a while for the rain to get there, giving the undertaker and his assistant enough time to get Pete McLaren's body down from the gallows and cart it off to be placed in a plain pine coffin. Ace and Chance watched from the boardwalk in front of the marshal's office as the wagon carrying the coffin trundled up the hill toward the cemetery.

"They'll have to hurry to get that box in the ground before the storm gets here," Chance said. "I wouldn't want to be filling in a grave in a pouring rain. You'd be racing to get it covered up before it flooded."

"McLaren's beyond caring now," Ace said.

"True." Chance shivered as another peal of thunder rolled down from the mountains.

"Let's go down to the stable and check on the horses," Ace suggested.

Glancing toward the dark clouds scudding through the sky, they walked hurriedly along the street. When they reached the livery stable, they found Crackerjack trying to calm some of the horses spooked by the thunder. The Jensen brothers' mounts seemed calm. They were used to the sound of guns going off, so real thunder didn't bother them.

"Gonna be a real gully washer, boys,"

Crackerjack greeted Ace and Chance. "A pur-dee toad-strangler." Lightning flashed and thunder rumbled. "Tater wagon's rollin' over."

"You don't get many storms like this around here, do you?" Ace asked.

"Once ever' two or three years, I reckon. We're safe enough here in town from floodin', but all the arroyos in these parts will be runnin' bank deep before the day's over, I'll bet."

"Maybe it'll just make a lot of racket and then not amount to anything," Chance said.

Crackerjack shook his head. "Not this storm. My achin' joints are tellin' me it's gonna be a bad one."

The rain started while Ace and Chance were walking back to the hotel. Big drops splattered into the dust in the street, more and more of them falling with each passing second. The brothers broke into a run as the rain began falling in earnest, like someone pouring out a giant bucket over the town. The skies opened up in a deluge the likes of which the citizens of Lone Pine hadn't seen in quite a while. The rain fell in blinding sheets felt like they could pound a person into the ground.

Both young men were soaked by the time they reached the hotel porch.

"Looks like Crackerjack's joints were right," Chance said as he took off his hat and wiped water off his face.

"Let's go inside and get some dry duds on," Ace suggested.

• • •

After toweling off and donning fresh clothes, they went back down to the lobby.

Colonel Howden stood by the front windows watching the downpour. "You fellows weren't planning on leaving town right away, were you?"

"No, not for a while yet," Ace said. "I don't know how long we would have stayed around if all this hadn't happened, but we're in no hurry to leave." For his part, he hoped to get to know Meredith Emory better, without all the violence and drama that the clash with Pete McLaren had caused. He suspected that Chance felt the same way about Fontana Dupree.

At the moment, neither of them wanted to go back out into that storm, so he nodded toward a checkerboard set up on a table in a corner of the lobby and asked Chance, "Interest you in a game?"

"Well, you can't really bet on checkers . . . but I suppose it's a better way to pass the time than nothing."

Over in the Melodian, Fontana sat with a glass of wine in front of her and listened to the rain falling outside. The atmosphere in the saloon was subdued. Men at the bar and the tables conversed quietly. Orrie was reading a month-old Denver newspaper.

Hank Muller pulled out a chair at her table

293

and lowered himself into it without waiting for an invitation. There was little if any formality between the two of them. They had been friends for quite a while. Muller had never expressed any lustful interest in her, for which Fontana was glad. As he had told her once, he enjoyed her singing on a personal level, and having her around was good for business, so he didn't want to do anything to jeopardize that.

"You look a mite down in the mouth," he commented.

Fontana shrugged and toyed with her glass. "I thought it might make me feel better once McLaren got what was coming to him . . . but it really didn't."

"It takes a while. The pain of Dolly's death will fade sooner or later, and then you'll be glad that justice was done."

"I'm glad now. But like I said, it doesn't really help much."

Muller frowned. "McLaren sure seemed to think he'd get out of hanging somehow. Makes me worry a little that he knew something the rest of us don't."

"Like what?"

"I don't know," the saloonkeeper replied with a shake of his head. "Maybe this storm's just given me the fantods."

The glass in the saloon's windows shook a little as more thunder crashed.

Meredith Emory said, "If this keeps up, we'll have to do a story about Lone Pine washing away in a flood."

"If Lone Pine washes away, we won't be here to do a story about anything, now will we?" her brother asked with a gentle smile.

Meredith laughed. "No, I suppose that's right." She grew more serious as she went on. "Lee, I don't think I've ever seen anything quite so terrible."

They were sitting at their desks in the newspaper office with nothing to do at the moment other than wait out the storm.

Emory leaned back in his chair and clasped his hands together in front of his stomach. "I've witnessed hangings before, and it's never pleasant. This one may have been worse than usual because of all the violence that preceded it. McLaren's attitude—and the weather—didn't help matters."

"I hope I never see another one."

"I hope there's never a need for another hanging here in Lone Pine"—Emory smiled faintly—"but I wouldn't count on it. The frontier is still a long way from being tamed. Anyway, civilization is often just a veneer."

"I suppose."

They fell silent in the gloom of the office, which was broken only by a single lamp. The shadows inside and out grew more oppressive as the clouds thickened and the sky grew ever more dark.

Miguel Soriano poured himself a cup of coffee from the pot staying warm on the stove. The office door was open, and a chilly gust passed through the marshal's office.

He had been trying not to think about what had happened that morning, but it was impossible to keep the memories out of his mind. *The pounding of his heart as he climbed to the gallows platform, the feel of the lever in his hands, the moment just before he had released the trapdoor . . . seemingly endless, yet less than the blink of an eye . . . the piercing crack when Pete McLaren's neck had broken . . .*

Miguel had ended a man's life . . . not that it was his fault. He knew no one was to blame for McLaren's fate except McLaren himself. And as a lawman who carried a gun and knew he might be called on to use it to defend himself and others, Miguel knew that sometimes killing was necessary. He would lose no sleep over McLaren's death.

But it was easy to imagine that cold wind sweeping through the office as McLaren's spirit, come back to taunt him one last time. He even thought for a second that he heard a contemptuous laugh.

Miguel wasn't the superstitious sort, but he had grown up hearing talk among the old women of his family about ghosts and witches and restless, evil spirits. A shiver went through him as he carried his cup over to the door to close it. He started to swing it shut, then paused abruptly.

The rain was falling so hard he could barely see the buildings across the street, but for a split second he thought he had glimpsed something in the street during a lightning flash.

A man on horseback?

In the torrential downpour, it was difficult to be sure. Then the lightning flickered again, and he didn't see anything.

He put it down to the strain he had been under during the past week and closed the door.

Down at the livery stable, Crackerjack Sawyer used his pitchfork to throw some hay down from the loft. Just under the roof, the roar of the rain was almost deafening, though the old-timer thought he heard something—a fleeting fragment of a voice—over the racket. He went over to the opening through which hay was lifted into the loft and pushed back the door.

He couldn't see anything outside except the sheets of rain, but again he thought he heard someone speaking. He shook his head. That was loco. "Who would be out and about in a storm like this? Nobody in his right mind, that's who."

He went back over to the ladder and tossed the pitchfork down, then followed, climbing down with a spryness that belied his years. As his feet touched the hard-packed ground, a couple horses in the stalls spooked again and started bumping and kicking against the slats.

Crackerjack turned toward them. "Settle down, you blasted high-strung varmints. There ain't a blamed thing to worry about—"

Something crashed down on the back of his head and sent him plummeting into a darkness thicker than that closing in outside.

"It's the middle of the afternoon, but it looks like night out there," Chance said as he and Ace finished another checker game. "I'm ahead on the number of games won, by the way."

"There's nothing riding on it," Ace pointed out.

"No, but I like to keep track anyway."

Ace chuckled. "Another game?"

"Maybe in a few minutes." Chance stood up and stretched to get the kinks out of his back. "I've been sitting too long."

Colonel Howden came into the lobby through the door that led back into his living quarters. "You boys want some coffee? I just brewed a pot."

"That sounds good," Ace said as he stood up, too.

"I'll bring it out here."

As Howden went back into the rear of the hotel, Chance said from the front window, "Ace, come over here for a minute."

"Something wrong?" Ace asked as he joined his brother. He saw the frown on Chance's face.

"I don't know. I thought I saw something out there."

"You did see something. A whole lot of rain."

Chance shook his head. "No, it was more than that. Just for a second, I would have sworn I saw a couple men walking along the boardwalk over there by the Melodian."

"So?"

"I think they were carrying rifles."

Ace frowned, too. "Maybe they were, but that doesn't have to mean anything bad." He didn't sound like he was completely convinced of that, however.

"I think we should go check it out."

"We're not deputies anymore, remember?" Ace reminded his brother. "Actually, we never were. We were just volunteers."

"That never stopped us from mixing in where there was trouble."

Chance had a point there, Ace knew. And if Chance, with his carefree nature, was worried about something, there was probably genuine cause for concern.

"You want to make sure Fontana's all right, don't you?"

"I wouldn't mind," Chance admitted.

"Let's go upstairs and get our slickers and then take a look around town."

Chance nodded.

They were headed for the stairs when Colonel Howden reappeared carrying a tray with three steaming coffee cups on it. "Here you go—" He stopped abruptly as he saw the intent expressions on the brothers' faces and the brisk way they were moving.

"Sorry, Colonel," Ace said. "We have to step out for a few minutes."

"In this weather?"

"We shouldn't be gone long. Maybe the coffee won't be too cold by the time we get back."

With that, Ace and Chance hurried upstairs to fetch their rain gear.

Orrie went over to the table where Fontana and Muller were sitting. "Would you like to sing something, Miss Dupree? I'm sort of getting bored, just sitting around and listening to it rain. I've already read everything I can lay my hands on."

"Might not be a bad idea," Muller said. "This place is blasted gloomy. It needs something to perk it up a mite."

Fontana didn't feel much like singing. She had considered skipping it entirely, but Muller and Orrie were her friends. She could tell they wanted her to. "All right. I want to go up to my room first and change into something else." She looked down at the dark gown she had worn to Pete McLaren's hanging that morning. "If I'm going to sing, I want to be wearing something more appropriate. More cheerful."

"Good idea," Orrie said, grinning. "While you're gone, I'll pick out a couple songs. A couple of bouncy tunes will make a big difference in here, I'll bet."

Maybe they would make a difference in the way she felt, too, Fontana thought as she climbed the stairs to the Melodian's second floor. As she reached the landing and turned toward her room, she caught a glimpse of movement down at the end of the hall. It was shadowy where the corridor made a right-angle turn and led back to the rear stairs.

Fontana frowned. All the girls were downstairs, and none of the bartenders lived up there. No one else did except her and Hank Muller . . . and he was downstairs, too.

No one should have been lurking around on the second floor. Thinking somebody might have decided to use the storm as cover for sneaking in to see what they could steal, she thought to turn back and fetch Muller, then abruptly decided to have a look for herself. She wasn't afraid of a sneak thief. Besides, she thought she might have imagined it and didn't want Muller to think she was going crazy and seeing things that weren't there.

She strode along the hall and turned the corner. "Is someone there?" She saw right away there wasn't, that the short, narrow corridor was empty.

Then one of the shadows close beside her moved. A hand clamped over her mouth and an arm looped around her waist to jerk her back against a solid, muscular form.

Orrie sat at the piano, noodling around on the keys. The notes were so quiet nobody in the room was really paying attention to them. He found playing like that soothing. It allowed him to work his way up to real tunes.

He had picked out a couple comic opera tunes that Fontana seemed to have enjoyed singing in the past. He liked playing them, and listeners usually responded to them. As soon as she came back down, they would lift the spirits of the people, even on the dark, rainy afternoon that had followed a hanging. Time to put all that in the past.

A huge crash of thunder made Orrie jerk his head around toward the door.

Standing there, illuminated by lightning, was a tall man in a long, black duster and a broad-brimmed black hat. He was silhouetted by the flash so that nothing was visible of his face except piercing, burning eyes.

Chapter Thirty-four

Rain sluiced down over Ace and Chance as they walked across the street. Mud sucked at their boots with each step. Water dripped from the brims of their hats. Cold trickles somehow found their way underneath the yellow slickers they wore.

The frequent lightning lit up the street well enough for them to look around and see that no one else was moving. Lifting his voice to be heard above the rain, Chance said, "I must have imagined I saw a couple hombres with rifles. Nobody's out here. Everybody else in town has too much sense to be out in this miserable weather."

"Well, we're already out here, so we might as well go on over to the saloon and make sure everything's all right," Ace said.

"I admit, I'll feel better once I see Fontana for myself." Chance grinned under the dripping brim of his hat. "Of course, seeing Fontana always makes me feel better."

They turned toward the Melodian. The light coming from the saloon's front windows and entrance was nothing but a vague yellow blob in the downpour. Before Ace and Chance could start toward it, someone hailed them from behind.

They turned and saw another slicker-clad shape coming toward them. Ace recognized Miguel Soriano's voice as the marshal called, "Ace? Chance? Is that you?"

"It's us, Marshal," Ace replied. "What are you doing out here?"

"I could ask the same of you two," Miguel said as he came up to them. "I thought I saw someone moving around a little while ago. I started to figure I was seeing things and tried not to worry about it, but it nagged at me until I decided to make sure. Reckon it was you boys I saw."

"How long ago was this?"

"Ten or fifteen minutes, I'd say."

Ace shook his head. "It wasn't us. We haven't been out here that long. Chance thought he saw somebody, too."

"A couple men with rifles," Chance added.

"The man I saw was on horseback . . . I thought," Miguel said. "Now I'm not sure of anything."

An uneasy feeling stirred in Ace's gut, and he knew it didn't have anything to do with the midday meal he had eaten. "We were going to walk down to the saloon. Want to come with us?"

"Yeah, I sure will. Anybody who would come out in weather like this might be up to no good."

The three young men turned toward the saloon again.

•••

Fontana struggled against the grip of the man holding her but had no chance of breaking free. He was too strong. The big hand pressed over her mouth completely shut off any outcry she might have made.

"Take it easy, girl," a deep voice said in her ear. "Nobody's lookin' to hurt you. Not yet, anyway."

That didn't make her feel any better as the man forced her back around the corner and along the corridor toward the landing. From the corner of her eye, she could see down into the main room of the saloon below. As the lightning flashed, she saw how the glare caught the tall man standing in the entrance. He pushed the batwings aside and moved into the saloon with a catlike stride.

Enough lamps were burning in the saloon for her to get a good look at the man's face as he lifted his head to peer up the stairs toward her. His rugged features were deeply tanned and weathered from years of exposure. Pale hair poked out from under his black hat. His eyes were deep-set, and Fontana felt their power even from the distance.

Silence had fallen over the saloon. Everyone was staring at the newcomer. He had the same sort of compelling fascination that a snake held for a bird or a small animal.

Hank Muller broke that silence by stepping

away from the bar and saying hoarsely, "What do you want?" That wasn't the way he normally greeted customers—but everyone in the Melodian sensed that this was no normal customer.

The man smiled, but the expression was colder than the winds that had swept in with the rain. "Lookin' for a little shelter from the storm, Hank."

"Do I know you?" Muller demanded.

From the landing, Fontana could tell he was trying to put up a brave front but was as spooked as everybody else in here.

"It's been a good long while, but we've met," admitted the stranger in black.

No one had yet noticed Fontana and her captor at the top of the stairs. All eyes were on the man who had just come into the place. That changed as the man holding her began to force her down the stairs. Muller's eyes swung in that direction.

So did Orrie's. The little piano player exclaimed, "My God!"

Muller took a step toward the stairs, but the stranger's hand went swiftly under the long duster he wore and came out gripping a revolver. He thrust the long barrel at the saloonkeeper and barked, "Stay where you are, Muller. I don't want to shoot you, but I will if I have to."

The stranger had stepped far enough into the room that a couple tables were behind him. Men sitting at those tables could have jumped him, but the menace radiating from him was so powerful that they tried to flee, leaping to their feet and heading for the door.

The batwings parted, and they stopped short. Trying to back up, they practically fell over their own feet. Several more men moved into the saloon, all of them wielding rifles or handguns. They were hard-faced men wearing dusters similar to that of the man who was undeniably their leader.

The man in black smiled at Muller, "You startin' to figure out who I am, Hank?"

"Good Lord," Muller breathed out. "You're *Otis McLaren.*"

"Never expected to see me again, did you? At least, you were *hoping* you'd never see me again. But I'll bet my little brother warned you I'd be back." McLaren's smile disappeared, replaced by a bleak expression that scored deep trenches in his cheeks. "I just made it a little too late, that's all."

Fontana could tell that Muller was scared, and she didn't blame him. She was terrified.

But Muller wasn't the sort to back down. He squared his shoulders and asked, "What the hell do you want?"

"Justice." McLaren turned his head just slightly and added, "Bring 'em in."

More members of the outlaw's gang entered the saloon. A couple pushed a stumbling figure ahead of them. Solomon Horton lost his balance and fell to his knees. One of the men grabbed his arm, jerked him roughly to his feet again, and dragged him to Otis McLaren.

Another had a limp form draped over his shoulder. He bent and let his burden roll down to the floor. Fontana recognized Crackerjack Sawyer, but she couldn't tell if the old livery-man was dead or merely unconscious.

The boss outlaw went on. "My brother's lawyer got word to me what was goin' on. Pete told him where he could get in touch with me, but I didn't make it in time to save Pete. All I can do now . . . is avenge him." McLaren turned and pressed the gun muzzle against the side of Horton's head.

The lawyer trembled so hard he would have fallen again if not for the other man's grip on his arm.

"You didn't keep Pete alive long enough for me to get here," McLaren said. "But don't worry, Mr. Lawyer Man. You're still good for something, so I'm not gonna blow your brains out . . . if you tell me the name of every man on the jury that convicted my brother."

"I-I'm sorry —"

"Don't be sorry." McLaren eared back the revolver's hammer. "Just talk."

"You . . . you've got two of the jury members right here. Muller and that old man from the livery stable—"

"Horton, you son of a bitch," Muller broke in. "You've got no more guts than an old yellow dog."

"He'll kill me!" Horton cried.

McLaren said, "That's right. I damn sure will. Tell me the others."

"There was Lee Emory . . . he's the editor of the newspaper . . . and Colonel Howden over at the hotel . . ." More names spilled from Horton's slack mouth until he finished with "And . . . and two boys from out of town . . . they're brothers, their name is Jensen—"

"That's twelve," McLaren said. "And I haven't forgotten about the judge who sentenced Pete to hang, or the prosecutor, or the marshal who arrested him."

Horton said, "It . . . it was Hoyt Dixon who arrested him. He's the man your brother shot."

"Well, somebody else put him *back* in jail, didn't they?"

"Miguel Soriano. He's the deputy who took over as marshal—"

"All right. A greaser marshal, eh? Things really have changed around here. And then there's old José. We were trail partners once, before he got old and fat. Your letter said he was part of the reason Pete was behind bars to start with. They're all gonna die, but we'll start with the jury. They're the ones who found Pete guilty." McLaren's lips drew back from his teeth in a vicious grimace. "Twelve men who are gonna die just like he did."

"Boss," one of the outlaws said from the entrance. "Somebody's comin'."

Still half a block from the Melodian, Ace, Chance, and Miguel were close enough to make out a few shapes moving around against the light from inside the saloon. Ace didn't think anything of that, since he expected the place to have at least a few customers, even on such a stormy afternoon.

A sudden flash of lightning revealed an unexpected sight, however. A man stood in the entrance with one of the batwings pushed back, peering at them. The lightning reflected off the barrel of the gun he held in his hand.

"Who the hell—" Miguel began.

"Look out!" Ace said as the gun in the man's hand jerked up and spouted flame.

Even as the shot roared out, Ace and Chance had instinctively leaped apart. Ace's shoulder rammed into Miguel and knocked him aside, as well. The bullet passed between the Jensen brothers with a flat *whap!* audible even over the steady roar of the rain.

Miguel staggered from the collision with Ace but didn't fall down. Ace stayed on his feet although his boots slipped in a puddle. Chance sprawled in the mud but scrambled back up again.

"Spread out!" Miguel called to the brothers.

All three struggled against the slickers to get their guns out, but by the time they reached cover—Miguel behind a parked wagon, Ace behind an overflowing rain barrel, and Chance kneeling at the corner of a porch—they had their Colts in hand.

They didn't know who had taken that shot at them, and anyway, they couldn't start blazing away at the saloon. There were bound to be innocent people in there who would be in danger from a stray slug.

Chapter Thirty-five

McLaren lunged to the door, grabbed his man by the collar, and jerked him back, throwing him to the floor. "Damn it, Pittman. Why'd you open fire? I wasn't ready to tell the town we were here yet."

The outlaw called Pittman clearly didn't like being manhandled, but he wasn't going to argue with McLaren. He seemed to have more sense than that. "Sorry, Otis," he said as he got to his feet. "I saw three tough-looking hombres, and they were heading this way, so I thought—"

"That was your mistake," McLaren said. "You leave the thinkin' to me, like usual."

All the townspeople in the saloon were too

scared to make a sound, so everyone heard the shout from outside.

"Hold your fire! This is Marshal Soriano! Throw down your gun and come out with your hands over your head!"

McLaren grinned coldly at Pittman. "You reckon I ought to send you out, since you're the one who opened the ball?"

Without waiting for an answer, McLaren turned and went to the entrance, stopping far enough back from the batwings that he couldn't be seen easily from outside. "Marshal Soriano . . . you're just the man I want to talk to." McLaren's voice was so cold and dead, it sounded like it came from inside a grave.

"I'm not talking to anybody until you come out with your hands up!"

"Oh, I reckon you will," McLaren said. "Unless you want us to start shootin' folks in here. There are sixteen of us, so I don't reckon it'd take very long to wipe out the whole lot of 'em." He motioned for the outlaw holding Fontana to bring her over from the stairs.

As she was turned over to McLaren, she got her first good look at her captor. He was a big man with a thatch of coarse black hair, a hooked nose, and high cheekbones. Mostly Indian, but his pale blue eyes indicated he had a little white blood in him, too. And pure evil, no matter what his heritage, as she could tell from one glance at him.

The marshal didn't answer McLaren for several seconds. Then he called, "Take it easy in there. No need for any more shooting. Just tell me who you are and what you want."

"That's easy. My name's Otis McLaren . . . and I want revenge for my brother!"

From where he crouched behind the wagon, Miguel looked over at Ace and Chance. They had all heard the voice from inside the saloon quite plainly.

"McLaren warned us his brother would be back," Miguel said, quietly enough that the Jensen brothers could hear him but the men inside the saloon could not. "I don't think anybody really believed him, though."

"Looks like he was telling the truth," Ace said. "Maybe we can circle around behind the place and get in from the back."

As if he had heard them after all, Otis McLaren shouted, "And by the way, Marshal, if you and your friends are thinkin' about tryin' any tricks, you'd be advised not to! I got a pretty little gal here who'll be the first one to die if you do!"

A second later, a scream rang out.

"Fontana!" Chance cried, ready to spring out from behind the porch.

Ace shot him a look that made him pause. "Stay down, blast it. You getting gunned down won't help Fontana, and you know it."

Miguel called toward the saloon, "No tricks,

313

I swear! Just don't hurt anybody, McLaren!"

"Oh, I'll hurt people, all right, you can count on that! Startin' with the twelve men who sent my brother to the gallows! I got two of 'em in here already, but you'd better round up the other ten and send them in here, or the floors of this saloon will be runnin' with blood!" McLaren's hand was still wrapped up in Fontana's hair where he had grabbed and twisted it to make her scream. He leered down at her and said, "You better hope that Mex lawman listens to me, gal, because I meant every word I said."

Huddled next to him, she didn't doubt that for a second. McLaren was crazy . . . crazy mean. And the men he had brought to Lone Pine with him probably weren't any better.

She didn't think the marshal would cooperate with McLaren's warped lust for vengeance. She hoped he wouldn't, anyway, although the thought of how McLaren would react to being defied terrified her.

McLaren let go of her hair and gave her a shove that sent her slumping to the floor. He turned back to the batwings and called, "What's it gonna be, Marshal?"

"Let those people in there go, McLaren!" Miguel replied. "They didn't have anything to do with what happened to your brother!"

"Two of 'em did, like I told you! Hell, if you're gonna stall, we'll just start with them!"

McLaren turned, pointed his revolver at Hank Muller, and went on. "Since the old-timer's still out cold, we'll start with you, Muller." He nodded to his men. "You boys know what to do."

Fontana cried, "No!" as she lunged up from the floor and grabbed at McLaren's arm, trying to pull the gun down. Muller was her friend and had always treated her decently. She fought for him without thinking.

But only for a moment.

McLaren's other arm came up and his hand cracked across her face in a backhanded blow that jerked her head around and made her topple to the floor again.

"You bastard!" Orrie yelled as he lunged toward McLaren instinctively.

Close by and within easy reach, the outlaw who'd captured Fontana upstairs lashed out with a gun, smashing it into the back of Orrie's head and driving him off his feet. He landed on the sawdust-littered floor and didn't move. Blood leaked from his head, forming a little crimson pool in the sawdust.

With an ugly grin, McLaren said, "Now, if there's not gonna be any more dramatics, let's get on with it."

Two of the outlaws closed in on Hank Muller.

A burly man who had survived a long time in a tough business, he wasn't going to just let them do whatever they wanted without putting up a fight. He lashed out at the first man who came within reach of his fists and actually connected with the punch, but then the second man slugged him in the belly. A third joined the fight, got an arm around Muller's neck from behind, and dragged him backwards. For a long moment, fists crashed into his head and body again and again.

"Don't kill him," McLaren said. "You know better than that. Don't even knock him out. I want him to be awake for every second of what's gonna happen to him."

The outlaws beat the fight out of Muller but left him conscious, as McLaren had commanded. The saloonkeeper hung loosely in their grip, his head drooping forward and blood dripping from his smashed nose and mouth. His eyes were open and filled with helpless rage.

McLaren nodded to his men again. The ones holding Muller wrestled him toward the back of the room where the second floor balcony over-hung the area where the piano stood. Another outlaw took the rope looped over his shoulder and started fashioning a noose at the end of it. Another walked up the stairs and along the balcony.

"No," Fontana said in a hollow voice from where she half-lay on the floor. "No!"

"He's got it comin'," McLaren said flatly. "If it was good enough for my brother, it's good enough for him."

Several of the men who had been drinking in the saloon before the fresh hell walked in moved to stand up, unable to contain themselves in the face of the new horror. Members of McLaren's band who weren't busy with Muller turned their guns on the citizens, and they had no choice but to sit down again. Their faces were twisted in a mixture of fury and revulsion.

Muller began cursing in a thin voice, but that was cut off when the outlaw with the rope looped it around his neck and drew it tight. He threw it up to the man on the balcony, who caught it and looped it around a couple thick balusters that supported the railing along the edge of the balcony. He dropped the end of the rope back down to the others.

McLaren told one of his men, "Keep an eye on the street out there," then walked over to face Muller. "You know you deserve this for what you did. Pete was a good kid."

"He was . . . a vicious killer," Muller croaked, forcing the words out past the rope pulled tight around his neck. "He gunned down . . . Marshal Dixon . . . and an innocent girl. He got . . . a fair trial. That was . . . more than he deserved. Should've been . . . gunned down . . . like the mad dog he was!"

"You've said your piece," McLaren grated. "Hope you're satisfied with it, because those were your last words, you son of a bitch." He nodded to his men. "Get it done."

Those holding Muller let go of him and stepped back as four outlaws hauled on the rope. Muller's hands went to the strand around his neck and pawed at it, but it was too tight. He couldn't get his fingers under it. With grunts of effort, the men heaved on the rope, and Muller's feet came up off the floor.

He began kicking and jerking, and almost instantly his face turned bright red. The men pulled harder on the rope and lifted him more until his feet were a good eight inches off the floor. His face was purple, his eyes wide and protruding until it seemed they would pop right out of their sockets like grapes.

"I sentence you to hang by the neck until you're dead," McLaren intoned.

The outlaws held on tight as Muller continued to struggle for breath. His legs flailed wildly in the air. He tried to reach above his head and grasp the rope so he could pull himself up and relieve the terrible pressure on his throat, but he didn't have the strength. The brutal beating he had endured had made sure of that. His hands slipped away from the rope, and gradually his struggles grew weaker. His swollen face took on a bluish tinge, and his tongue poked grotesquely from his mouth.

Finally, after a few minutes that seemed like an

eternity, he hung there limply, his arms dangling at his sides. The sharp reek of evacuated bowels filled the air around him. His eyes were still open, but they stared straight ahead sightlessly.

Fontana's sobs were the only sound in the room until McLaren said, "Tie that rope to the piano and leave him there. It ought to hold him up." He turned to look at the horror-stricken townspeople who had been snared in his web. "I want you all to see him! Take a good look! This is what happens to people who cross Otis McLaren!" He kicked the still senseless form of Crackerjack Sawyer. "As soon as this old geezer wakes up so he'll know what's going on, he's got the same thing in store for him. I ain't leavin' here until there are twelve dead men hangin' from that balcony! That'll be their gallows!"

Chapter Thirty-six

There had been no more shouts from inside the saloon since McLaren's ultimatum. Ace glanced over at Chance and could tell from the strained look on his brother's face that Chance was having a hard time controlling his emotions. His anger, and his fear for Fontana, might make him do something foolish.

As much as Ace hated the thought of splitting up, it might be the best thing. "Chance!"

"What?"

"From where you are, you can back off without them getting a good look at you from inside the saloon. Do that and head down to the newspaper office."

"What the hell for? You really think a reporter is what we need right now?"

"The three of us are no match for McLaren and his men. If it comes down to a fight, we're going to need all the help we can get. Lee can help you spread the word. Gather all the reinforcements you can, but don't just come marching back up the street with them. We've got to be careful and not let McLaren know what we're doing."

"I'm not a damn fool," Chance snapped. "I won't tip him off. Not as long as he's got Fontana for a hostage."

Despite Chance's mention of Fontana, Ace could tell she wasn't the only thing on his brother's mind. Chance had started thinking about fighting back, which was the best thing for him. For all of them, really. No matter what, they couldn't give in to Otis McLaren's demands. It was unlikely the vicious outlaw would honor any deal he made.

A much bigger chance was that McLaren would try to take his vengeance on the entire town. He might even try to burn Lone Pine to the ground . . . assuming the rain ever stopped, that is.

No sooner had that thought crossed Ace's mind

than he realized the downpour had slacked off considerably over the past few minutes. The thunder and lightning were farther away as the storm moved to the east. The sky overhead was lighter, although gloom still hung thickly over the town as the afternoon waned.

An evening of violence and death lay just ahead, unless Ace, Chance, and Miguel could figure out some way to turn the tables on Otis McLaren.

"Don't do anything crazy while I'm gone." Chance faded back into the shadows along the wall of the building where he had taken cover. In moments, he disappeared as he headed for the newspaper office.

From behind the wagon, Miguel asked, "You have some sort of plan, Ace?"

"Not yet," Ace admitted. "How about you?"

"I knew I wasn't the right man for this job," Miguel said in indirect answer to the question. "Marshal Dixon would have figured out something by now."

"Marshal Dixon probably never faced a crazy-mad killer with that big a gang behind him," Ace pointed out. "Chance has gone to round up some of the other folks in town. We'll even up the odds before we try anything."

"There aren't enough fighting men in town to even up those odds. Not when you consider the sort of men McLaren must have with him."

"Then we'll just have to do the best we—"

Ace stopped short as he realized somebody was coming out of the saloon.

Chance hated being wet and filthy, and under other circumstances he might have been angry at Otis McLaren for causing him to fall in the muddy street and probably ruin his clothes. However, he would have gladly taken a bath in a hog wallow if it meant Fontana would be free.

He had barely gotten the opportunity to do more than admire her from a distance, like all the other men who listened to her sing and appreciated her beauty. But the few conversations they had shared, the frank looks that had passed between them, told Chance the potential was there for more. Much more.

If she lived through the ordeal.

The rain had tapered off to nothing more than a steady drizzle by the time he reached the newspaper office. The front door was locked, and no one answered when Chance hammered his fist on the panel.

Knowing that Lee and Meredith Emory had their living quarters in a small house behind the newspaper office, Chance circled around the building and saw lights burning in the windows. He knocked on the door, and Meredith opened it a few moments later.

"Chance!" she exclaimed in surprise at the sight

of the muddy, bedraggled figure on the doorstep. "What in the world—"

"Did you hear the shot earlier?"

"Shot? I—No, I don't know what you're talking about."

Chance didn't explain but asked another question. "Is your brother here?"

"Of course. Lee!" Meredith stepped back and told Chance, "Come in."

"I'll drip water on your floor," he warned.

"Somehow I have a feeling that's going to be the least of our concerns."

Lee Emory came into the room through an open doorway. "Chance? What are you doing here? You look like you've been swimming in the mud."

"Close enough. There's trouble down at the Melodian. Bad trouble." Chance paused. "Otis McLaren has come to town after all, just like his brother threatened. He's taken over the saloon and is holding everyone in it hostage, including Fontana."

"Good Lord! We have to help them. I have an old gun in the closet—"

"A gun with which you're a terrible shot," Meredith interrupted him. "Lee, you know you're a better fighter with words than you ever were with bullets."

"Maybe," Emory admitted with a grimace. "Why did you come here, Chance?"

"Because you can help spread the word. Let the

town know what's going on. Warn the men they may need to protect their families and help us fight the gang McLaren brought with him."

"What does he *want?*" Meredith asked.

"He's demanding that the town turn over the twelve jurors from his brother's trial. He claims to have two of them already. I suppose Hank Muller is one of them, but I don't know who the other one is."

Meredith put a hand to her mouth in horror. "He plans to kill all the jurors?" Her frightened gaze went to her brother.

"For a start," Chance said. "I don't know what he intends to do after that, but I reckon it won't be anything good."

"Otis McLaren is a madman," Emory said. "He may plan to wipe out the whole town to avenge his no-good brother."

Chance nodded. "I wouldn't put it past him."

Meredith said, "Lee, you're not going anywhere *near* that saloon."

Her brother smiled faintly. "That's where you're wrong. I'll do what you ask, Chance, and help you round up some reinforcements, but I'll be taking along that gun anyway."

"Lee, I told you—"

"This town has been our home for a long time, Meredith. These people are our friends and neighbors. I'm not going to turn my back on them." He lifted a hand to stop her when she tried to protest again. "But I'm not going to just waltz in there like a lamb going to slaughter, either. Don't worry about that. Otis McLaren's going to find that he's got a bigger fight on his hands than he bargained for, and I'm going to be part of it."

"I hope you're right, Lee," Chance said, "because there are a lot of lives riding on us."

Ace wiped rain from his eyes as he watched the batwings swing open and a man step slowly and uncertainly through them. He stumbled toward the edge of the boardwalk with his hands held up in front of him.

"Don't shoot!" the man called. "For God's sake, don't shoot!"

Ace recognized Solomon Horton, although the lawyer looked rumpled instead of dapper and appeared to have lost all his smug self-confidence.

"Horton, what the hell are you doing?" Miguel asked.

"He . . . he sent me out here to talk to you. McLaren did, I mean. He sent me."

"Stop babbling. You've got a message from him?"

"Yeah, I . . . He told me to tell you . . . He's going to hang all twelve jurors, just like Pete was strung up. He already . . . Oh, God! He already killed Hank Muller!" Horton covered his face with his hands, as if by doing that he could shut out all the terrible images that were playing in his mind. The shudder that went through him proved that he couldn't. He lowered his hands and went on. "They put a rope around his neck and hauled him up under the balcony. He . . . he strangled to death while . . . while we all watched . . ."

"That's what he plans to do to all the jurors?" The strain in Miguel's voice testified to the depth of the horror he was experiencing.

"Yes. He has Crackerjack Sawyer in there, and he says he'll do the same to him as soon as Crackerjack wakes up. They knocked him out earlier, when they first rode into town."

From behind the rain barrel, Ace asked, "How does McLaren know who the jurors are?"

Horton swallowed hard. "I . . . I told him. I had to! He put a gun to my head! He would have killed me if I didn't answer his questions."

"I'm guessing you're the reason he's here," Miguel said.

"I didn't have any choice. Pete wrote a letter to him, told me where to send it. He said his brother would get it and come to help him. I was afraid not to. You . . . you know what Pete was like!"

"You son of a bitch." Miguel's voice was choked. "You betrayed the whole town. What else does McLaren say he's going to do?"

"Once he's finished with the jurors, he's going

to kill you and . . . and the judge . . . and Timothy Buchanan. I don't know if he plans to . . . hang you . . . but he says you have to pay for what happened to Pete, too. He's even going to kill old José."

"And if we don't cooperate with him? If the jurors don't turn themselves over to him?"

"He'll kill everybody in the saloon," Horton said. "Then he'll start on the rest of the town. And he won't stop until everybody in Lone Pine is dead and the town is just . . . is just smoldering ashes . . ."

Ace figured that was what McLaren planned to do anyway, whether he got any cooperation or not. Once the killing started, the orgy of blood and death would continue until the entire settlement was wiped off the map. It would be one of the worst massacres in the history of the frontier.

With that bleak prospect facing them, Ace thought they might as well go ahead and fight. It was a matter of figuring out the best way to go about that battle.

"What do you want me to tell him?" Horton asked miserably.

"Tell him we've got to have some time to think it over," Miguel said. "And we'll need his word that if he gets what he wants, he won't hurt anybody else."

Ace knew Miguel was stalling for time. It was

the only thing they could do until they had time to mount some sort of counterattack.

Holding his hands up again, Horton turned toward the batwings. "They said—"

"I heard what they said," Otis McLaren growled from inside the saloon. A gun barrel was thrust over the top of the batwings and blasted orange flame from its muzzle.

Horton cried out in shock and pain as the bullet slammed into his chest and knocked him backwards. He fell off the boardwalk and landed in the street as mud splashed up around him. The rain turned the front of his shirt pink as blood welled from the wound. The lawyer's arms and legs twitched a couple of times, and then he lay still.

The gun barrel disappeared. "Reckon now you know I mean business," McLaren called, "even though a damn lawyer ain't much of a loss. He should've done more to help Pete. Do I get those other ten jurors . . . or do I start throwing bodies out into the street?"

Chapter Thirty-seven

Fontana sat with her back against the bar and Orrie's head cradled in her lap. The wound on the piano player's head had stopped bleeding, but there was a lot of dried blood on his face. He hadn't regained consciousness. His chest rose and fell fairly steadily, though, so at least he was still alive.

That was more than could be said for Hank Muller. Fontana was careful to keep her eyes averted from the horrible sight of the saloon-keeper hanging from the balcony. She knew she would never be able to erase from her memory the image of Muller's face as he died. It would haunt her for as long as she lived.

Muller wasn't the only one who had died. From where Fontana sat, she could look under the batwings at the entrance and see a little of the dark, motionless shape that was Solomon Horton's body. She knew that Horton had brought his own fate on himself by representing Pete McLaren and contacting Otis McLaren, but she felt a little sorry for him anyway. Otis McLaren had gunned him down viciously . . . the same way McLaren did everything, apparently.

So far he hadn't killed anyone else, but she knew it was only a matter of time.

McLaren's men had herded all the prisoners in front of the bar and ordered them to sit down on the floor. That way they were in a nice, compact group and could be slaughtered with ease. That was what was waiting for all of them, unless somebody came up with a plan to stop the killing. Miguel Soriano and the Jensen brothers were still out there on the loose. Fontana had placed her faith in them.

Crackerjack Sawyer had been grabbed by the ankles and dragged over to the bar. The old liveryman was still unconscious, like Orrie. They had hit him so hard he might never wake up.

Considering what McLaren had planned for him, that was the kindest alternative.

The man who had captured Fontana upstairs seemed to be McLaren's second in command. She had heard McLaren call him Gyp. Maybe he wasn't mostly Indian after all. Maybe he was a Gypsy. She had run across them from time to time.

It didn't really matter, she told herself. The blood of a cold-blooded killer ran in his veins, and that was really the only heritage that was important.

Gyp went over to McLaren and asked, "How much longer are you gonna wait, boss? It'll be dark outside soon, especially with all those clouds. That'll make it easier for those bastards to try to sneak up on us."

The rain had all but stopped, but a thick overcast still hung in the sky.

A harsh laugh came from McLaren. He was sitting at a table with his long legs stretched out in front of him and crossed at the ankles. His high-topped boots were midnight black just like the rest of his outfit. "They're not going to try anything. They don't have the guts. You forget, Gyp, I lived in this settlement for a long time. I know the sort of cowards you'll find here. They never stood up to me back then, did they? Hell, that's one reason I left and never came back until now. I was tired of all the crawlin' and grovelin' they did! It made me sick."

"You been gone from here a long time, though, Otis. Maybe folks have changed."

McLaren let out a disgusted snort and shook his head. "A place doesn't change that much."

"They put your brother on trial and strung him up. That don't sound like grovelin' to me."

McLaren's head snapped up. For a second Fontana thought Gyp had gone too far. She wouldn't have been surprised to see McLaren's gun come out with the speed of a striking snake and spout death at his segundo.

But the dark rage on McLaren's rugged face eased, and he said, "It's a hell of a lot easier to pass judgment in a trial than it is to stand up to a man who's eager to kill you. They thought once they hanged Pete, they wouldn't have anything else to worry about. I reckon they're figuring out by now that they were wrong."

A few feet away from where Fontana sat with Orrie, Crackerjack stirred. His eyelids began to flutter. He hadn't moved much yet, nor had he made a sound, but she could tell he was starting to come to.

Moving slowly in the hope that she wouldn't draw any attention from McLaren's men, she reached over and rested a hand on Crackerjack's shoulder. She squeezed lightly. As long as McLaren didn't realize he was conscious, the old liveryman was safe.

If he let out a groan or tried to sit up, he was doomed. McLaren would hang him from the balcony, just as he had Hank Muller.

Crackerjack's eyes opened. Fontana squeezed harder on his shoulder. He turned his head to look toward her, but his eyes were bleary and unfocused. She shook her head a little, praying that he would see her and be able to tell what she meant by the gesture. She couldn't move too much, or McLaren's men would notice what was going on and her efforts would backfire.

Crackerjack didn't say anything. His eyes closed until they were slits, but Fontana could tell he was looking around as best he could and trying to figure out what was going on.

Over at the table where McLaren was sitting, Gyp asked, "So how much more time are you gonna give them?"

"Not long," McLaren promised. "Don't worry, Gyp. Before the night's over, you'll get what you want."

Gyp turned his head to stare long and hard at Fontana. She felt her blood turn to ice in her veins as he said, "I'm lookin' right at what I want, boss."

Ace and Miguel had retreated from their cover when Chance came back with Lee Emory, and the four men were having a council of war in the alcove that housed the entrance to Donald Barr's general store. Barr had poked his head out to see what was going on, taken one look at the grim faces of the four men, and closed and locked the door, pulling down the shade that blocked them from seeing inside.

"I think it's safe to say we won't be getting any help from him," Emory commented with a disgusted expression on his face.

"You can't blame Mr. Barr for being scared," Miguel said. "He's just a storekeeper. He works hard, but he's not a fighter."

"Neither am I, but I'm here." Emory hefted the old rifle he carried. "Although my sister may think I'm mad."

Ace said, "Comes a time in most folks' lives when they have to stand up and fight, whether they want to or not. The world doesn't really give 'em a choice."

"You're wise beyond your years, Ace," Emory said.

"We've just run into more than our share of trouble," Chance explained. "He's not really that smart."

Ace let that go. If ribbing him made Chance forget for a moment that Fontana was in danger, that was a good thing.

"I'm the marshal of this town," Miguel said. "I ought to be the one to deal with this problem."

"Not by yourself," Emory said. "You wouldn't stand a chance. There are more than a dozen killers in there. They outnumber us, what, four to one?"

"Colonel Howden will help," Ace said. "He's not going to let anything happen to Mr. Sawyer if he can prevent it."

"You really think so?" Chance asked. "Those two old-timers are still fighting the Civil War!"

"Yeah, but I think they're friends, even though they'd never admit it. And if anything happened to Crackerjack, who would the colonel feud with?"

Chance shrugged. "You've got a point there." His face tightened. "But we've got to stop standing around and talking about it. I know you got McLaren to put off killing anybody else right now, but there's no telling how long that'll last. It could turn into a bloodbath in there with-out any warning."

"You're right," Miguel said. "Mr. Emory, you and Chance see how many volunteers you can round up. We'll figure out a plan of attack once we know how many men we'll have to work with."

Ace said, "It would be better if you went along with Mr. Emory, Marshal. Like you said, you're the law here in Lone Pine now. Folks will be more likely to listen to you. Chance and I can hold down the fort here, and if any more trouble starts in the saloon—"

"We'll be going in there, one way or another,"

Chance promised. His face was set in grim lines.

Miguel considered the suggestion for a moment, then nodded. "All right. We'll be back. But if we hear any shots from this part of town, we won't waste any time getting here."

He and Emory left the alcove and hurried along the boardwalk, away from the saloon. Ace eased out where he could get a better look up and down the street. He didn't see anyone moving. In fact, Lone Pine would have looked deserted if not for a few lights burning in windows here and there. The hanging that morning had put everyone in a somber mood, and then the torrential storm had given the citizens even more reason to stay inside and hunker down.

Some of them might have even figured out that a gang of bloodthirsty killers was in town and were lying low because of that. Ace was confident the word would spread quickly once Miguel and Emory started recruiting volunteers to fight McLaren's gang. Then people really would hunker down and pray to come through the oncoming night alive.

"At least nobody's suggested we ought to give ourselves up to McLaren," Chance said.

"Surrendering doesn't come easy to hombres like us," Ace said.

"That's right. We're Jensens, even if we're not *those* Jensens. We've got that same stubbornness, though." Chance shook his head. "And I don't believe for a second surrendering would do any good. It wouldn't save Fontana or any of the other folks in there. McLaren's a rabid dog. Once he starts killing in earnest, he won't stop until there's nobody left to kill."

Ace couldn't disagree with that, but he thought one other thing would stop the killing.

Like a rabid dog, Otis McLaren had to be put down.

Chapter Thirty-eight

Thankfully, Crackerjack Sawyer hadn't moved, and as Gyp leered at Fontana, she patted the old-timer's shoulder gently and pulled her hand away. She hoped it looked like she'd been making an affectionate gesture, rather than trying to warn Crackerjack not to let on that he was awake.

She returned Gyp's stare levelly. During her years of working in saloons as a singer, she had dealt with many lecherous admirers. She was an expert at turning them away with an icy look. That might not work with Gyp, she knew, but she wasn't going to let him know how scared she was.

After a moment he turned away and started talking to McLaren again. Relief went through Fontana, not only for herself but for Crackerjack, as well. It looked like she had postponed the gruesome fate McLaren had planned for him.

Crackerjack's luck—all their luck—might run out at any time, though.

A while later, Orrie finally stirred. Like Crackerjack, who was still feigning unconsciousness, the first sign of awareness in the piano player was the fluttering of his eyelids. Then he shifted his head a little in Fontana's lap and groaned. Fontana didn't try to stop him, since McLaren didn't bear any particular grudge against him.

When he opened his eyes and looked up at her, he whispered, "Wha . . . what happened . . . ?"

"Just lie there and rest," she told him quietly. "You got knocked out. But you're going to be all right." She hoped that was true. Although she had no way of knowing how much damage the blow to the head had done, at least he seemed fairly coherent.

He said, "McLaren . . . ?"

"He and his men are still here."

Orrie turned his head a little more, and as he stiffened, Fontana knew he must have spotted Hank Muller's body hanging from the balcony. Orrie started to get up, but Fontana put her hands on his shoulders and held him down.

"There's nothing you can do for Hank now," she said as she leaned over closer to Orrie.

"That bastard's . . . gonna kill all of us."

"He may try, but this isn't over yet, Orrie. There are folks out there in town who are going to help us."

"W-who?"

"Miguel Soriano. Ace and Chance Jensen. And there are bound to be others willing to fight."

Orrie sighed and closed his eyes. For a second, Fontana thought he had passed out again, but then he murmured, "When the time comes, put a gun in my hand. I'll fight. I can do more than play the piano, you know."

So could she, Fontana thought. And if she got a chance, she would have no trouble pulling the trigger.

Shapes came out of the gloom and turned into Miguel, Lee Emory, and about a dozen other men. Ace recognized Colonel Charles Howden and a few of the other men who had been on Pete McLaren's jury.

"These are all the volunteers we could find," Miguel reported.

Howden added, "Our numbers are few, but our hearts are those of lions."

Emory said, "I've been thinking. Maybe we could convince McLaren to trade the hostages for one or two of us. I know I'd be willing to risk going in there if it meant some or all of those other folks would be safe."

"Your sister wouldn't agree with that," Ace said. "And I don't think it would do a bit of good, either. You can't think of McLaren as a reasonable man."

"What he did to Hank Muller is proof of that," Chance added.

"He'd just kill you and demand that the rest of the jury surrender, too," Ace went on. "You'd be throwing your life away, Lee."

Emory sighed. "I suppose you're right." He looked over at Miguel. "So what's your plan, Marshal?"

"If we attack the saloon head-on, those outlaws will wipe us out," Miguel said. "But if we could get in the back and take them by surprise—"

"Even if we do that, there'll be a lot of lead flying around," Chance interrupted. "Too much. Some of the hostages are bound to be hit."

"There'll be a risk, all right," Ace said. "But not doing anything is certain death for all of them."

"Surely, McLaren will have the back door guarded," Emory pointed out. "Even if we can fight our way in that way, we won't have any element of surprise on our side."

"That's why we've got to have a distraction," Ace said. "I was thinking I'd turn myself over to McLaren."

Chance stared at him while Emory said sharply, "Wait a minute. I suggest surrendering and you act like I'm crazy, but now you're going to do it and it's a good idea?"

"No offense, Lee, but I reckon I've had more experience handling this sort of trouble than you have."

"Not enough to allow you to fight off more than a dozen hardened killers!"

"Ace could hold his own for a while, I'll bet, but Lee's right. It's crazy." Chance paused. "That's why I'm going in with you."

"Now hold on," Miguel began.

"Hey, if two of us surrender, that cuts the odds in half, right?" Chance said.

Ace shook his head. "I can't let you do that."

"I don't see how you can stop me. You may have been born a few minutes before me, but that doesn't make you the boss, Ace."

"You're both insane," Emory said.

Ace held up a hand. "Wait a minute. What I had in mind was waiting until the rest of you could get in position to storm the back of the saloon. When the time is right, I'll cause a ruckus—"

Chance cleared his throat.

Ace looked at his brother and saw that he'd be wasting time and energy arguing with him. "*We'll* cause a ruckus, and that way McLaren and his men won't know you're busting in until it's too late."

"It'll still be extremely dangerous for everyone involved, including the hostages," Emory said.

"Yes," Ace said, "it will. But it may be the only way to keep McLaren from burning down the town and slaughtering everyone in it."

A bleak silence followed that statement. None

of the men gathered there could dispute what Ace had said.

"All right," Miguel finally said. "Give us fifteen minutes. Then do whatever you think is best, Ace. Just try to stay alive, both of you, until we can get in there to give you a hand."

"That's the plan," Ace replied. He left unsaid the thought that plans often went awry, but he was sure it was in everyone's head as the rest of the men slipped off into the shadows.

Ace and Chance checked their guns. Each of them thumbed a cartridge into the cylinder, filling the chamber that was normally left empty so the hammer could rest on it. Ace didn't really expect it to come down to a shootout between he and his brother and McLaren's whole gang. That could end only one way, with both Jensen brothers dead.

But if that was what was going to happen, they wanted to be able to give as good an account of themselves as they could . . . and to send as many outlaws ahead of them to Hell as possible.

"Doc would be mad at us, you know," Chance said as he slid his revolver back into its holster. "We're playing a sucker's game here."

"Sometimes when the stakes are high enough, you don't have any choice."

"They couldn't be any higher," Chance said. "With Fontana in there . . ."

"I know. And if we don't stop McLaren, it won't be long until Meredith is in danger, too, along with everyone else in Lone Pine. We're doing the right thing, Chance."

"Yeah. I just hope I get a crack at McLaren before it's over."

"I might just get a crack at him first," Ace said.

Before they could continue the good-natured joshing to break the tension, a raised voice cut through the gathering night.

"Hey, Marshal, you still out there? Or did you run off and leave these folks you swore to protect?"

Those harsh tones belonged to Otis McLaren, Ace knew. He stepped up to the front corner of the alcove and called along the boardwalk, "What do you want, McLaren?"

"You ain't Soriano," the outlaw replied.

Ace hesitated. He hated to say anything bad about Miguel, even though it would be a lie, but that might be the best thing. "You're right, McLaren. He left town. You scared him off."

"Doesn't matter. I'll find the greaser bastard sooner or later . . . when I'm through here."

"That doesn't sound good," Chance whispered.

Ace ignored his brother's comment and said again, "What do you want?"

"You know damn well what I want! I want the sons of bitches responsible for my brother's hanging, and I'm sick and tired of waitin' for them! Send them in now, or I'm gonna let one of my friends have that pretty little gal who was yelling earlier. He's mighty anxious to get to know her better."

342

Chance said, "Fontana!" and started to lunge past Ace.

Ace caught hold of his brother's arm and stopped him. "Hold on," he said urgently. "Miguel and the others haven't had time to get ready yet."

"I don't care! If those bastards are going to hurt Fontana—"

Ace overrode his protest, calling along the boardwalk, "We've been trying to talk to all the jurors and convince them to do the right thing. You've got to give us a little more time, McLaren—"

"You're outta time!" the outlaw rasped. "I'm turnin' the girl over to my pard Gyp in sixty seconds." McLaren paused, then asked, "Who the hell are you, anyway?"

"Ace Jensen."

"Jensen! You're one of the jurors . . . you and your brother!"

Chance raised his voice. "I'm here, too, McLaren! You leave Miss Dupree alone!"

McLaren laughed. "Only one way to stop it! You want to save her for a little while, you and your brother get in here—*now!*"

Ace and Chance glanced at each other. It was too soon, but the decision had been taken out of their hands.

"All right, McLaren!" Ace called. "We're coming in!"

Chapter Thirty-nine

As terrified as Fontana was of McLaren, Gyp, and the other outlaws, when she heard Ace's response to McLaren's threat, her heart sank. Ace and Chance would be walking into a trap, with certain death awaiting them. They were willing to risk that to try to save her.

Knowing that made her resolve that if she got the chance, she would risk her life to save them. It was only fair. "Orrie," she said quietly, "do you think you feel strong enough to sit up?"

"I . . . I reckon."

Fontana slid her arm around his shoulders to help him as he lifted himself to a sitting position with his back against the bar.

He moaned and closed his eyes for a moment. "The room's spinning around all crazylike."

"Just hold on," Fontana told him. "It'll settle down."

"Yeah." Orrie swallowed hard, blinked a few times. "It's not quite as bad now. I got one hell of a wallop, didn't I?"

"Yes, and that's just one more score I have to even with those monsters." Fontana's voice was low and hard with anger.

Orrie cast a worried glance at her. "Wait a minute. Just what are you plannin' on doing?"

"I'm not sure yet. But if I have a chance to get my hands on a gun, I'm going to show them that a woman can pull a trigger just as well as a man."

For a moment Orrie didn't reply, but then he said, "I reckon they plan on killing all of us anyway, so there's no point in tellin' you to be careful, is there?"

"Not one damn bit," Fontana said with a faint smile.

Orrie looked down at his own right hand and flexed it. "I haven't held a gun for a long time," he murmured, "but I suppose it's like playing the piano. You never really forget how, do you?"

"Let's hope not." She caught her breath as the batwings slowly swung open and Ace and Chance Jensen stepped into the saloon.

Miguel led his small force through the alleys of Lone Pine, circling to come up behind the Melodian. Not a bit of daylight remained in the sky, and back there it was positively stygian. The men had to feel their way along, which slowed them down. He hoped the Jensen brothers wouldn't wind up staging their distraction too early.

Miguel stopped short as a large, dark shape suddenly loomed up in front of him. He could barely see it, but even so he could tell it was big. Had a cow gotten loose in the storm and started roaming around?

He heard heavy breathing and knew it wasn't a cow but rather a human being.

Ace and Chance stopped short as a dozen guns were pointed at them and hammers clicked back with a sinister metallic sound. A tall, white-haired man dressed all in black, including a long duster, swaggered toward them with a pearl-handled revolver in his hand. Ace saw the family resemblance to Pete McLaren and knew he was looking at Otis McLaren.

The outlaw's upper lip curled in a sneer. "You're the Jensen brothers?"

"That's right." Ace was able to keep his voice calm and level, although it took an effort. He wasn't sure he and Chance had ever been in a worse fix.

"Why, you ain't nothin' but a couple damn kids!"

"We're men full-grown," Chance said. "Don't ever doubt it, McLaren."

The notorious bad man took a quick step toward them and raised the gun as if he were about to slash at Chance's head with it. Chance didn't flinch.

McLaren controlled the reaction and said, "You know who I am, eh?"

"It's pretty obvious you're the boss here." Ace didn't want to mention the resemblance to Pete, since being reminded of his brother might push McLaren over the edge. Ace wanted to keep the outlaw talking for as long as possible to give Miguel, Emory, and the others a chance to launch their attack on the saloon. "And we've been talking to you for a while, so we recognize your voice."

"Then you know it doesn't pay to cross me." McLaren gestured curtly with the gun in his hand. "Get rid of those irons. Do it slow and easy, though."

Carefully, Ace and Chance slid their guns out of their holsters. Following McLaren's commands, they placed the weapons on the floor and then kicked them away. One of McLaren's men stepped forward and scooped them up.

Chance looked across the room, spotted Fontana sitting on the floor with her back to the bar, next to the piano player Orrie, and called to her, "Fontana, are you all right?"

Before she could answer, McLaren stepped closer in front of Chance, blocking his view of the young woman. "Don't you worry about the gal, boy. You'd do better worrying about what I've got in store for *you*."

Ace and Chance had both seen Hank Muller's body dangling from the balcony. Now, at McLaren's not-so-veiled threat, they couldn't keep their eyes from going back to the dead man. With his bluish-purple face, protruding tongue, and bulging, glassy eyes, Muller was a hideous sight. Ace managed not to shudder as he thought about the agonizing death the saloonkeeper had suffered, but it wasn't easy. He knew Chance felt the same way.

Pushing what had happened to Muller out of his mind, Ace said, "We surrendered like you wanted, McLaren. How about letting Miss Dupree and the other women go?"

McLaren let out a contemptuous snort. "What sort of idiot do you take me for, kid? None of these hostages are going anywhere until I have everything I want. That's twelve jurors hangin' from that balcony, and when that's done I want the judge and the marshal and the prosecutor, too." McLaren shrugged. "Not sure there'll be room to string them up, though. Maybe I'll just shoot 'em, or turn my pard Gyp loose on them with his knife. He's mighty handy with a blade, Gyp is."

Ace saw one of the outlaws grinning and figured the dark-faced hombre was Gyp. The cruelty etched on the man's face was chilling.

"You can't really expect the rest of the jurors to just walk in here and give themselves up," Chance said.

"Why not?" McLaren snapped. "You did. Maybe they've got loved ones in here they'd like to save. For damn sure, they've got families out in the town, and by now I expect everybody in Lone Pine knows what's going to happen if I don't get what I want. I'll kill everybody and burn down the whole settlement if that's what it takes to get justice for my brother."

"Your brother already got what was coming to him," Chance said, unable to control himself. He wasn't as cool and calculating as his brother, and when his rage boiled up, it had to go somewhere.

Unfortunately, Otis McLaren was the same way, and he had the odds on his side. He took a quick step forward and hooked his left fist into Chance's belly. It was a vicious blow that sunk McLaren's fist almost to the wrist. As the breath gusted out of Chance's lungs and he bent over, McLaren lifted his left fist and brought it down like a hammer on the young man's head. Chance crumpled to the floor.

Even though Ace knew how important it was to draw things out, he almost launched himself at McLaren, trembling a little as he fought to control the urge.

McLaren stepped back and grinned at Ace. "Want to tear my head off, don't you, boy? I hurt your brother, and now you want to hurt me. I reckon you *do* understand how it was with me and Pete, don't you?"

"Don't compare us to the two of you," Ace said tightly. "We're not good-for-nothing outlaws."

"Kid, you're just askin' for worse than you're already gonna get." McLaren waved his gun barrel at Chance. "Get him on his feet."

Ace helped his brother up.

Standing again, Chance glared at McLaren and muttered, "Mighty brave with a gun in your hand and more than a dozen men at your back, aren't you?"

"I'd say I'm mighty smart to have a gun in my hand and men at my back, while you . . . you got nothin'." The arrogant grin on McLaren's face faded away as he went on. "Don't you ever say nothin' bad about my brother again, you understand? You keep mouthin' off, and I'll make sure you die last . . . and you'll have to watch what happens to that girl you're fond of before you die, too."

"All right," Chance muttered. "Whatever you say. Just leave her alone."

"We'll see." McLaren turned his back on the Jensen brothers, a deliberately taunting move, and walked over to the bar where Fontana and Orrie sat. Chance leaned forward, but Ace put a hand on his arm to stop him from doing something foolish. McLaren reached down and grasped Fontana's arm to drag her to her feet. She tried to flinch away from him, but his fingers clamped cruelly on her flesh.

Orrie caught hold of McLaren's arm. "Leave her alone!" he cried.

McLaren kicked him in the chest, driving him back against the bar. Orrie gasped and turned pale as he slid down to the floor.

Miguel brought up his gun and ordered in a harsh whisper, "Hold it, mister, whoever you are."

"Miguel? Do not shoot! It is José."

"José? What the hell are you doing here? What do you want?" Miguel asked. "Were you looking for me?"

"No, but fate has brought us together, amigo." The fat cantina owner held something in his hand.

Miguel figured it was the ancient cap-and-ball pistol he had seen José take out and show off when he'd had too much of his own tequila and started reminiscing about his days as a bandito.

"I know that Otis McLaren is in the saloon." José paused. "I have come to kill him."

Lee Emory said, "I thought the two of you were old friends."

"There was a time when we rode together, Señor Emory, this is true. But I would not call us amigos. Do you know why I left his gang?" José didn't wait for an answer. "Because he was a bad man. *Muy malo*! *El loco*! A madman, señors. One never knew when Otis might fly into a rage, and when he did, he was as likely to kill one of his own men as anyone else. My poor nerves, they could not stand it. So I came back here and opened my cantina and have lived in peace ever since."

"Until now," Miguel said.

"*Sí*. Now Otis is back, and I know he bears me ill will because of what happened to his *hermano*. There is only one way to save my life . . . and that is to kill him first." José looked around at the other men. "That is what you intend to do as well, no?"

"That's the plan," Emory said.

"Then I will join you! We fight for our town and our lives and the lives of those we love!"

"You're welcome to come along," Miguel said. "We're going in the back of the saloon while the Jensen brothers create a distraction by surrendering to McLaren."

José caught his breath. "They go in there alone, just the two of them? Into the hands of that monster?"

"That's the plan."

"Then may *El Señor Dios* be with them," José said as he crossed himself with the hand holding the gun. "They will need all the help they can get!"

Chapter Forty

McLaren pulled Fontana over to the Jensen brothers. "Here's your sweetie, kid," he said to Chance. "You can see for yourself that she's not hurt. You want to keep her that way?"

Chance glared. "You know I do, damn it."

"Then here's what you're gonna do. I could have my boys string you up right now, like they did with Muller, but that'd be too quick. I want you to suffer. Pete was locked up for days, and I don't like to think about how miserable he must've been. So you're gonna hurt, too, and my boys are gonna see to it." McLaren turned his head. "Gyp, you and Sinton come here."

Gyp ambled forward, joined by another of the outlaws. Sinton was almost as broad as he was tall, but there was nothing soft and fat about him. He was built like a boulder and looked to be about as solid as one.

"You want me to take my knife to these two little bastards, boss?" Gyp asked with a blood-thirsty eagerness in his voice.

"Not yet," McLaren said. "I want you to teach 'em a lesson, though. You can beat them within an inch of their lives . . . but don't kill them. I want their lives choked out by a noose, the way Muller's was." The outlaw's voice caught a little as he added, "The way my little brother's was."

"Pete didn't choke to death," Chance said. "His neck snapped when he dropped."

For a second Ace thought McLaren was going to shoot Chance then and there, but again the killer controlled the urge. He stepped back and nodded. Gyp and Sinton took off their gun belts and handed them to other members of the gang, then advanced on Ace and Chance with grins on their faces and their fists balled, ready to deal out punishment.

That was a good thing, Ace told himself. It would give the men outside more time. They could get in position to launch their attack while Ace and Chance were battling the two bruisers.

All they had to do was stay alive for a while. McLaren had ordered his men not to kill the Jensen brothers, but you never could tell what would happen in a fight.

With a sudden snarl, Gyp lunged at Chance, and Sinton was right behind him, barreling toward Ace.

The Jensen brothers had found themselves in plenty of rough-and-tumble brawls over the years, but Ace didn't know if they had ever faced two such ruthless opponents.

Sinton spread long, apelike arms as he closed in. Ace knew if he allowed himself to be caught in that dangerous embrace, Sinton would try to crush him and might be able to snap his ribs. A quick dart to his left took Ace out of the path of Sinton's charge, but he realized a second too late that it had been a feint. Sinton's right arm swung toward him in a blindingly fast back-hand that smashed across the side of Ace's head like a tree trunk. Ace flew off his feet and landed on an empty table that collapsed into rubble underneath him.

At the same time, Gyp threw a flurry of short but powerful punches aimed at Chance's head and body. Chance was able to block most of them, but a couple times one of Gyp's fists got through and crashed into him. One blow caught Chance on the jaw, the other in the solar plexus. He staggered back under the impact and fought to stay on his feet. He knew that if he went down, Gyp would start tromping and kicking.

Sinton leaned over to pluck Ace from the debris of the destroyed table. However, Ace grabbed one of the broken chair legs and brought the makeshift club up and around in a sweeping blow that landed on Sinton's right ear. Sinton howled in pain and staggered back.

Chance caught his balance before he fell, but he backpedaled anyway to draw Gyp in. He fell for it and crowded close enough that Chance was able to shoot a straight left between the outlaw's hands and land it solidly on his nose. Blood spurted hotly across Chance's knuckles as he felt the satisfying shiver of the impact run up his arm. Gyp was stopped in his tracks, and Chance took advantage of the opportunity to hook a right into the man's belly.

Sinton recovered quickly from the blow to the head and batted the chair leg aside as Ace tried to strike again. With his other hand he groped for Ace's throat as he forced the younger man back toward the bar. Ace blocked the attempt and lifted an uppercut that caught Sinton's beard-stubbled chin and rocked his head back, but it didn't slow his attack much.

Rather than stand and trade punches with Chance, Gyp lowered his shoulder and plowed into him. Their legs tangled, and they both went down, landing hard on the floor. Gyp tried to roll on top, but Chance got an elbow up, rammed it against the side of Gyp's head, and levered the outlaw to the side. A swift roll brought Chance on top, and he dug his right knee in Gyp's belly before the man could writhe away.

Sinton looped his other arm around in a wind-milling punch that came crashing down on Ace's right shoulder like a sledgehammer. The blow had been aimed at the top of his skull, and if it had landed there it would have driven Ace's head down between his shoulders and probably crushed his spine. As it was, his arm and shoulder went numb. He knew he couldn't fight Sinton one-handed, so he twisted away from the man and tried to put some distance between them while he recovered.

Chance had Gyp pinned to the floor and smashed his fists into Gyp's face. More blood flew. Gyp jerked his left leg up, got the calf in front of Chance's throat, and threw him off. Chance slid through the sawdust and came to a stop against the legs of a table. A few feet away, Gyp scrambled up and dived after him. Quickly,

Chance overturned the table. Unable to stop, Gyp plowed into it headfirst.

Sinton went after Ace with surprising speed and agility for a man built like he was. Ace fended him off while shaking his right arm to get some feeling back into it. His retreat was cut off when his back hit the bar. Sinton's piggish eyes lit up with anticipation. He had Ace trapped and expected to keep the younger man pinned against the bar while he pounded him to raw meat.

Gyp was stunned by the collision with the table. Chance pushed himself up, clubbed his hands together, and leaped toward his opponent as he brought his arms up and then down. The powerful blow landed on the back of Gyp's neck and drove his face against the floor, doing even more damage to his already pulped and bloody nose. Gyp groaned, tried to get up, and couldn't make it. He slumped back down.

Against the bar, Ace forced his right arm to work enough that he was able to grasp the hardwood with both hands and pull himself up as Sinton closed in on him. Ace drew his knees up and lashed out with both legs in a mule kick that landed on Sinton's chest. Sinton wasn't ready for that. He flew backwards and landed on his head. Like Gyp before him, that stunned him. His groggy efforts to get up came to no avail. With his breath rasping in his throat, he lay there, unable to continue the fight.

All during the battle, the other outlaws had been shouting encouragement to their comrades. A shocked silence fell over the saloon as the men stared at the fallen Gyp and Sinton. They had come out on the losing end of the fight.

Not that Ace and Chance were in that much better shape. As they looked at each other, both battered and breathing heavily, a quick grin passed between them. They were still in deadly danger and so were all the other citizens of Lone Pine trapped in the saloon, but for a moment, at least, they were triumphant.

McLaren still had hold of Fontana's arm. He looked disgusted, and he expressed that by giving her a shove that sent her stumbling toward Chance. "Here. You like the bitch so much, you can say good-bye to her."

Fontana caught her balance and turned to face McLaren. "They beat your men!"

He laughed. "You didn't think that little fracas meant anything, did you? Those two weren't fighting for their lives. They're still gonna die. They might not have suffered as much as I hoped they would, but it don't change anything." McLaren gestured toward Gyp and Sinton and told his men, "Get those two on their feet."

Still being covered by several of the outlaws, Chance moved over to Fontana and took her in his arms. "I've been wanting to do this ever since I laid eyes on you, but I sure wish it had been under different circumstances."

"So do I," she said as she wrapped her arms around his neck and hugged him.

Chance pressed his lips to her throat and slid the kiss up next to her ear. "Don't show any reaction," he breathed, just loud enough for her and no one else to hear.

Fontana stiffened slightly.

Chance noticed but hoped none of the outlaws had. "Miguel and some other folks are going to be busting in here any minute. When all hell breaks loose, get behind the bar or some other cover and stay there until it's over."

She murmured, "You're sure?"

"Yep."

"But will they be in time . . . to save you and Ace?"

Chance didn't have an answer for that question.

But it was starting to look more unlikely as Otis McLaren grasped Fontana's shoulder and jerked her away from him. "That's enough. It's time for the two of you Jensen boys to dance on air."

Chapter Forty-one

With José joining their group, they were still out-numbered, Miguel reflected as they approached the back of the Melodian, but every gun helped, he supposed. Would the element of surprise be enough to swing the advantage their way?

He doubted it, but with any luck, they would be able to kill Otis McLaren and quite a few of the outlaws before they were wiped out them-selves. With McLaren dead, it was a lot less likely the others would carry through on his plan. They would probably be content to light a shuck out of Lone Pine as fast as they could. The town would be safe, even though the price paid for that safety would be high.

First was the matter of getting inside the saloon.

Miguel stopped his companions and eased forward in the shadows to take a look at the back of the building. He figured the door was locked, but it wouldn't surprise him if McLaren had posted a guard or two back there, as well.

Sure enough, after a minute or so Miguel spotted a figure leaning against the wall next to a stack of empty liquor crates. The man had something tucked under his arm. Miguel knew it had to be a rifle or shotgun.

As far as he could tell, there was only one sentry. In his arrogance, McLaren probably believed he had nothing to worry about where the townspeople were concerned. He would remember when the settlement had been called Buzzard's Roost and he had ridden high, wide, and hand-some around there, with everybody too scared to stand up to him.

McLaren was going to learn that a few things had changed.

"Do you see anything?" Lee Emory whispered as he moved up silently beside Miguel.

"One guard," Miguel whispered, pointing toward the man beside the crates. "If we can get past him without him giving an alarm, we might be able to get inside without that bunch of outlaws knowing it."

José joined the two of them in time to hear what Miguel said. He leaned closer and told them, "Let me take care of him."

"You?" Emory said. "No offense, José, but—"

"No, señor, I know what I am doing. See?" Something metallic gleamed for a split second on the fat man's right hand. "A flask of tequila. That bandito will smell it and believe I am just a *borracho*." José paused. "I have much experience being drunk."

"It might work," Emory said. "You'd have to be pretty quick, though."

"That I can do as well, señor, when I have to."

José added in a prayerful tone, "At least I hope so, if El Señor Dios wills it."

Miguel thought for a moment, then said, "Give it a try. But if you think he's catching on too soon, just keep going and we'll try something else, *comprende*?"

"*Sí.*" José unscrewed the cap from the flask and began splashing the potent liquor over the front of his shirt.

Miguel figured José hadn't brought the tequila with him tonight specifically for the ploy, but it was good thinking anyway. The tequila was strong enough that the guard would be able to smell it as José approached.

When he was ready, José took a deep breath and then started toward the back of the saloon in a stumbling walk, weaving back and forth a little for added effect. Between the unsteady gait and the reek of tequila, he definitely seemed to be drunk.

Miguel saw the guard straighten from his casual pose as José approached. The man leveled the rifle in his hands and snapped, "Hold it right there, mister."

"Wha . . ." José staggered to a halt. "Is . . . is someone there?"

"Good Lord," the outlaw said. "José, is that you?"

Miguel frowned. He hadn't considered the possibility that the sentry had been with

McLaren's gang for so long he would remember José.

Something else occurred to Miguel then, a thought that sent ice down his spine. What if José decided to try to save himself from McLaren's vengeance by betraying the group of townspeople hidden in the dark alley next to the saloon? All he had to do was point them out, and the guard could open fire. That would bring the rest of the gang and ruin everything.

Instead José mumbled, "Do . . . do I know you, señor?"

"It's me, you fat ol' fool. Ned Byers."

"Ned! Mi amigo Ned! What are you doing here?"

"You ain't heard what's goin' on?" Byers asked with suspicion edging into his voice.

"I have heard nothing. I have been"—José hiccupped very realistically—"in my cantina all day."

"Yeah, you smell like it, all right," Byers said with a note of disgust. "You didn't know Otis was back in town with all the boys?"

"Otis? My old compadre Otis? I must see him and say hello."

"Yeah, he wants to see you, too. He's got some other business to take care of first, but he'll get around to you. Why don't you go on in?"

"Into the saloon? This is where Otis is?"

"Yeah. Hang on a minute." Byers stepped to the door and rapped quietly on it.

In the shadows, Miguel held his breath. They might not have to bust the back door down after all. That could be a big stroke of luck for them . . . but if something went wrong, it could spell disaster.

The door opened, and Byers told one of the outlaws inside, "Look who's here. It's ol' José his ownself. Otis is gonna be mighty happy to see him."

"I would not be sure of that, Ned." José swung his good arm around, taking Byers by surprise. Having slid the cap and ball pistol out from where it was tucked behind the sash around his waist, José smashed it against Byers's skull with enough force to stretch him out on the ground.

"What the hell!" exclaimed the outlaw just inside the door.

"Not another sound, amigo," José said as he pointed the revolver at the man's face and eared back the hammer. "This old hogleg, she will blow your head clean off your shoulders if I pull the trigger. Get your hands up and come with me." He backed away from the door.

The outlaw went with him, arms half-lifted. A few feet out the door, he suddenly muttered, "The hell with this," and dropped his arms. His hand clawed at the gun on his hip.

José pulled the trigger, but the hammer snapped harmlessly as the old revolver misfired. The outlaw's gun came up and flame spouted from its muzzle as the roar of the shot filled the alley behind the saloon.

Fontana put her hands against Otis McLaren's chest and cried, "No! You can't hang them!"

"You've got that wrong, girl. I can do any damn thing I want." McLaren laughed and hefted the pearl-handled revolver. "This gun says I can, and so do the guns of these fellas with me."

She continued to clutch at him. "But if you spare them, I . . . I'll do anything you want."

McLaren laughed harshly. "I reckon you'll do that anyway, whether I hang those little bastards or not. Anyway, I sort of promised you to Gyp." He laughed again. "Although he ain't in much shape to handle anything else right now, even a sweet little morsel like you."

It was true that Gyp wasn't in very good shape. He had to have help standing up, and blood dripped from his nose and mouth as his head drooped forward.

At McLaren's words, though, he lifted his head and snarled. "I'll be in . . . a lot better shape . . . when those two Jensens are danglin' there next to Muller!"

"Let's get at it, then." McLaren nodded to his men, several of whom closed in around Ace and Chance.

In the alley behind the Melodian, José reeled back as the gunman fired. Miguel lunged toward them from the corner. He didn't want to use his gun unless he had to. One shot might go overlooked inside the saloon, depending on what was happening in there. A whole flurry of them was bound to be noticed.

Miguel left his feet in a diving tackle that sent him crashing into the man who had just shot José. They fell to the trash-littered ground in the alley and Miguel made a desperate grab for the gun with his left hand. His fingers closed around the cylinder and clamped down tight on it, which meant it couldn't turn and the outlaw couldn't fire.

A second later, Miguel's right fist slammed into the man's face. He went limp, and Miguel was able to wrench the gun out of his hand.

Miguel stood up and looked around to see Lee Emory supporting José. Colonel Howden and the other men were there, too, ready to charge into the saloon through the rear entrance.

"A couple of you tie this man up and gag him." Miguel gave the low-voiced order. "José, how bad are you hurt?"

"It is nothing, Marshal," the fat man replied, although his voice was thin from pain. "The bullet, she hit me in the same shoulder as before, so I will not even need another sling!"

Miguel nodded. "You're going to stay out here and cover our backs. Somebody give him a gun that actually works."

"This old *pistola*, it has never let me down before," José said in mournful tones. "I can still help you—"

"I told you, you're going to watch our back. Anyway, you've done plenty. You got us in there where we need to be, and from the looks of it, they didn't notice that shot." Miguel drew the pistol he had jammed back into its holster before he tackled the outlaw. "Let's go. Quiet and careful."

Ace had hoped the fight took enough time to give Miguel and the others a chance to get in position and launch their attack. That didn't seem to be the case, so all he and Chance could do was put up a fight against overwhelming odds.

Fontana suddenly screamed and threw herself at McLaren. She clawed at his face, raking her fingernails down his weathered cheeks. With that going on, everybody in the room paused to look at the two of them, and Orrie chose that moment to lurch up from his place against the bar, even though he was obviously in great pain from being kicked by McLaren earlier. Lunging at the outlaw nearest to him, he grabbed the man's gun arm, shoved it toward the ceiling, and rammed into the man as hard as he could.

Unfortunately, Orrie wasn't very big and didn't weigh much, so he wasn't able to knock the outlaw off his feet. The man caught himself, wrenched his arm free, and fired at point-blank range. Orrie doubled over as the slug punched into his middle.

McLaren cursed as he tried to fend off Fontana's attack. He brought his left arm around in a backhand that slammed into her head. Her rich brown hair came loose from its pins and fell around her face in disarray as she toppled to the floor.

"By God, that's enough!" he bellowed. Looking around, he saw Orrie lying crumpled on the floor in a spreading pool of blood, and then pointed his gun at Fontana.

Chance lunged toward him, and so did Ace, but some of McLaren's men grabbed them and held them back.

The bloody scratches Fontana had given him stood out against McLaren's cheeks. His finger whitened on the trigger just for a second, but he held off. Instead of shooting Fontana, he grated, "I reckon the music's over."

Chapter Forty-two

With Emory, the colonel, and the other men at his back, Miguel stepped through the doorway. They hurried to the door on the other side of the room then crept through a short hallway with Hank Muller's office to the left. Stopping at the closed door at the end of the hall, Miguel wrapped his left hand around the doorknob, turned it carefully, and opened the door slightly.

Some sort of commotion was going on inside the saloon, and he hated to think what it might be. On the other hand, the Jensen brothers were supposed to create a distraction. From the sound of it, they most likely had succeeded.

As Miguel eased the door open a little farther, a harsh voice shouted, "Hang 'em!"

The time for stealth was over. He threw the door open and charged into the saloon with flame spurting from the gun in his hand.

The brutal command echoed in the air as gunthunder crashed. The man holding Ace's left arm cried out and let go, falling away with crimson flowers blooming on his shirt where bullets had torn into him.

Ace knew there was only one logical explanation for the sudden turn of events, and sure enough, he saw Miguel Soriano had burst into the room, gun blazing.

Even though he was battered, bruised, and weary from the fight, Ace knew it was the only chance he and his brother had. With one arm free, he twisted away from the other outlaw holding him and brought his left fist whistling around in a powerful punch that landed solidly on the man's jaw. That broke his grip, and Ace was loose.

Chance took advantage of the same opportunity Ace had and turned on the men holding him. He managed to drive an elbow in the belly of one man and hooked a foot behind the knee of the other, then jerked and made the outlaw topple.

At the same time, Lee Emory, Colonel Howden, and the other members of the group from Lone Pine poured into the saloon and opened fire on McLaren's gang. The fact that all the hostages had been forced to sit down against the bar came in handy. Although mostly out of the line of fire to start with, most hunkered lower, stretching out on the floor.

Not Fontana, though. She surged up and leaped at Otis McLaren to wrestle with him for his gun. She was no match for the brutal outlaw leader. He slammed a fist in her face and she staggered backwards.

A few yards away, Chance glanced over his shoulder at Fontana as she reeled away from McLaren. He dived at her and knocked her to the floor an instant before bullets sizzled through the space where she had been. "I thought I told you to get down and stay down!" he yelled over the crash of guns.

"They killed Orrie!"

"They'll pay for it," Chance promised. He got a hand on the floor, pushed himself up a little, then grabbed one of the outlaws around the legs and upended him. The back of the man's head smacked against the floor when he landed, and he didn't move again.

Chance ripped the gun out of the man's hand, rolled over, and came up triggering. Another member of McLaren's gang went over backwards as the shots ripped through him.

The chaos of flaming death filled the saloon. Men on both sides were falling as slugs whipped back and forth. Ace scooped two fallen revolvers from the floor and came up on a knee as the guns roared and bucked in his hands. From the corner of his eye he saw Sinton drawing a bead on him and twisted in that direction, firing just as the burly outlaw squeezed off a shot. Ace felt the warm breath of the bullet as it went past his cheek. Sinton doubled over as both of Ace's bullets buried themselves in his ample gut.

A few yards away, Chance had another target and was about to fire again when something crashed against his back and knocked him forward.

An arm looped around his neck and closed on his throat like a vise. "Now I'll kill you, you son of a bitch!" Gyp rasped in Chance's ear as he tried to crush the young man's windpipe.

Gyp had caught him without much air in his lungs. Explosions were already going off behind Chance's eyes, and a red haze descended over his sight. He stumbled forward with Gyp hanging on to him, then thrust a foot back and tangled it with the outlaw's feet. Chance planted his other leg and drove forward. He twisted as they both fell so Gyp wouldn't land on top of him.

The impact loosened Gyp's hold but didn't break it. Chance was able to gulp down enough air to keep himself from passing out. He twisted far enough to reach back and get his hand on Gyp's face. His fingers dug for the outlaw's eyes. Gyp jerked his head back, but he couldn't get away from Chance. He bellowed in pain and let go. He had to, or else Chance would have dragged his eyes right out of their sockets.

Chance writhed around and slashed the edge of his hand across Gyp's throat, making it his turn to gasp for breath. Chance hit him again . . . using the gun in his other hand. The blow landed with a crunching sound as bone shattered. Gyp spasmed once, then straightened out and lay still. His eyes rolled up and began to glaze over.

He wouldn't molest Fontana or any other woman ever again.

The battle had given Crackerjack Sawyer the chance to stop pretending to be unconscious. He had scrambled to his feet when the fighting started and leaped onto the bar, rolling over it to land on the other side. Grabbing a full bottle of whiskey by the neck, he leaned over the hardwood and smashed the bottle over the head of an outlaw who came within reach. The blow took the hardcase by surprise, and he folded up, out cold.

Crackerjack snatched another bottle from the back bar and waited for a second victim to come within reach. His eyes widened, though, as he spotted one of the outlaws aiming a gun at Howden's back. Crackerjack drew back his arm and let fly. The whiskey bottle smacked against the outlaw's head and laid him out.

"You're welcome, you damn Yankee!" Crackerjack yelled at the colonel.

Howden looked over his shoulder in surprise, then in a blur of motion brought his rifle to his shoulder and fired. Crackerjack jerked back, then realized Howden hadn't been aiming at him. He looked to his left along the bar and saw one of the outlaws wilting with a hand pressed to his chest where blood welled out of a bullet hole.

"Same to you, Johnny Reb!" Howden called. "That varmint was about to ventilate you!"

The two old-timers looked at each other for a second, then both nodded. It was all the gesture either of them needed.

Miguel's left arm hung limp at his side, blood dripping down it from the wound where a slug had knocked out a chunk of meat from the upper arm. His right arm was still fine, though, and the gun in that hand blasted at the outlaws until the hammer fell on an empty chamber. Reloading one-handed would be difficult, so he waded into the fray with the gun rising and falling as he struck out with it. A couple more of McLaren's men went down. Miguel didn't know if he had knocked them out or cracked their skulls and killed them, and he didn't care. All that mattered was that they were out of the fight.

The gunfire had begun to die out. A few more

shots blasted, then an echoing silence fell over the saloon. Ace looked around, saw to his great relief that Chance was still on his feet and apparently unharmed except for some scrapes and bruises, and then took stock of the situation.

All of McLaren's gang huddled in bloody heaps on the floor except for a couple who had thrown their guns down and surrendered. Several of the townsmen from Lone Pine had been killed or badly wounded in the frantic battle, but Miguel, Lee Emory, Colonel Howden, and Crackerjack Sawyer were still standing. Miguel was wounded, and so was Emory, who had to lean on his rifle to hold him up. The right leg of his trousers was stained with blood where he'd been winged.

Chance helped Fontana to her feet.

She threw her arms around his neck and hung on tightly to him, burying her face against his chest. "Is it over?" she asked in a voice hoarse from the clouds of powder smoke that hung in the air. "Is it really over?"

"Looks like it is," Chance told her.

Ace wasn't so sure. His eyes quickly searched the bodies scattered on the floor for one wearing a long black duster, but he didn't find any. He opened his mouth to ask if anyone had seen what happened to Otis McLaren . . .

But before he could get the words out, a terrified scream ripped through the night outside, and Ace figured he had his answer.

Chapter Forty-three

"My God!" Lee Emory cried in a voice wracked by pain and fear. "That sounded like Meredith!"

Ace thought so, too, and was already dashing toward the batwings. He slapped through them onto the boardwalk, only to be greeted by the roar of a shot and the flat *whap!* of a bullet passing close by his ear.

He dived to the planks and rolled off them as another slug struck the boardwalk and threw splinters into the air. He landed on his belly and looked up to see Otis McLaren backing away. The outlaw's left arm was around Meredith Emory's neck as he dragged her along with him like a human shield.

Ace had no idea how Meredith had gotten herself captured by McLaren, but that wasn't important at the moment. Since McLaren was still shooting at him, he scrambled along the muddy street and threw himself behind a water trough. He looked back at the saloon. Chance and Emory were pushing through the batwings.

The newspaperman yelled, "Meredith!"

"Stay back!" Ace shouted. "Hold your fire!" He didn't want anyone blazing away at McLaren and hitting Meredith instead.

McLaren didn't have to worry about that. He

slammed a pair of shots at the Melodian's entrance, and Chance and Emory ducked back barely in time to avoid them.

A harsh laugh floated along the street. "Damn. Looks like all the sheep livin' here have got more guts than I expected. I never figured they'd even put up a fight, let alone get the best of my boys."

"When people are fighting for their homes and loved ones, they're liable to surprise you," Ace called back. "Let Meredith go, McLaren. She never did anything to hurt you or your brother. You've got no grudge against her."

"The hell with that! She's gonna get me outta here. I didn't mind killin' to avenge Pete, but I sure never figured on dyin' to do it!" McLaren continued backing away.

Ace couldn't get a shot from where he was without taking too big a risk of hitting Meredith. He tried to figure out what McLaren's plan was.

Ace glanced around, looking for getaway horses, but saw none tied at the hitch racks. The earlier storm had prompted men to put their mounts out of the weather and the gang had left their horses down at the livery stable. Anyway, McLaren was going in the other direction. Maybe he thought that if he could reach the hills outside of town, he could lose any pursuers there, especially if he kept Meredith with him as a hostage.

Ace didn't want to let things get that far. He was gathering his strength and courage to charge McLaren and try to dodge the outlaw's bullets until he was close enough to tackle the man when a large shape suddenly moved out of an alley mouth behind McLaren.

"Otis, *mi amigo!*" José called as he put his head down and charged.

McLaren rasped a curse, and José crashed into him like a maddened bull.

The collision staggered McLaren. As he tried to catch his balance, Meredith twisted in his grip and got a hand under his chin, shoving it up and back. That broke McLaren's hold on her. She dived away from him, sprawling in the muddy street out of the line of fire.

Ace surged up from behind the water trough and triggered a shot. McLaren threw lead back at him, then turned and ran. Ace charged after him. Hearing boots slap against the muddy street, he glanced over and saw that Chance had sprinted out of the saloon to join him.

McLaren twisted and fired back at them as he fled, but the shots went wild. The duster flapped around him like a pair of giant black wings. The Jensen brothers held their fire, knowing their shots would be more accurate if they closed in first.

A chill went through Ace as he realized McLaren's path was going to take him right to the gallows where his brother had been hanged that morning. The trapdoor was still down, and the rope with its noose on the end still hung through the opening where it had been ever since Pete McLaren's corpse was removed.

Otis McLaren ducked behind the thirteen steps and used them for cover. Ace and Chance slid to a stop as the outlaw's bullet whined between them. Ace lifted both guns and fired as the revolver in Chance's hand blasted.

McLaren staggered back, his gun hand sagging. Clearly, at least one of the Jensen brothers' bullets had gone between the gallows steps and found its target. McLaren brushed against the hang rope and reached up with his free hand to grab the noose and hold himself up.

Ace and Chance fired again as McLaren tried to raise his gun. The outlaw jerked back as the slugs pounded into him, then he leaned forward. He'd been hanging on to the noose with his left hand. That arm went through the loop as life fled from his body. The rope caught him and held him up for a second, then his arm slid out of it and he splashed facedown in the mud underneath the gallows.

He didn't get up again.

Ace covered McLaren as Chance eased up and checked the body.

"Dead," Chance reported, and Ace finally lowered his guns.

They turned and trudged back up the street toward the crowd gathered in front of the Melodian. Meredith was there, having run to join her brother. Lee Emory stood leaning on the rifle while his other arm was tight around his sister's shoulders. Miguel was beside them, a rag tied around his wounded arm as a makeshift bandage. José, Crackerjack, Colonel Howden, and the other townspeople who had joined in the battle waited for the Jensen brothers. Judge Ordway and Timothy Buchanan watched from the boardwalk.

Miguel said, "Is he—?"

"He's dead," Ace said. "No more McLarens to threaten Lone Pine."

Pete and Otis has been responsible for a lot of death and suffering before justice had finally ended both of their lawless careers. All too often, Ace reflected, justice extracted a large price.

But it was a price that had to be paid.

Fontana hurried forward to meet Chance and put a hand on his arm. "You're all right?"

"Yeah. I'm sorry about Orrie."

"He was a good man. A lot braver than anybody ever expected."

"You'll have to find another piano player."

"I will," she said, her voice thick with emotion. "One of these days. When I feel up to singing again."

Chance put an arm around her and drew her against him, letting her rest her head on his shoulder.

"This arm's going to make it hard for me to keep up with all the marshal duties for a while," Miguel said to Ace. "You sure I can't interest you and your brother in those deputy badges?"

"We'll be glad to lend a hand," Ace said with a tired smile. He looked at Meredith and saw her smiling back at him. "I reckon we'll be around here for a while . . . but let's keep it unofficial." Badges would just make it harder to leave when the time finally came to move on.

One thing Ace was sure of—sooner or later the Jensen boys would just have to drift.

About the Authors

WILLIAM W. JOHNSTONE is the *New York Times* and *USA Today* bestselling author of over 300 books, including the series Preacher: The First Mountain Man; MacCallister; Luke Jensen, Bounty Hunter; Flintlock; Those Jensen Boys!; Savage Texas; Matt Jensen, the Last Mountain Man; and The Family Jensen. His thrillers include *Tyranny, Stand Your Ground, Suicide Mission,* and *Black Friday.*

Visit his website at www.williamjohnstone.net.

Being the all-around assistant, typist, researcher, and fact-checker to one of the most popular western authors of all time, **J. A. JOHNSTONE** learned from the master, Uncle William W. Johnstone.

The elder Johnstone began tutoring J.A. at an early age. After-school hours were often spent retyping manuscripts or researching his massive American Western History library as well as the more modern wars and conflicts. J.A. worked hard—and learned.

"Every day with Bill was an adventure story in itself. Bill taught me all he could about the art of storytelling. *'Keep the historical facts accurate,'* he would say. *'Remember the readers—and as your grandfather once told me, I am telling you now: Be the best J. A. Johnstone you can be.'* "

Center Point Large Print
600 Brooks Road / PO Box 1
Thorndike, ME 04986-0001 USA

(207) 568-3717

US & Canada:
1 800 929-9108
www.centerpointlargeprint.com